MURDER IN THE MEWS

ALSO BY AGATHA CHRISTIE

Mysteries
The Man in the Brown Suit
The Secret of Chimneys
The Seven Dials Mystery
The Mysterious Mr Quin
The Sittaford Mystery
The Hound of Death
The Listerdale Mystery
Why Didn't They Ask Evans?
Parker Pyne Investigates
Murder Is Easy
And Then There Were None
Towards Zero
Death Comes as the End
Sparkling Cyanide
Crooked House
They Came to Baghdad
Destination Unknown
Spider's Web *
The Unexpected Guest *
Ordeal by Innocence
The Pale Horse
Endless Night
Passenger To Frankfurt
Problem at Pollensa Bay
While the Light Lasts

Poirot
The Mysterious Affair at Styles
The Murder on the Links
Poirot Investigates
The Murder of Roger Ackroyd
The Big Four
The Mystery of the Blue Train
Black Coffee *
Peril at End House

Lord Edgware Dies
Murder on the Orient Express
Three-Act Tragedy
Death in the Clouds
The ABC Murders
Murder in Mesopotamia
Cards on the Table
Murder in the Mews
Dumb Witness
Death on the Nile
Appointment with Death
Hercule Poirot's Christmas
Sad Cypress
One, Two, Buckle My Shoe
Evil Under the Sun
Five Little Pigs
The Hollow
The Labours of Hercules
Taken at the Flood
Mrs McGinty's Dead
After the Funeral
Hickory Dickory Dock
Dead Man's Folly
Cat Among the Pigeons
The Adventure of the Christmas Pudding
The Clocks
Third Girl
Hallowe'en Party
Elephants Can Remember
Poirot's Early Cases
Curtain: Poirot's Last Case

Marple
The Murder at the Vicarage
The Thirteen Problems
The Body in the Library
The Moving Finger

A Murder Is Announced
They Do It with Mirrors
A Pocket Full of Rye
4.50 from Paddington
The Mirror Crack'd from Side to Side
A Caribbean Mystery
At Bertram's Hotel
Nemesis
Sleeping Murder
Miss Marple's Final Cases

Tommy & Tuppence
The Secret Adversary
Partners in Crime
N or M?
By the Pricking of My Thumbs
Postern of Fate

Published as Mary Westmacott
Giant's Bread
Unfinished Portrait
Absent in the Spring
The Rose and the Yew Tree
A Daughter's a Daughter
The Burden

Memoirs
An Autobiography
Come, Tell Me How You Live
The Grand Tour

Play and Stories
Akhnaton
The Mousetrap and Other Plays
The Floating Admiral †
Star Over Bethlehem
Hercule Poirot and the Greenshore Folly

* novelized by Charles Osborne   † contributor

Agatha Christie®

Murder in the Mews

and Other Stories

HarperCollins*Publishers*

Agatha Christie

HarperCollins*Publishers* Ltd
1 London Bridge Street
London SE1 9GF
www.harpercollins.co.uk

This paperback edition 2018

First published in Great Britain by
Collins, The Crime Club 1937

Agatha Christie® Poirot® Murder in the Mews™
Copyright © 1937 Agatha Christie Limited. All rights reserved.
www.agathachristie.com

A catalogue record for this book is
available from the British Library

ISBN 978-0-00-816492-8 (PB)
ISBN 978-0-00-825537-4 (POD PB)

Set in Sabon LT Std by Palimpsest Book Production Limited,
Falkirk, Stirlingshire

Find out more about HarperCollins and the environment at
www.harpercollins.co.uk/green

To my old friend
Sybil Heeley
with affection

Contents

MURDER IN THE MEWS

CHAPTER 1

'Penny for the guy, sir?'

A small boy with a grimy face grinned ingratiatingly.

'Certainly not!' said Chief Inspector Japp. 'And, look here, my lad—'

A short homily followed. The dismayed urchin beat a precipitate retreat, remarking briefly and succinctly to his youthful friends:

'Blimey, if it ain't a cop all togged up!'

The band took to its heels, chanting the incantation:

> *Remember, remember*
> *The fifth of November*
> *Gunpowder treason and plot.*
> *We see no reason*
> *Why gunpowder treason*
> *Should ever be forgot.*

The chief inspector's companion, a small, elderly man with an egg-shaped head and large, military-looking moustaches, was smiling to himself.

'*Très bien*, Japp,' he observed. 'You preach the sermon very well! I congratulate you!'

'Rank excuse for begging, that's what Guy Fawkes' Day is!' said Japp.

'An interesting survival,' mused Hercule Poirot. 'The fireworks go up—crack—crack—long after the man they commemorate and his deed are forgotten.'

The Scotland Yard man agreed.

'Don't suppose many of those kids really know who Guy Fawkes was.'

'And soon, doubtless, there will be confusion of thought. Is it in honour or in execration that on the fifth of November the *feu d'artifice* are sent up? To blow up an English Parliament, was it a sin or a noble deed?'

Japp chuckled.

'Some people would say undoubtedly the latter.'

Turning off the main road, the two men passed into the comparative quiet of a mews. They had been dining together and were now taking a short cut to Hercule Poirot's flat.

As they walked along the sound of squibs was still heard periodically. An occasional shower of golden rain illuminated the sky.

'Good night for a murder,' remarked Japp with professional interest. 'Nobody would hear a shot, for instance, on a night like this.'

'It has always seemed odd to me that more criminals do not take advantage of the fact,' said Hercule Poirot.

'Do you know, Poirot, I almost wish sometimes that *you* would commit a murder.'

'*Mon cher!*'

'Yes, I'd like to see just how you'd set about it.'

'My dear Japp, *if* I committed a murder you would not have the least chance of seeing—how I set about it! You would not even be aware, probably, that a murder had been committed.'

Japp laughed good-humouredly and affectionately.

'Cocky little devil, aren't you?' he said indulgently.

At half-past eleven the following morning, Hercule Poirot's telephone rang.

''Allo? 'Allo?'

'Hullo, that you, Poirot?'

'*Oui, c'est moi.*'

'Japp speaking here. Remember we came home last night through Bardsley Gardens Mews?'

'Yes?'

'And that we talked about how easy it would be to shoot a person with all those squibs and crackers and the rest of it going off?'

'Certainly.'

'Well, there was a suicide in that mews. No. 14. A young widow—Mrs Allen. I'm going round there now. Like to come?'

'Excuse me, but does someone of your eminence, my dear friend, usually get sent to a case of suicide?'

'Sharp fellow. No—he doesn't. As a matter of fact our doctor seems to think there's something funny about this. Will you come? I kind of feel you ought to be in on it.'

'Certainly I will come. No. 14, you say?'

'That's right.'

Poirot arrived at No. 14 Bardsley Gardens Mews almost at the same moment as a car drew up containing Japp and three other men.

No. 14 was clearly marked out as the centre of interest. A big circle of people, chauffeurs, their wives, errand boys, loafers, well-dressed passers-by and innumerable children were drawn up all staring at No. 14 with open mouths and a fascinated stare.

A police constable in uniform stood on the step and did his best to keep back the curious. Alert-looking young men with cameras were busy and surged forward as Japp alighted.

'Nothing for you now,' said Japp, brushing them aside. He nodded to Poirot. 'So here you are. Let's get inside.'

They passed in quickly, the door shut behind them and they found themselves squeezed together at the foot of a ladder-like flight of stairs.

A man came to the top of the staircase, recognized Japp and said:

'Up here, sir.'

Japp and Poirot mounted the stairs.

The man at the stairhead opened a door on the left and they found themselves in a small bedroom.

'Thought you'd like me to run over the chief points, sir.'

'Quite right, Jameson,' said Japp. 'What about it?'

Divisional Inspector Jameson took up the tale.

'Deceased's a Mrs Allen, sir. Lived here with a friend—a Miss Plenderleith. Miss Plenderleith was away staying in the country and returned this morning. She let herself in with her key, was surprised to find no one about. A woman usually comes in at nine o'clock to do for them. She went upstairs first into her own room (that's this room) then across the landing to her friend's room. Door was locked on the inside. She rattled the handle, knocked and called, but couldn't get any answer. In the end getting alarmed she rang up the police station. That was at ten forty-five. We came along at once and forced the door open. Mrs Allen was lying in a heap on the ground shot through the head. There was an automatic in her hand—a Webley .25—and it looked a clear case of suicide.'

'Where is Miss Plenderleith now?'

'She's downstairs in the sitting-room, sir. A very cool, efficient young lady, I should say. Got a head on her.'

'I'll talk to her presently. I'd better see Brett now.'

Accompanied by Poirot he crossed the landing and entered the opposite room. A tall, elderly man looked up and nodded.

'Hallo, Japp, glad you've got here. Funny business, this.'

Japp advanced towards him. Hercule Poirot sent a quick searching glance round the room.

It was much larger than the room they had just quitted. It had a built-out bay window, and whereas the other room had been a bedroom pure and simple, this was emphatically a bedroom disguised as a sitting-room.

The walls were silver and the ceiling emerald green. There were curtains of a modernistic pattern in silver and green. There was a divan covered with a shimmering emerald green silk quilt and numbers of gold and silver cushions. There was a tall antique walnut bureau, a walnut tallboy, and several modern chairs of gleaming chromium. On a low glass table there was a big ashtray full of cigarette stubs.

Delicately Hercule Poirot sniffed the air. Then he joined Japp where the latter stood looking down at the body.

In a heap on the floor, lying as she had fallen from one of the chromium chairs, was the body of a young woman of perhaps twenty-seven. She had fair hair and delicate features. There was very little make-up on the face. It was a pretty, wistful, perhaps slightly stupid face. On the left side of the head was a mass of congealed blood. The fingers of the right hand were clasped round a small pistol. The woman was dressed in a simple frock of dark green high to the neck.

'Well, Brett, what's the trouble?'

Japp was looking down also at the huddled figure.

'Position's all right,' said the doctor. 'If she shot herself she'd probably have slipped from the chair into just that position. The door was locked and the window was fastened on the inside.'

'That's all right, you say. Then what's wrong?'

'Take a look at the pistol. I haven't handled it—waiting for the fingerprint men. But you can see quite well what I mean.'

Together Poirot and Japp knelt down and examined the pistol closely.

'I see what you mean,' said Japp rising. 'It's in the curve of her hand. It *looks* as though she's holding it—but as a matter of fact she *isn't* holding it. Anything else?'

'Plenty. She's got the pistol in her *right* hand. Now take a look at the wound. The pistol was held close to the head just above the left ear—the *left* ear, mark you.'

'H'm,' said Japp. 'That does seem to settle it. She couldn't hold a pistol and fire it in that position with her right hand?'

'Plumb impossible, I should say. You might get your arm round but I doubt if you could fire the shot.'

'That seems pretty obvious then. Someone else shot her and tried to make it look like suicide. What about the locked door and window, though?'

Inspector Jameson answered this.

'Window was closed and bolted, sir, but although the door was locked *we haven't been able to find the key.*'

Japp nodded.

'Yes, that was a bad break. Whoever did it locked the door when he left and hoped the absence of the key wouldn't be noticed.'

Poirot murmured:

'*C'est bête, ça!*'

'Oh, come now, Poirot, old man, you mustn't judge everybody else by the light of your shining intellect! As a matter of fact that's the sort of little detail that's quite apt to be overlooked. Door's locked. People break in. Woman found dead—pistol in her hand—clear case of suicide—she locked herself in to do it. They don't go hunting about for keys. As a matter of fact, Miss Plenderleith's sending for the police was lucky. She might have got one or two of the chauffeurs to come and burst in the door—and then the key question would have been overlooked altogether.'

'Yes, I suppose that is true,' said Hercule Poirot. 'It would have been many people's natural reaction. The police, they are the last resource, are they not?'

He was still staring down at the body.

'Anything strike you?' Japp asked.

The question was careless but his eyes were keen and attentive.

Hercule Poirot shook his head slowly.

'I was looking at her wrist-watch.'

He bent over and just touched it with a finger-tip. It was a dainty jewelled affair on a black moiré strap on the wrist of the hand that held the pistol.

'Rather a swell piece that,' observed Japp. 'Must have cost money!' He cocked his head inquiringly at Poirot. 'Something in that maybe?'

'It is possible—yes.'

Poirot strayed across to the writing-bureau. It was the kind that has a front flap that lets down. This was daintily set out to match the general colour scheme.

There was a somewhat massive silver inkstand in the centre, in front of it a handsome green lacquer blotter. To the left of the blotter was an emerald glass pen-tray containing a silver penholder—a stick of green sealing-wax, a pencil and two stamps. On the right of the blotter was a movable calendar giving the day of the week, date and month. There was also a little glass jar of shot and standing in it a flamboyant green quill pen. Poirot seemed interested in the pen. He took it out and looked at it but the quill was innocent of ink. It was clearly a decoration—nothing more. The silver penholder with the ink-stained nib was the one in use. His eyes strayed to the calendar.

'Tuesday, November fifth,' said Japp. 'Yesterday. That's all correct.'

He turned to Brett.

'How long has she been dead?'

'She was killed at eleven thirty-three yesterday evening,' said Brett promptly.

Then he grinned as he saw Japp's surprised face.

'Sorry, old boy,' he said. 'Had to do the super doctor of fiction! As a matter of fact eleven is about as near as I can put it—with a margin of about an hour either way.'

'Oh, I thought the wrist-watch might have stopped—or something.'

'It's stopped all right, but it's stopped at a quarter past four.'

'And I suppose she couldn't have been killed possibly at a quarter past four.'

'You can put that right out of your mind.'

Poirot had turned back the cover of the blotter.

'Good idea,' said Japp. 'But no luck.'

The blotter showed an innocent white sheet of

blotting-paper. Poirot turned over the leaves but they were all the same.

He turned his attention to the waste-paper basket.

It contained two or three torn-up letters and circulars. They were only torn once and were easily reconstructed. An appeal for money from some society for assisting ex-service men, an invitation to a cocktail party on November 3rd, an appointment with a dressmaker. The circulars were an announcement of a furrier's sale and a catalogue from a department store.

'Nothing there,' said Japp.

'No, it is odd . . .' said Poirot.

'You mean they usually leave a letter when it's suicide?'

'Exactly.'

'In fact, one more proof that it *isn't* suicide.'

He moved away.

'I'll have my men get to work now. We'd better go down and interview this Miss Plenderleith. Coming, Poirot?'

Poirot still seemed fascinated by the writing-bureau and its appointments.

He left the room, but at the door his eyes went back once more to the flaunting emerald quill pen.

CHAPTER 2

At the foot of the narrow flight of stairs a door gave admission to a large-sized living-room—actually the converted stables. In this room, the walls of which were finished in a roughened plaster effect and on which hung etchings and woodcuts, two people were sitting.

One, in a chair near the fireplace, her hand stretched out to the blaze, was a dark efficient-looking young woman of twenty-seven or eight. The other, an elderly woman of ample proportions who carried a string bag, was panting and talking when the two men entered the room.

'—and as I said, Miss, such a turn it gave me I nearly dropped down where I stood. And to think that this morning of all mornings—'

The other cut her short.

'That will do, Mrs Pierce. These gentlemen are police officers, I think.'

'Miss Plenderleith?' asked Japp, advancing.

The girl nodded.

'That is my name. This is Mrs Pierce who comes in to work for us every day.'

The irrepressible Mrs Pierce broke out again.

'And as I was saying to Miss Plenderleith, to think that this morning of all mornings, my sister's Louisa Maud should have been took with a fit and me the only one handy and as I say flesh and blood is flesh and blood, and I didn't think Mrs Allen would mind, though I never likes to disappoint my ladies—'

Japp broke in with some dexterity.

'Quite so, Mrs Pierce. Now perhaps you would take Inspector Jameson into the kitchen and give him a brief statement.'

Having then got rid of the voluble Mrs Pierce, who departed with Jameson talking thirteen to the dozen, Japp turned his attention once more to the girl.

'I am Chief Inspector Japp. Now, Miss Plenderleith, I should like to know all you can tell me about this business.'

'Certainly. Where shall I begin?'

Her self-possession was admirable. There were no signs of grief or shock save for an almost unnatural rigidity of manner.

'You arrived this morning at what time?'

'I think it was just before half-past ten. Mrs Pierce, the old liar, wasn't here, I found—'

'Is that a frequent occurrence?'

Jane Plenderleith shrugged her shoulders.

'About twice a week she turns up at twelve—or not at all. She's supposed to come at nine. Actually, as I say, twice a week she either "comes over queer," or else some member of her family is overtaken by sickness. All these daily women are like that—fail you now and again. She's not bad as they go.'

'You've had her long?'

'Just over a month. Our last one pinched things.'

'Please go on, Miss Plenderleith.'

'I paid off the taxi, carried in my suitcase, looked round for Mrs P., couldn't see her and went upstairs to my room. I tidied up a bit then I went across to Barbara—Mrs Allen—and found the door locked. I rattled the handle and knocked but could get no reply. I came downstairs and rang up the police station.'

'*Pardon!*' Poirot interposed a quick, deft question. 'It did not occur to you to try and break down the door—with the help of one of the chauffeurs in the mews, say?'

Her eyes turned to him—cool, grey-green eyes. Her glance seemed to sweep over him quickly and appraisingly.

'No, I don't think I thought of that. If anything was wrong, it seemed to me that the police were the people to send for.'

'Then you thought—*pardon, mademoiselle*—that there *was* something wrong?'

'Naturally.'

'Because you could not get a reply to your knocks? But possibly your friend might have taken a sleeping draught or something of that kind—'

'She didn't take sleeping draughts.'

The reply came sharply.

'Or she might have gone away and locked her door before going?'

15

'Why should she lock it? In any case she would have left a note for me.'

'And she did not—leave a note for you? You are quite sure of that?'

'Of course I am sure of it. I should have seen it at once.'

The sharpness of her tone was accentuated.

Japp said:

'You didn't try and look through the keyhole, Miss Plenderleith?'

'No,' said Jane Plenderleith thoughtfully. 'I never thought of that. But I couldn't have seen anything, could I? Because the key would have been in it?'

Her inquiring gaze, innocent, wide-eyed, met Japp's. Poirot smiled suddenly to himself.

'You did quite right, of course, Miss Plenderleith,' said Japp. 'I suppose you'd no reason to believe that your friend was likely to commit suicide?'

'Oh, no.'

'She hadn't seemed worried—or distressed in any way?'

There was a pause—an appreciable pause before the girl answered.

'No.'

'Did you know she had a pistol?'

Jane Plenderleith nodded.

'Yes, she had it out in India. She always kept it in a drawer in her room.'

'H'm. Got a licence for it?'

'I imagine so. I don't know for certain.'

'Now, Miss Plenderleith, will you tell me all you can

about Mrs Allen, how long you've known her, where her
relations are—everything in fact.'

Jane Plenderleith nodded.

'I've known Barbara about five years. I met her first
travelling abroad—in Egypt to be exact. She was on her
way home from India. I'd been at the British School in
Athens for a bit and was having a few weeks in Egypt
before going home. We were on a Nile cruise together. We
made friends, decided we liked each other. I was looking
at the time for someone to share a flat or a tiny house
with me. Barbara was alone in the world. We thought we'd
get on well together.'

'And you did get on well together?' asked Poirot.

'Very well. We each had our own friends—Barbara was
more social in her likings—my friends were more of the
artistic kind. It probably worked better that way.'

Poirot nodded. Japp went on:

'What do you know about Mrs Allen's family and her
life before she met you?'

Jane Plenderleith shrugged her shoulders.

'Not very much really. Her maiden name was Armitage,
I believe.'

'Her husband?'

'I don't fancy that he was anything to write home about.
He drank, I think. I gather he died a year or two after the
marriage. There was one child, a little girl, which died when
it was three years old. Barbara didn't talk much about her
husband. I believe she married him in India when she was
about seventeen. Then they went off to Borneo or one of

the God-forsaken spots you send ne'er-do-wells to—but as it was obviously a painful subject I didn't refer to it.'

'Do you know if Mrs Allen was in any financial difficulties?'

'No, I'm sure she wasn't.'

'Not in debt—anything of that kind?'

'Oh, no! I'm sure she wasn't in that kind of a jam.'

'Now there's another question I must ask—and I hope you won't be upset about it, Miss Plenderleith. Had Mrs Allen any particular man friend or men friends?'

Jane Plenderleith answered coolly:

'Well, she was engaged to be married if that answers your question.'

'What is the name of the man she was engaged to?'

'Charles Laverton-West. He's M.P. for some place in Hampshire.'

'Had she known him long?'

'A little over a year.'

'And she has been engaged to him—how long?'

'Two—no—nearer three months.'

'As far as you know there has not been any quarrel?'

Miss Plenderleith shook her head.

'No. I should have been surprised if there had been anything of that sort. Barbara wasn't the quarrelling kind.'

'How long is it since you last saw Mrs Allen?'

'Friday last, just before I went away for the weekend.'

'Mrs Allen was remaining in town?'

'Yes. She was going out with her fiancé on the Sunday, I believe.'

'And you yourself, where did you spend the weekend?'

'At Laidells Hall, Laidells, Essex.'

'And the name of the people with whom you were staying?'

'Mr and Mrs Bentinck.'

'You only left them this morning?'

'Yes.'

'You must have left very early?'

'Mr Bentinck motored me up. He starts early because he has to get to the city by ten.'

'I see.'

Japp nodded comprehendingly. Miss Plenderleith's replies had all been crisp and convincing.

Poirot in his turn put a question.

'What is your own opinion of Mr Laverton-West?'

The girl shrugged her shoulders.

'Does that matter?'

'No, it does not matter, perhaps, but I should like to have your opinion.'

'I don't know that I've thought about him one way or the other. He's young—not more than thirty-one or two—ambitious—a good public speaker—means to get on in the world.'

'That is on the credit side—and on the debit?'

'Well,' Miss Plenderleith considered for a moment or two. 'In my opinion he's commonplace—his ideas are not particularly original—and he's slightly pompous.'

'Those are not very serious faults, mademoiselle,' said Poirot, smiling.

'Don't you think so?'

Her tone was slightly ironic.

'They might be to you.'

He was watching her, saw her look a little disconcerted. He pursued his advantage.

'But to Mrs Allen—no, she would not notice them.'

'You're perfectly right. Barbara thought he was wonderful— took him entirely at his own valuation.'

Poirot said gently:

'You were fond of your friend?'

He saw the hand clench on her knee, the tightening of the line of the jaw, yet the answer came in a matter-of-fact voice free from emotion.

'You are quite right. I was.'

Japp said:

'Just one other thing, Miss Plenderleith. You and she didn't have a quarrel? There was no upset between you?'

'None whatever.'

'Not over this engagement business?'

'Certainly not. I was glad she was able to be so happy about it.'

There was a momentary pause, then Japp said:

'As far as you know, did Mrs Allen have any enemies?'

This time there was a definite interval before Jane Plenderleith replied. When she did so, her tone had altered very slightly.

'I don't know quite what you mean by enemies?'

'Anyone, for instance, who would profit by her death?'

'Oh, no, that would be ridiculous. She had a very small income anyway.'

'And who inherits that income?'

Jane Plenderleith's voice sounded mildly surprised as she said:

'Do you know, I really don't know. I shouldn't be surprised if I did. That is, if she ever made a will.'

'And no enemies in any other sense?' Japp slid off to another aspect quickly. 'People with a grudge against her?'

'I don't think anyone had a grudge against her. She was a very gentle creature, always anxious to please. She had a really sweet, lovable nature.'

For the first time that hard, matter-of-fact voice broke a little. Poirot nodded gently.

Japp said:

'So it amounts to this—Mrs Allen has been in good spirits lately, she wasn't in any financial difficulty, she was engaged to be married and was happy in her engagement. There was nothing in the world to make her commit suicide. That's right, isn't it?'

There was a momentary silence before Jane said:

'Yes.'

Japp rose.

'Excuse me, I must have a word with Inspector Jameson.' He left the room.

Hercule Poirot remained *tête à tête* with Jane Plenderleith.

CHAPTER 3

For a few minutes there was silence.

Jane Plenderleith shot a swift appraising glance at the little man, but after that she stared in front of her and did not speak. Yet a consciousness of his presence showed itself in a certain nervous tension. Her body was still but not relaxed. When at last Poirot did break the silence the mere sound of his voice seemed to give her a certain relief. In an agreeable everyday voice he asked a question.

'When did you light the fire, mademoiselle?'

'The fire?' Her voice sounded vague and rather absent-minded. 'Oh, as soon as I arrived this morning.'

'Before you went upstairs or afterwards?'

'Before.'

'I see. Yes, naturally . . . And it was already laid—or did you have to lay it?'

'It was laid. I only had to put a match to it.'

There was a slight impatience in her voice. Clearly she suspected him of making conversation. Possibly that was what he was doing. At any rate he went on in quiet conversational tones.

'But your friend—in her room I noticed there was a gas fire only?'

Jane Plenderleith answered mechanically.

'This is the only coal fire we have—the others are all gas fires.'

'And you cook with gas, too?'

'I think everyone does nowadays.'

'True. It is much labour saving.'

The little interchange died down. Jane Plenderleith tapped on the ground with her shoe. Then she said abruptly:

'That man—Chief Inspector Japp—is he considered clever?'

'He is very sound. Yes, he is well thought of. He works hard and painstakingly and very little escapes him.'

'I wonder—' muttered the girl.

Poirot watched her. His eyes looked very green in the firelight. He asked quietly:

'It was a great shock to you, your friend's death?'

'Terrible.'

She spoke with abrupt sincerity.

'You did not expect it—no?'

'Of course not.'

'So that it seemed to you at first, perhaps, that it was impossible—that it could not be?'

The quiet sympathy of his tone seemed to break down Jane Plenderleith's defences. She replied eagerly, naturally, without stiffness.

'That's just it. Even if Barbara *did* kill herself, I can't imagine her *killing herself that way*.'

'Yet she had a pistol?'

Jane Plenderleith made an impatient gesture.

'Yes, but that pistol was a—oh! a hang over. She'd been in out-of-the-way places. She kept it out of habit—not with any other idea. I'm sure of that.'

'Ah! and why are you sure of that?'

'Oh, because of the things she said.'

'Such as—?'

His voice was very gentle and friendly. It led her on subtly.

'Well, for instance, we were discussing suicide once and she said much the easiest way would be to turn the gas on and stuff up all the cracks and just go to bed. I said I thought that would be impossible—to lie there waiting. I said I'd far rather shoot myself. And she said no, she could never shoot herself. She'd be too frightened in case it didn't come off and anyway she said she'd hate the bang.'

'I see,' said Poirot. 'As you say, it is odd . . . Because, as you have just told me, *there was a gas fire in her room.*'

Jane Plenderleith looked at him, slightly startled.

'Yes, there was . . . I can't understand—no, I can't understand why she didn't do it that way.'

Poirot shook his head.

'Yes, it seems—odd—not natural somehow.'

'The whole thing doesn't seem natural. I still can't believe she killed herself. I suppose it *must* be suicide?'

'Well, there is one other possibility.'

'What do you mean?'

Poirot looked straight at her.

'It might be—murder.'

'Oh, no?' Jane Plenderleith shrank back. 'Oh no! What a horrible suggestion.'

'Horrible, perhaps, but does it strike you as an impossible one?'

'But the door was locked on the inside. So was the window.'

'The door was locked—yes. But there is nothing to show if it were locked from the inside or the outside. You see, *the key was missing.*'

'But then—if it is missing . . .' She took a minute or two. 'Then it must have been locked from the *outside*. Otherwise it would be somewhere in the room.'

'Ah, but it may be. The room has not been thoroughly searched yet, remember. Or it may have been thrown out of the window and somebody may have picked it up.'

'Murder!' said Jane Plenderleith. She turned over the possibility, her dark clever face eager on the scent. 'I believe you're right.'

'But if it were murder there would have been a motive. Do you know of a motive, mademoiselle?'

Slowly she shook her head. And yet, in spite of the denial, Poirot again got the impression that Jane Plenderleith was deliberately keeping something back. The door opened and Japp came in.

Poirot rose.

'I have been suggesting to Miss Plenderleith,' he said, 'that her friend's death was not suicide.'

Japp looked momentarily put out. He cast a glance of reproach at Poirot.

'It's a bit early to say anything definite,' he remarked. 'We've always got to take all possibilities into account, you understand. That's all there is to it at the moment.'

Jane Plenderleith replied quietly.

'I see.'

Japp came towards her.

'Now then, Miss Plenderleith, have you ever seen this before?'

On the palm of his hand he held out a small oval of dark blue enamel.

Jane Plenderleith shook her head.

'No, never.'

'It's not yours nor Mrs Allen's?'

'No. It's not the kind of thing usually worn by our sex, is it?'

'Oh! so you recognize it.'

'Well, it's pretty obvious, isn't it? That's half of a man's cuff link.'

CHAPTER 4

'That young woman's too cocky by half,' Japp complained.

The two men were once more in Mrs Allen's bedroom. The body had been photographed and removed and the fingerprint man had done his work and departed.

'It would be unadvisable to treat her as a fool,' agreed Poirot. 'She most emphatically is *not* a fool. She is, in fact, a particularly clever and competent young woman.'

'Think she did it?' asked Japp with a momentary ray of hope. 'She might have, you know. We'll have to get her alibi looked into. Some quarrel over this young man—this budding M.P. She's rather *too* scathing about him, I think! Sounds fishy. Rather as though she were sweet on him herself and he'd turned her down. She's the kind that would bump anyone off if she felt like it, and keep her head while she was doing it, too. Yes, we'll have to look into that alibi. She had it very pat and after all Essex isn't very far away. Plenty of trains. Or a fast car. It's worth while finding out if she went to bed with a headache for instance last night.'

'You are right,' agreed Poirot.

'In any case,' continued Japp, 'she's holding out on us.

Eh? Didn't you feel that too? That young woman knows something.'

Poirot nodded thoughtfully.

'Yes, that could be clearly seen.'

'That's always a difficulty in these cases,' Japp complained. 'People *will* hold their tongues—sometimes out of the most honourable motives.'

'For which one can hardly blame them, my friend.'

'No, but it makes it much harder for *us*,' Japp grumbled.

'It merely displays to its full advantage your ingenuity,' Poirot consoled him. 'What about fingerprints, by the way?'

'Well, it's murder all right. No prints whatever on the pistol. Wiped clean before being placed in her hand. Even if she managed to wind her arm round her head in some marvellous acrobatic fashion she could hardly fire off a pistol without hanging on to it and she couldn't wipe it after she was dead.'

'No, no, an outside agency is clearly indicated.'

'Otherwise the prints are disappointing. None on the door-handle. None on the window. Suggestive, eh? Plenty of Mrs Allen's all over the place.'

'Did Jameson get anything?'

'Out of the daily woman? No. She talked a lot but she didn't really know much. Confirmed the fact that Allen and Plenderleith were on good terms. I've sent Jameson out to make inquiries in the mews. We'll have to have a word with Mr Laverton-West too. Find out where he was and what he was doing last night. In the meantime we'll have a look through her papers.'

He set to without more ado. Occasionally he grunted and tossed something over to Poirot. The search did not take long. There were not many papers in the desk and what there were were neatly arranged and docketed.

Finally Japp leant back and uttered a sigh.

'Not very much, is there?'

'As you say.'

'Most of it quite straightforward—receipted bills, a few bills as yet unpaid—nothing particularly outstanding. Social stuff—invitations. Notes from friends. These—' he laid his hand on a pile of seven or eight letters—'and her cheque book and passbook. Anything strike you there?'

'Yes, she was overdrawn.'

'Anything else?'

Poirot smiled.

'Is it an examination that you put me through? But yes, I noticed what you are thinking of. Two hundred pounds drawn to self three months ago—and two hundred pounds drawn out yesterday—'

'And nothing on the counterfoil of the cheque book. No other cheques to self except small sums—fifteen pounds the highest. And I'll tell you this—there's no such sum of money in the house. Four pounds ten in a handbag and an odd shilling or two in another bag. That's pretty clear, I think.'

'Meaning that she paid that sum away yesterday.'

'Yes. Now who did she pay it to?'

The door opened and Inspector Jameson entered.

'Well, Jameson, get anything?'

'Yes, sir, several things. To begin with, nobody actually heard the shot. Two or three women say they did because they want to think they did—but that's all there is to it. With all those fireworks going off there isn't a dog's chance.'

Japp grunted.

'Don't suppose there is. Go on.'

'Mrs Allen was at home most of yesterday afternoon and evening. Came in about five o'clock. Then she went out again about six but only to the post box at the end of the mews. At about nine-thirty a car drove up—Standard Swallow saloon—and a man got out. Description about forty-five, well set up military-looking gent, dark blue overcoat, bowler hat, toothbrush moustache. James Hogg, chauffeur from No. 18 says he's seen him calling on Mrs Allen before.'

'Forty-five,' said Japp. 'Can't very well be Laverton-West.'

'This man, whoever he was, stayed here for just under an hour. Left at about ten-twenty. Stopped in the doorway to speak to Mrs Allen. Small boy, Frederick Hogg, was hanging about quite near and heard what he said.'

'And what did he say?'

'"*Well, think it over and let me know.*" And then she said something and he answered: "*All right. So long.*" After that he got in his car and drove away.'

'That was at ten-twenty,' said Poirot thoughtfully.

Japp rubbed his nose.

'Then at ten-twenty Mrs Allen was still alive,' he said. 'What next?'

'Nothing more, sir, as far as I can learn. The chauffeur

at No. 22 got in at half-past ten and he'd promised his kids to let off some fireworks for them. They'd been waiting for him—and all the other kids in the mews too. He let 'em off and everybody around about was busy watching them. After that everyone went to bed.'

'And nobody else was seen to enter No. 14?'

'No—but that's not to say they didn't. Nobody would have noticed.'

'H'm,' said Japp. 'That's true. Well, we'll have to get hold of this "military gentleman with the toothbrush moustache." It's pretty clear that he was the last person to see her alive. I wonder who he was?'

'Miss Plenderleith might tell us,' suggested Poirot.

'She might,' said Japp gloomily. 'On the other hand she might not. I've no doubt she could tell us a good deal if she liked. What about you, Poirot, old boy? You were alone with her for a bit. Didn't you trot out that Father Confessor manner of yours that sometimes makes such a hit?'

Poirot spread out his hands.

'Alas, we talked only of gas fires.'

'Gas fires—gas fires.' Japp sounded disgusted. 'What's the matter with you, old cock? Ever since you've been here the only things you've taken an interest in are quill pens and waste-paper baskets. Oh, yes, I saw you having a quiet look into the one downstairs. Anything in it?'

Poirot sighed.

'A catalogue of bulbs and an old magazine.'

'What's the idea, anyway? If anyone wants to throw away an incriminating document or whatever it is you have in mind they're not likely just to pitch it into a waste-paper basket.'

'That is very true what you say there. Only something quite unimportant would be thrown away like that.'

Poirot spoke meekly. Nevertheless Japp looked at him suspiciously.

'Well,' he said. 'I know what I'm going to do next. What about you?'

'*Eh bien*,' said Poirot. 'I shall complete my search for the unimportant. There is still the dustbin.'

He skipped nimbly out of the room. Japp looked after him with an air of disgust.

'Potty,' he said. 'Absolutely potty.'

Inspector Jameson preserved a respectful silence. His face said with British superiority: 'Foreigners!'

Aloud he said:

'So that's Mr Hercule Poirot! I've heard of him.'

'Old friend of mine,' explained Japp. 'Not half as balmy as he looks, mind you. All the same he's getting on now.'

'Gone a bit gaga as they say, sir,' suggested Inspector Jameson. 'Ah well, age will tell.'

'All the same,' said Japp, 'I wish I knew what he was up to.'

He walked over to the writing-table and stared uneasily at an emerald green quill pen.

CHAPTER 5

Japp was just engaging his third chauffeur's wife in conversation when Poirot, walking noiselessly as a cat, suddenly appeared at his elbow.

'Whew, you made me jump,' said Japp. 'Got anything?'

'Not what I was looking for.'

Japp turned back to Mrs James Hogg.

'And you say you've seen this gentleman before?'

'Oh, yes sir. And my husband too. We knew him at once.'

'Now look here, Mrs Hogg, you're a shrewd woman, I can see. I've no doubt that you know all about everyone in the mews. And you're a woman of judgment—unusually good judgment, I can tell that—' Unblushingly he repeated this remark for the third time. Mrs Hogg bridled slightly and assumed an expression of superhuman intelligence. 'Give me a line on those two young women—Mrs Allen and Miss Plenderleith. What were they like? Gay? Lots of parties? That sort of thing?'

'Oh, no sir, nothing of the kind. They went out a good bit—Mrs Allen especially—but they're *class*, if you know what I mean. Not like some as I could name down the other end. I'm sure the way that Mrs Stevens goes on—if

33

she *is* a Mrs at all which I doubt—well I shouldn't like to tell you what goes on there—I—'

'Quite so,' said Japp, dexterously stopping the flow. 'Now that's very important what you've told me. Mrs Allen and Miss Plenderleith were well liked, then?'

'Oh yes, sir, very nice ladies, both of them—especially Mrs Allen. Always spoke a nice word to the children, she did. Lost her own little girl, I believe, poor dear. Ah well, I've buried three myself. And what I say is—'

'Yes, yes, very sad. And Miss Plenderleith?'

'Well, of course she was a nice lady too, but much more abrupt if you know what I mean. Just go by with a nod, she would, and not stop to pass the time of day. But I've nothing against her—nothing at all.'

'She and Mrs Allen got on well together?'

'Oh, yes sir. No quarrelling—nothing like that. Very happy and contented they were—I'm sure Mrs Pierce will bear me out.'

'Yes, we've talked to her. Do you know Mrs Allen's fiancé by sight?'

'The gentleman she's going to marry? Oh, yes. He's been here quite a bit off and on. Member of Parliament, they do say.'

'It wasn't he who came last night?'

'No, sir, it was *not*.' Mrs Hogg drew herself up. A note of excitement disguised beneath intense primness came into her voice. 'And if you ask me, sir, what you are thinking is all *wrong*. Mrs Allen wasn't *that* kind of lady, I'm sure. It's true there *was* no one in the house, but I do *not* believe anything of the kind—I said so to Hogg only this morning. "No, Hogg," I said, "Mrs Allen was a lady—a real lady—so don't go suggesting things"—knowing what a man's mind is, if you'll excuse my mentioning it. Always coarse in their ideas.'

Passing this insult by, Japp proceeded:

'You saw him arrive and you saw him leave—that's so, isn't it?'

'That's so, sir.'

'And you didn't hear anything else? Any sounds of a quarrel?'

'No, sir, nor likely to. Not, that is to say, that such things couldn't be heard—because the contrary to that is well known—and down the other end the way Mrs Stevens goes for that poor frightened maid of hers is common talk—and one and all we've advised her not to stand it, but there, the wages is good—temper of the devil she may have but pays for it—thirty shillings a week . . .'

Japp said quickly:

'But you didn't hear anything of the kind at No. 14?'

'No, sir. Nor likely to with fireworks popping off here, there and everywhere and my Eddie with his eyebrows singed off as near as nothing.'

'This man left at ten-twenty—that's right, is it?'

'It might be, sir. I couldn't say myself. But Hogg says so and he's a very reliable, steady man.'

'You actually saw him leave. Did you hear what he said?'

'No, sir. I wasn't near enough for that. Just saw him from my window, standing in the doorway talking to Mrs Allen.'

'See her too?'

'Yes, sir, she was standing just inside the doorway.'

'Notice what she was wearing?'

'Now really, sir, I couldn't say. Not noticing particularly as it were.'

Poirot said:

'You did not even notice if she was wearing day dress or evening dress?'

'No, sir, I can't say I did.'

Poirot looked thoughtfully up at the window above and then across to No. 14. He smiled and for a moment his eye caught Japp's.

'And the gentleman?'

'He was in a dark-blue overcoat and a bowler hat. Very smart and well set up.'

Japp asked a few more questions and then proceeded to his next interview. This was with Master Frederick Hogg, an impish-faced, bright-eyed lad, considerably swollen with self-importance.

'Yes, sir. I heard them talking. "*Think it over and let me know*," the gent said. Pleasant like, you know. And then she said something and he answered, "*All right. So long.*" And he got into the car—I was holding the door open but he didn't give me nothing,' said Master Hogg with a slight tinge of depression in his tone. 'And he drove away.'

'You didn't hear what Mrs Allen said?'

'No, sir, can't say I did.'

'Can you tell me what she was wearing? What colour, for instance?'

'Couldn't say, sir. You see, I didn't really see her. She must have been round behind the door.'

'Just so,' said Japp. 'Now look here, my boy, I want you to think and answer my next question very carefully. If you don't know and can't remember, say so. Is that clear?'

'Yes, sir.'

Master Hogg looked at him eagerly.

'Which of 'em closed the door, Mrs Allen or the gentleman?'

'The front door?'

'The front door, naturally.'

The child reflected. His eyes screwed themselves up in an effort of remembrance.

'Think the lady probably did—No, she didn't. He did. Pulled it to with a bit of a bang and jumped into the car quick. Looked as though he had a date somewhere.'

'Right. Well, young man, you seem a bright kind of shaver. Here's sixpence for you.'

Dismissing Master Hogg, Japp turned to his friend. Slowly with one accord they nodded.

'Could be!' said Japp.

'There are possibilities,' agreed Poirot.

His eyes shone with a green light. They looked like a cat's.

CHAPTER 6

On re-entering the sitting-room of No. 14, Japp wasted no time in beating about the bush. He came straight to the point.

'Now look here, Miss Plenderleith, don't you think it's better to spill the beans here and now. It's going to come to that in the end.'

Jane Plenderleith raised her eyebrows. She was standing by the mantelpiece, gently warming one foot at the fire.

'I really don't know what you mean.'

'Is that quite true, Miss Plenderleith?'

She shrugged her shoulders.

'I've answered all your questions. I don't see what more I can do.'

'Well, it's my opinion you could do a lot more—if you chose.'

'That's only an opinion, though, isn't it, Chief Inspector?'

Japp grew rather red in the face.

'I think,' said Poirot, 'that mademoiselle would appreciate better the reason for your questions if you told her just how the case stands.'

'That's very simple. Now then, Miss Plenderleith, the facts

are as follows. Your friend was found shot through the head with a pistol in her hand and the door and the window fastened. That looked like a plain case of suicide. *But it wasn't suicide*. The medical evidence alone proves that.'

'How?'

All her ironic coolness had disappeared. She leaned forward—intent—watching his face.

'The pistol was in her hand—*but the fingers weren't grasping it*. Moreover there were *no fingerprints at all* on the pistol. And the angle of the wound makes it impossible that the wound should have been self-inflicted. Then again, she left no letter—rather an unusual thing for a suicide. And though the door was locked the key has not been found.'

Jane Plenderleith turned slowly and sat down in a chair facing them.

'So that's it!' she said. 'All along I've felt it was *impossible* that she should have killed herself! I was right! She *didn't* kill herself. Someone else killed her.'

For a moment or two she remained lost in thought. Then she raised her head brusquely.

'Ask me any questions you like,' she said. 'I will answer them to the best of my ability.'

Japp began:

'Last night Mrs Allen had a visitor. He is described as a man of forty-five, military bearing, toothbrush moustache, smartly dressed and driving a Standard Swallow saloon car. Do you know who that is?'

'I can't be sure, of course, but it sounds like Major Eustace.'

39

'Who is Major Eustace? Tell me all you can about him?'

'He was a man Barbara had known abroad—in India. He turned up about a year ago, and we've seen him on and off since.'

'He was a friend of Mrs Allen's?'

'He behaved like one,' said Jane dryly.

'What was her attitude to him?'

'I don't think she really liked him—in fact, I'm sure she didn't.'

'But she treated him with outward friendliness?'

'Yes.'

'Did she ever seem—think carefully, Miss Plenderleith—afraid of him?'

Jane Plenderleith considered this thoughtfully for a minute or two. Then she said:

'Yes—I think she was. She was always nervous when he was about.'

'Did he and Mr Laverton-West meet at all?'

'Only once, I think. They didn't take to each other much. That is to say, Major Eustace made himself as agreeable as he could to Charles, but Charles wasn't having any. Charles has got a very good nose for anybody who isn't well—quite—quite.'

'And Major Eustace was not—what you call—quite—quite?' asked Poirot.

The girl said dryly:

'No, he wasn't. Bit hairy at the heel. Definitely not out of the top drawer.'

'Alas—I do not know those two expressions. You mean to say he was not the *pukka sahib*?'

A fleeting smile passed across Jane Plenderleith's face, but she replied gravely, 'No.'

'Would it come as a great surprise to you, Miss Plenderleith, if I suggested that this man was blackmailing Mrs Allen?'

Japp sat forward to observe the result of his suggestion.

He was well satisfied. The girl started forward, the colour rose in her cheeks, she brought down her hand sharply on the arm of her chair.

'So that was it! What a fool I was not to have guessed. Of course!'

'You think the suggestion feasible, mademoiselle?' asked Poirot.

'I was a fool not to have thought of it! Barbara's borrowed small sums off me several times during the last six months. And I've seen her sitting poring over her pass-book. I knew she was living well within her income, so I didn't bother, but, of course, if she was paying out sums of money—'

'And it would accord with her general demeanour—yes?' asked Poirot.

'Absolutely. She was nervous. Quite jumpy sometimes. Altogether different from what she used to be.'

Poirot said gently:

'Excuse me, but that is not just what you told us before.'

'That was different,' Jane Plenderleith waved an impatient hand. 'She wasn't *depressed*. I mean she wasn't feeling

41

suicidal or anything like that. But blackmail—yes. I wish she'd told *me*. I'd have sent him to the devil.'

'But he might have gone—not to the devil, but to Mr Charles Laverton-West?' observed Poirot.

'Yes,' said Jane Plenderleith slowly. 'Yes . . . that's true . . .'

'You've no idea of what this man's hold over her may have been?' asked Japp.

The girl shook her head.

'I haven't the faintest idea. I can't believe, knowing Barbara, that it could have been anything really serious. On the other hand—' she paused, then went on. 'What I mean is, Barbara was a bit of a simpleton in some ways. She'd be very easily frightened. In fact, she was the kind of girl who would be a positive gift to a blackmailer! The nasty brute!'

She snapped out the last three words with real venom.

'Unfortunately,' said Poirot, 'the crime seems to have taken place the wrong way round. It is the victim who should kill the blackmailer, not the blackmailer his victim.'

Jane Plenderleith frowned a little.

'No—that is true—but I can imagine circumstances—'

'Such as?'

'Supposing Barbara got desperate. She may have threatened him with that silly little pistol of hers. He tries to wrench it away from her and in the struggle he fires it and kills her. Then he's horrified at what he's done and tries to pretend it was suicide.'

'Might be,' said Japp. 'But there's a difficulty.'

She looked at him inquiringly.

'Major Eustace (if it was him) left here last night at ten-twenty and said goodbye to Mrs Allen on the doorstep.'

'Oh,' the girl's face fell. 'I see.' She paused a minute or two. 'But he might have come back later,' she said slowly.

'Yes, that is possible,' said Poirot.

Japp continued:

'Tell me, Miss Plenderleith, where was Mrs Allen in the habit of receiving guests, here or in the room upstairs?'

'Both. But this room was used for more communal parties or for my own special friends. You see, the arrangement was that Barbara had the big bedroom and used it as a sitting-room as well, and I had the little bedroom and used this room.'

'If Major Eustace came by appointment last night, in which room do you think Mrs Allen would have received him?'

'I think she would probably bring him in here.' The girl sounded a little doubtful. 'It would be less intimate. On the other hand, if she wanted to write a cheque or anything of that kind, she would probably take him upstairs. There are no writing materials down here.'

Japp shook his head.

'There was no question of a cheque. Mrs Allen drew out two hundred pounds in cash yesterday. And so far we've not been able to find any trace of it in the house.'

'And she gave it to that brute? Oh, poor Barbara! Poor, poor Barbara!'

Poirot coughed.

'Unless, as you suggest, it was more or less an accident, it still seems a remarkable fact that he should kill an apparently regular source of income.'

'Accident? It wasn't an accident. He lost his temper and saw red and shot her.'

'That is how you think it happened?'

'Yes.' She added vehemently, 'It was murder—*murder*!'

Poirot said gravely:

'I will not say that you are wrong, mademoiselle.'

Japp said:

'What cigarettes did Mrs Allen smoke?'

'Gaspers. There are some in that box.'

Japp opened the box, took out a cigarette and nodded. He slipped the cigarette into his pocket.

'And you, mademoiselle?' asked Poirot.

'The same.'

'You do not smoke Turkish?'

'Never.'

'Nor Mrs Allen?'

'No. She didn't like them.'

Poirot asked:

'And Mr Laverton-West. What did he smoke?'

She stared hard at him.

'Charles? What does it matter what he smoked? You're not going to pretend that *he* killed her?'

Poirot shrugged his shoulders.

'A man has killed the woman he loved before now, mademoiselle.'

Jane shook her head impatiently.

'Charles wouldn't kill anybody. He's a very careful man.'

'All the same, mademoiselle, it is the careful men who commit the cleverest murders.'

She stared at him.

'But not for the motive you have just advanced, M. Poirot.'

He bowed his head.

'No, that is true.'

Japp rose.

'Well, I don't think that there's much more I can do here. I'd like to have one more look round.'

'In case that money should be tucked away somewhere? Certainly. Look anywhere you like. And in my room too—although it isn't likely Barbara would hide it there.'

Japp's search was quick but efficient. The living-room had given up all its secrets in a very few minutes. Then he went upstairs. Jane Plenderleith sat on the arm of a chair, smoking a cigarette and frowning at the fire. Poirot watched her.

After some minutes, he said quietly:

'Do you know if Mr Laverton-West is in London at present?'

'I don't know at all. I rather fancy he's in Hampshire with his people. I suppose I ought to have wired him. How dreadful. I forgot.'

'It is not easy to remember everything, mademoiselle, when a catastrophe occurs. And after all, the bad news, it will keep. One hears it only too soon.'

'Yes, that's true,' the girl said absently.

Japp's footsteps were heard descending the stairs. Jane went out to meet him.

'Well?'

Japp shook his head.

'Nothing helpful, I'm afraid, Miss Plenderleith. I've been over the whole house now. Oh, I suppose I'd better just have a look in this cupboard under the stairs.'

He caught hold of the handle as he spoke, and pulled.

Jane Plenderleith said:

'It's locked.'

Something in her voice made both men look at her sharply.

'Yes,' said Japp pleasantly. 'I can see it's locked. Perhaps you'll get the key.'

The girl was standing as though carved in stone.

'I—I'm not sure where it is.'

Japp shot a quick glance at her. His voice continued resolutely pleasant and off-hand.

'Dear me, that's too bad. Don't want to splinter the wood, opening it by force. I'll send Jameson out to get an assortment of keys.'

She moved forward stiffly.

'Oh,' she said. 'One minute. It might be—'

She went back into the living-room and reappeared a moment later holding a fair-sized key in her hand.

'We keep it locked,' she explained, 'because one's umbrellas and things have a habit of getting pinched.'

'Very wise precaution,' said Japp, cheerfully accepting the key.

He turned it in the lock and threw the door open. It was dark inside the cupboard. Japp took out his pocket flashlight and let it play round the inside.

Poirot felt the girl at his side stiffen and stop breathing for a second. His eyes followed the sweep of Japp's torch.

There was not very much in the cupboard. Three umbrellas—one broken, four walking sticks, a set of golf clubs, two tennis racquets, a neatly-folded rug and several sofa cushions in various stages of dilapidation. On the top of these last reposed a small, smart-looking attaché-case.

As Japp stretched out a hand towards it, Jane Plenderleith said quickly:

'That's mine. I—it came back with me this morning. So there can't be anything there.'

'Just as well to make quite sure,' said Japp, his cheery friendliness increasing slightly.

The case was unlocked. Inside it was fitted with shagreen brushes and toilet bottles. There were two magazines in it but nothing else.

Japp examined the whole outfit with meticulous attention. When at last he shut the lid and began a cursory examination of the cushions, the girl gave an audible sigh of relief.

There was nothing else in the cupboard beyond what was plainly to be seen. Japp's examination was soon finished.

He relocked the door and handed the key to Jane Plenderleith.

'Well,' he said, 'that concludes matters. Can you give me Mr Laverton-West's address?'

'Farlescombe Hall, Little Ledbury, Hampshire.'

'Thank you, Miss Plenderleith. That's all for the present. I may be round again later. By the way, mum's the word. Leave it at suicide as far as the general public's concerned.'

'Of course, I quite understand.'

She shook hands with them both.

As they walked away down the mews, Japp exploded:

'What the—the hell was there in that cupboard? There was *something*.'

'Yes, there was something.'

'And I'll bet ten to one it was something to do with the attaché-case! But like the double-dyed mutt I must be, I couldn't find anything. Looked in all the bottles—felt the lining—what the devil could it be?'

Poirot shook his head thoughtfully.

'That girl's in it somehow,' Japp went on. 'Brought that case back this morning? Not on your life, she didn't! Notice that there were two magazines in it?'

'Yes.'

'Well, one of them was for *last July*!'

CHAPTER 7

It was the following day when Japp walked into Poirot's flat, flung his hat on the table in deep disgust and dropped into a chair.

'Well,' he growled. '*She's* out of it!'

'Who is out of it?'

'Plenderleith. Was playing bridge up to midnight. Host, hostess, naval-commander guest and two servants can all swear to that. No doubt about it, we've got to give up any idea of her being concerned in the business. All the same, I'd like to know *why* she went all hot and bothered about that little attaché-case under the stairs. That's something in *your* line, Poirot. You like solving the kind of triviality that leads nowhere. The Mystery of the Small Attaché-Case. Sounds quite promising!'

'I will give you yet another suggestion for a title. The Mystery of the Smell of Cigarette Smoke.'

'A bit clumsy for a title. Smell—eh? Was *that* why you were sniffing so when we first examined the body? I saw you—*and* heard you! Sniff—sniff—sniff. Thought you had a cold in your head.'

'You were entirely in error.'

Japp sighed.

'I always thought it was the little grey cells of the brain. Don't tell me the cells of your nose are equally superior to anyone else's.'

'No, no, calm yourself.'

'*I* didn't smell any cigarette smoke,' went on Japp suspiciously.

'No more did I, my friend.'

Japp looked at him doubtfully. Then he extracted a cigarette from his pocket.

'That's the kind Mrs Allen smoked—gaspers. Six of those stubs were hers. *The other three were Turkish.*'

'Exactly.'

'Your wonderful nose knew that without looking at them, I suppose!'

'I assure you my nose does not enter into the matter. My nose registered nothing.'

'But the brain cells registered a lot?'

'Well—there were certain indications—do you not think so?'

Japp looked at him sideways.

'Such as?'

'*Eh bien*, there was very definitely something missing from the room. Also something added, I think . . . And then, on the writing-bureau . . .'

'I knew it! We're coming to that damned quill pen!'

'*Du tout*. The quill pen plays a purely negative role.'

Japp retreated to safer ground.

'I've got Charles Laverton-West coming to see me at

Scotland Yard in half an hour. I thought you might like to be there.'

'I should very much.'

'And you'll be glad to hear we've tracked down Major Eustace. Got a service flat in the Cromwell Road.'

'Excellent.'

'And we've got a little to go on there. Not at all a nice person, Major Eustace. After I've seen Laverton-West, we'll go and see him. That suit you?'

'Perfectly.'

'Well, come along then.'

At half-past eleven, Charles Laverton-West was ushered into Chief Inspector Japp's room. Japp rose and shook hands.

The M.P. was a man of medium height with a very definite personality. He was clean-shaven, with the mobile mouth of an actor, and the slightly prominent eyes that so often go with the gift of oratory. He was good-looking in a quiet, well-bred way.

Though looking pale and somewhat distressed, his manner was perfectly formal and composed.

He took a seat, laid his gloves and hat on the table and looked towards Japp.

'I'd like to say, first of all, Mr Laverton-West, that I fully appreciate how distressing this must be to you.'

Laverton-West waved this aside.

'Do not let us discuss my feelings. Tell me, Chief

Inspector, have you any idea what caused my—Mrs Allen to take her own life?'

'You yourself cannot help us in any way?'

'No, indeed.'

'There was no quarrel? No estrangement of any kind between you?'

'Nothing of the kind. It has been the greatest shock to me.'

'Perhaps it will be more understandable, sir, if I tell you that it was not suicide—but murder!'

'Murder?' Charles Laverton-West's eyes popped nearly out of his head. 'You say *murder*?'

'Quite correct. Now, Mr Laverton-West, have you any idea who might be likely to make away with Mrs Allen?'

Laverton-West fairly spluttered out his answer.

'No—no, indeed—nothing of the sort! The mere idea is—is *unimaginable*!'

'She never mentioned any enemies? Anyone who might have a grudge against her?'

'Never.'

'Did you know that she had a pistol?'

'I was not aware of the fact.'

He looked a little startled.

'Miss Plenderleith says that Mrs Allen brought this pistol back from abroad with her some years ago.'

'Really?'

'Of course, we have only Miss Plenderleith's word for that. It is quite possible that Mrs Allen felt herself to be in danger from some source and kept the pistol handy for reasons of her own.'

Charles Laverton-West shook his head doubtfully. He seemed quite bewildered and dazed.

'What is your opinion of Miss Plenderleith, Mr Laverton-West? I mean, does she strike you as a reliable, truthful person?'

The other pondered a minute.

'I think so—yes, I should say so.'

'You don't like her?' suggested Japp, who had been watching him closely.

'I wouldn't say that. She is not the type of young woman I admire. That sarcastic, independent type is not attractive to me, but I should say she was quite truthful.'

'H'm,' said Japp. 'Do you know a Major Eustace?'

'Eustace? Eustace? Ah, yes, I remember the name. I met him once at Barbara's—Mrs Allen's. Rather a doubtful customer in my opinion. I said as much to my—to Mrs Allen. He wasn't the type of man I should have encouraged to come to the house after we were married.'

'And what did Mrs Allen say?'

'Oh! she quite agreed. She trusted my judgment implicitly. A man knows other men better than a woman can do. She explained that she couldn't very well be rude to a man whom she had not seen for some time—I think she felt especially a horror of being *snobbish*! Naturally, as my wife, she would find a good many of her old associates well—unsuitable, shall we say?'

'Meaning that in marrying you she was bettering her position?' Japp asked bluntly.

Agatha Christie

Laverton-West held up a well-manicured hand.

'No, no, not quite that. As a matter of fact, Mrs Allen's mother was a distant relation of my own family. She was fully my equal in birth. But of course, in my position, I have to be especially careful in choosing my friends—and my wife in choosing hers. One is to a certain extent in the limelight.'

'Oh, quite,' said Japp dryly. He went on, 'So you can't help us in any way?'

'No indeed. I am utterly at sea. Barbara! Murdered! It seems incredible.'

'Now, Mr Laverton-West, can you tell me what your own movements were on the night of November fifth?'

'My movements? *My* movements?'

Laverton-West's voice rose in shrill protest.

'Purely a matter of routine,' explained Japp. 'We—er—have to ask everybody.'

Charles Laverton-West looked at him with dignity.

'I should hope that a man in my position might be exempt.'

Japp merely waited.

'I was—now let me see . . . Ah, yes. I was at the House. Left at half-past ten. Went for a walk along the Embankment. Watched some of the fireworks.'

'Nice to think there aren't any plots of that kind nowadays,' said Japp cheerily.

Laverton-West gave him a fish-like stare.

'Then I—er—walked home.'

'Reaching home—your London address is Onslow Square, I think—at what time?'

'I hardly know exactly.'

'Eleven? Half-past?'

'Somewhere about then.'

'Perhaps someone let you in.'

'No, I have my key.'

'Meet anybody whilst you were walking?'

'No—er—really, Chief Inspector, I *resent* these questions very much!'

'I assure you, it's just a matter of routine, Mr Laverton-West. They aren't personal, you know.'

The reply seemed to soothe the irate M.P.

'If that is all—'

'That is all for the present, Mr Laverton-West.'

'You will keep me informed—'

'Naturally, sir. By the way, let me introduce M. Hercule Poirot. You may have heard of him.'

Mr Laverton-West's eye fastened itself interestedly on the little Belgian.

'Yes—yes—I have heard the name.'

'Monsieur,' said Poirot, his manner suddenly very foreign. 'Believe me, my heart bleeds for you. Such a loss! Such agony as you must be enduring! Ah, but I will say no more. How magnificently the English hide their emotions.' He whipped out his cigarette case. 'Permit me—Ah, it is empty. Japp?'

Japp slapped his pockets and shook his head.

Laverton-West produced his own cigarette case, murmured, 'Er—have one of mine, M. Poirot.'

'Thank you—thank you.' The little man helped himself.

'As you say, M. Poirot,' resumed the other, 'we English do not parade our emotions. A stiff upper lip—that is our motto.'

He bowed to the two men and went out.

'Bit of a stuffed fish,' said Japp disgustedly. '*And* a boiled owl! The Plenderleith girl was quite right about him. Yet he's a good-looking sort of chap—might go down well with some woman who had no sense of humour. What about that cigarette?'

Poirot handed it over, shaking his head.

'Egyptian. An expensive variety.'

'No, that's no good. A pity, for I've never heard a weaker alibi! In fact, it wasn't an alibi at all . . . You know, Poirot, it's a pity the boot wasn't on the other leg. If *she'd* been blackmailing him . . . He's a lovely type for blackmail— would pay out like a lamb! Anything to avoid a scandal.'

'My friend, it is very pretty to reconstruct the case as you would like it to be, but that is not strictly our affair.'

'No, Eustace is our affair. I've got a few lines on him. Definitely a nasty fellow.'

'By the way, did you do as I suggested about Miss Plenderleith?'

'Yes. Wait a sec, I'll ring through and get the latest.'

He picked up the telephone receiver and spoke through it.

After a brief interchange he replaced it and looked up at Poirot.

'Pretty heartless piece of goods. Gone off to play golf. That's a nice thing to do when your friend's been murdered only the day before.'

Poirot uttered an exclamation.

'What's the matter now?' asked Japp.

But Poirot was murmuring to himself.

'Of course . . . of course . . . but naturally . . . What an imbecile I am—why, it leapt to the eye!'

Japp said rudely:

'Stop jabbering to yourself and let's go and tackle Eustace.'

He was amazed to see the radiant smile that spread over Poirot's face.

'But—yes—most certainly let us tackle him. For now, see you, I know everything—but everything!'

CHAPTER 8

Major Eustace received the two men with the easy assurance of a man of the world.

His flat was small, a mere *pied à terre*, as he explained. He offered the two men a drink and when that was refused he took out his cigarette case.

Both Japp and Poirot accepted a cigarette. A quick glance passed between them.

'You smoke Turkish, I see,' said Japp as he twirled the cigarette between his fingers.

'Yes. I'm sorry, do you prefer a gasper? I've got one somewhere about.'

'No, no, this will do me very well.' Then he leaned forward—his tone changed. 'Perhaps you can guess, Major Eustace, what it was I came to see you about?'

The other shook his head. His manner was nonchalant. Major Eustace was a tall man, good-looking in a somewhat coarse fashion. There was a puffiness round the eyes—small, crafty eyes that belied the good-humoured geniality of his manner.

He said:

'No—I've no idea what brings such a big gun as a

chief inspector to see me. Anything to do with my car?'

'No, it is not your car. I think you knew a Mrs Barbara Allen, Major Eustace?'

The major leant back, puffed out a cloud of smoke, and said in an enlightened voice:

'Oh, so that's it! Of course, I might have guessed. Very sad business.'

'You know about it?'

'Saw it in the paper last night. Too bad.'

'You knew Mrs Allen out in India, I think.'

'Yes, that's some years ago now.'

'Did you also know her husband?'

There was a pause—a mere fraction of a second—but during that fraction the little pig eyes flashed a quick look at the faces of the two men. Then he answered:

'No, as a matter of fact, I never came across Allen.'

'But you know something about him?'

'Heard he was by way of being a bad hat. Of course, that was only rumour.'

'Mrs Allen did not say anything?'

'Never talked about him.'

'You were on intimate terms with her?'

Major Eustace shrugged his shoulders.

'We were old friends, you know, old friends. But we didn't see each other very often.'

'But you did see her that last evening? The evening of November fifth?'

'Yes, as a matter of fact, I did.'

'You called at her house, I think.'

Major Eustace nodded. His voice took on a gentle, regretful note.

'Yes, she asked me to advise her about some investments. Of course, I can see what you're driving at—her state of mind—all that sort of thing. Well, really, it's very difficult to say. Her manner seemed normal enough and yet she *was* a bit jumpy, come to think of it.'

'But she gave you no hint as to what she contemplated doing?'

'Not the least in the world. As a matter of fact, when I said goodbye I said I'd ring her up soon and we'd do a show together.'

'You said you'd ring her up. Those were your last words?'

'Yes.'

'Curious. I have information that you said something quite different.'

Eustace changed colour.

'Well, of course, I can't remember the exact words.'

'My information is that what you actually said was, "*Well, think it over and let me know.*"'

'Let me see, yes I believe you're right. Not exactly that. I think I was suggesting she should let me know when she was free.'

'Not quite the same thing, is it?' said Japp.

Major Eustace shrugged his shoulders.

'My dear fellow, you can't expect a man to remember word for word what he said on any given occasion.'

'And what did Mrs Allen reply?'

'She said she'd give me a ring. That is, as near as I can remember.'

'And then you said, "*All right. So long.*"'

'Probably. Something of the kind anyway.'

Japp said quietly:

'You say that Mrs Allen asked you to advise her about her investments. *Did she, by any chance, entrust you with the sum of two hundred pounds in cash to invest for her?*'

Eustace's face flushed a dark purple. He leaned forward and growled out:

'What the devil do you mean by that?'

'Did she or did she not?'

'That's my business, Mr Chief Inspector.'

Japp said quietly:

'Mrs Allen drew out the sum of two hundred pounds in cash from her bank. Some of the money was in five-pound notes. The numbers of these can, of course, be traced.'

'What if she did?'

'*Was* the money for investment—or was it—blackmail, Major Eustace?'

'That's a preposterous idea. What next will you suggest?'

Japp said in his most official manner:

'I think, Major Eustace, that at this point I must ask you if you are willing to come to Scotland Yard and make a statement. There is, of course, no compulsion and you can, if you prefer it, have your solicitor present.'

'Solicitor? What the devil should I want with a solicitor? And what are you cautioning me for?'

Agatha Christie

'I am inquiring into the circumstances of the death of Mrs Allen.'

'Good God, man, you don't suppose—Why, that's nonsense! Look here, what happened was this. I called round to see Barbara by appointment—'

'That was at what time?'

'At about half-past nine, I should say. We sat and talked—'

'And smoked?'

'Yes, and smoked. Anything damaging in that?' demanded the major belligerently.

'Where did this conversation take place?'

'In the sitting-room. Left of the door as you go in. We talked together quite amicably, as I say. I left a little before half-past ten. I stayed for a minute on the doorstep for a few last words—'

'Last words—precisely,' murmured Poirot.

'Who are *you*, I'd like to know?' Eustace turned and spat the words at him. 'Some kind of damned dago! What are *you* butting in for?'

'I am Hercule Poirot,' said the little man with dignity.

'I don't care if you are the Achilles statue. As I say, Barbara and I parted quite amicably. I drove straight to the Far East Club. Got there at five and twenty to eleven and went straight up to the card-room. Stayed there playing bridge until one-thirty. Now then, put that in your pipe and smoke it.'

'I do not smoke the pipe,' said Poirot. 'It is a pretty *alibi* you have there.'

'It should be a pretty cast iron one anyway! Now then, sir,' he looked at Japp. 'Are you satisfied?'

'You remained in the sitting-room throughout your visit?'

'Yes.'

'You did not go upstairs to Mrs Allen's own boudoir?'

'No, I tell you. We stayed in the one room and didn't leave it.'

Japp looked at him thoughtfully for a minute or two. Then he said:

'How many sets of cuff links have you?'

'Cuff links? Cuff links? What's that got to do with it?'

'You are not bound to answer the question, of course.'

'Answer it? I don't mind answering it. I've got nothing to hide. And I shall demand an apology. There are these . . .' he stretched out his arms.

Japp noted the gold and platinum with a nod.

'And I've got these.'

He rose, opened a drawer and taking out a case, he opened it and shoved it rudely almost under Japp's nose.

'Very nice design,' said the chief inspector. 'I see one is broken—bit of enamel chipped off.'

'What of it?'

'You don't remember when that happened, I suppose?'

'A day or two ago, not longer.'

'Would you be surprised to hear that it happened *when you were visiting Mrs Allen*?'

'Why shouldn't it? I've not denied that I was there.' The major spoke haughtily. He continued to bluster, to act the part of the justly indignant man, but his hands were trembling.

Japp leaned forward and said with emphasis:

'Yes, but that bit of cuff link *wasn't found in the sitting-room*. It was found *upstairs* in Mrs Allen's boudoir—there in the room where she was killed, and where a man sat smoking *the same kind of cigarettes as you smoke*.'

The shot told. Eustace fell back into his chair. His eyes went from side to side. The collapse of the bully and the appearance of the craven was not a pretty sight.

'You've got nothing on me.' His voice was almost a whine. 'You're trying to frame me . . . But you can't do it. I've got an alibi . . . I never came near the house again that night . . .'

Poirot in his turn, spoke.

'No, you did not come near the house again . . . *You did not need to* . . . For perhaps Mrs Allen *was already dead when you left it*.'

'That's impossible—impossible—She was just inside the door—she spoke to me—People must have heard her—seen her . . .'

Poirot said softly:

'They heard *you* speaking to her . . . and pretending to wait for her answer and then speaking again . . . It is an old trick that . . . People may have *assumed* she was there, but they did not *see* her, because *they could not even say whether she was wearing evening dress or not—not even mention what colour she was wearing* . . .'

'My God—it isn't true—it isn't true—'

He was shaking now—collapsed . . .

Japp looked at him with disgust. He spoke crisply.

'I'll have to ask you, sir, to come with me.'

'You're arresting me?'

'Detained for inquiry—we'll put it that way.'

The silence was broken with a long, shuddering sigh. The despairing voice of the erstwhile blustering Major Eustace said:

'I'm sunk . . .'

Hercule Poirot rubbed his hands together and smiled cheerfully. He seemed to be enjoying himself.

CHAPTER 9

'Pretty the way he went all to pieces,' said Japp with professional appreciation, later that day.

He and Poirot were driving in a car along the Brompton Road.

'He knew the game was up,' said Poirot absently.

'We've got plenty on him,' said Japp. 'Two or three different aliases, a tricky business over a cheque, and a very nice affair when he stayed at the Ritz and called himself Colonel de Bathe. Swindled half a dozen Piccadilly tradesmen. We're holding him on that charge for the moment—until we get this affair finally squared up. What's the idea of this rush to the country, old man?'

'My friend, an affair must be rounded off properly. Everything must be explained. I am on the quest of the mystery you suggested. The Mystery of the Missing Attaché-Case.'

'The Mystery of the Small Attaché-Case—that's what I called it—It isn't missing that I know of.'

'Wait, *mon ami*.'

The car turned into the mews. At the door of No. 14, Jane Plenderleith was just alighting from a small Austin Seven. She was in golfing clothes.

She looked from one to the other of the two men, then produced a key and opened the door.

'Come in, won't you?'

She led the way. Japp followed her into the sitting-room. Poirot remained for a minute or two in the hall, muttering something about:

'*C'est embêtant*—how difficult to get out of these sleeves.'

In a moment or two he also entered the sitting-room minus his overcoat but Japp's lips twitched under his moustache. He had heard the very faint squeak of an opening cupboard door.

Japp threw Poirot an inquiring glance and the other gave a hardly perceptible nod.

'We won't detain you, Miss Plenderleith,' said Japp briskly.

'Only came to ask if you could tell us the name of Mrs Allen's solicitor.'

'Her solicitor?' The girl shook her head. 'I don't even know that she had one.'

'Well, when she rented this house with you, someone must have drawn up the agreement?'

'No, I don't think so. You see, I took the house, the lease is in my name. Barbara paid me half the rent. It was quite informal.'

'I see. Oh! well, I suppose there's nothing doing then.'

'I'm sorry I can't help you,' said Jane politely.

'It doesn't really matter very much.' Japp turned towards the door. 'Been playing golf?'

'Yes.' She flushed. 'I suppose it seems rather heartless to you. But as a matter of fact it got me down rather, being

67

Agatha Christie

here in this house. I felt I must go out and *do* something—tire myself—or I'd choke!'

She spoke with intensity.

Poirot said quickly:

'I comprehend, mademoiselle. It is most understandable—most natural. To sit in this house and think—no, it would not be pleasant.'

'So long as you understand,' said Jane shortly.

'You belong to a club?'

'Yes, I play at Wentworth.'

'It has been a pleasant day,' said Poirot.

'Alas, there are few leaves left on the trees now! A week ago the woods were magnificent.'

'It was quite lovely today.'

'Good afternoon, Miss Plenderleith,' said Japp formally. 'I'll let you know when there's anything definite. As a matter of fact we have got a man detained on suspicion.'

'What man?'

She looked at them eagerly.

'Major Eustace.'

She nodded and turned away, stooping down to put a match to the fire.

'Well?' said Japp as the car turned the corner of the mews.

Poirot grinned.

'It was quite simple. The key was in the door this time.'

'And—?'

Poirot smiled.

'*Eh, bien*, the golf clubs had gone—'

68

'Naturally. The girl isn't a fool, whatever else she is. *Anything else gone?*'

Poirot nodded his head.

'Yes, my friend—*the little attaché-case!*'

The accelerator leaped under Japp's foot.

'Damnation!' he said. 'I knew there was *something*. But what the devil is it? I searched that case pretty thoroughly.'

'My poor Japp—but it is—how do you say, "obvious, my dear Watson"?'

Japp threw him an exasperated look.

'Where are we going?' he asked.

Poirot consulted his watch.

'It is not yet four o'clock. We could get to Wentworth, I think, before it is dark.'

'Do you think she really went there?'

'I think so—yes. She would know that we might make inquiries. Oh, yes, I think we will find that she has been there.'

Japp grunted.

'Oh well, come on.' He threaded his way dexterously through the traffic. 'Though what this attaché-case business has to do with the crime I can't imagine. I can't see that it's got anything at all to do with it.'

'Precisely, my friend, I agree with you—it has nothing to do with it.'

'Then why—No, don't tell me! Order and method and everything nicely rounded off! Oh, well, it's a fine day.'

The car was a fast one. They arrived at Wentworth Golf Club a little after half-past four. There was no great congestion there on a week day.

Poirot went straight to the caddie-master and asked for Miss Plenderleith's clubs. She would be playing on a different course tomorrow, he explained.

The caddie-master raised his voice and a boy sorted through some golf clubs standing in a corner. He finally produced a bag bearing the initials, J.P.

'Thank you,' said Poirot. He moved away, then turned carelessly and asked, 'She did not leave with you a small attaché-case also, did she?'

'Not today, sir. May have left it in the clubhouse.'

'She was down here today?'

'Oh, yes, I saw her.'

'Which caddie did she have, do you know? She's mislaid an attaché-case and can't remember where she had it last.'

'She didn't take a caddie. She came in here and bought a couple of balls. Just took out a couple of irons. I rather fancy she had a little case in her hand then.'

Poirot turned away with a word of thanks. The two men walked round the clubhouse. Poirot stood a moment admiring the view.

'It is beautiful, is it not, the dark pine trees—and then the lake. Yes, the lake—'

Japp gave him a quick glance.

'That's the idea, is it?'

Poirot smiled.

'I think it possible that someone may have seen something. I should set the inquiries in motion if I were you.'

CHAPTER 10

Poirot stepped back, his head a little on one side as he surveyed the arrangement of the room. A chair here—another chair there. Yes, that was very nice. And now a ring at the bell—that would be Japp.

The Scotland Yard man came in alertly.

'Quite right, old cock! Straight from the horse's mouth. A young woman was seen to throw something into the lake at Wentworth yesterday. Description of her answers to Jane Plenderleith. We managed to fish it up without much difficulty. A lot of reeds just there.'

'And it was?'

'It was the attaché-case all right! But *why*, in heaven's name? Well, it beats me! Nothing inside it—not even the magazines. Why a presumably sane young woman should want to fling an expensively-fitted dressing-case into a lake—d'you know, I worried all night because I couldn't get the hang of it.'

'*Mon pauvre Japp*! But you need worry no longer. Here is the answer coming. The bell has just rung.'

George, Poirot's immaculate man-servant, opened the door and announced:

'Miss Plenderleith.'

The girl came into the room with her usual air of complete self-assurance. She greeted the two men.

'I asked you to come here—' explained Poirot. 'Sit here, will you not, and you here, Japp—because I have certain news to give you.'

The girl sat down. She looked from one to the other, pushing aside her hat. She took it off and laid it aside impatiently.

'Well,' she said. 'Major Eustace has been arrested.'

'You saw that, I expect, in the morning paper?'

'Yes.'

'He is at the moment charged with a minor offence,' went on Poirot. 'In the meantime we are gathering evidence in connection with the murder.'

'It *was* murder, then?'

The girl asked it eagerly.

Poirot nodded his head.

'Yes,' he said. 'It was murder. The wilful destruction of one human being by another human being.'

She shivered a little.

'Don't,' she murmured. 'It sounds horrible when you say it like that.'

'Yes—but it is horrible!'

He paused—then he said:

'Now, Miss Plenderleith, I am going to tell you just how I arrived at the truth in this matter.'

She looked from Poirot to Japp. The latter was smiling.

'He has his methods, Miss Plenderleith,' he said. 'I

humour him, you know. I think we'll listen to what he has to say.'

Poirot began:

'As you know, mademoiselle, I arrived with my friend at the scene of the crime on the morning of November the sixth. We went into the room where the body of Mrs Allen had been found and I was struck at once by several significant details. There were things, you see, in that room that were decidedly odd.'

'Go on,' said the girl.

'To begin with,' said Poirot, 'there was the smell of cigarette smoke.'

'I think you're exaggerating there, Poirot,' said Japp. '*I* didn't smell anything.'

Poirot turned on him in a flash.

'Precisely. *You did not smell any stale smoke. No more did I.* And that was very, very strange—for the door and the window were both closed and on an ashtray there were the stubs of no fewer than ten cigarettes. It was odd, very odd, that the room should smell—as it did, perfectly fresh.'

'So that's what you were getting at!' Japp sighed. 'Always have to get at things in such a tortuous way.'

'Your Sherlock Holmes did the same. He drew attention, remember, to the curious incident of the dog in the night-time—and the answer to that was there was no curious incident. The dog did nothing in the night-time. To proceed:

'The next thing that attracted my attention was a wrist-watch worn by the dead woman.'

'What about it?'

'Nothing particular about it, but it was worn on the *right* wrist. Now in my experience it is more usual for a watch to be worn on the left wrist.'

Japp shrugged his shoulders. Before he could speak, Poirot hurried on:

'But as you say, there is nothing very definite about *that*. Some people *prefer* to wear one on the right hand. And now I come to something really interesting—I come, my friends, to the writing-bureau.'

'Yes, I guessed that,' said Japp.

'That was really *very* odd—*very* remarkable! For two reasons. The first reason was that something was missing from that writing-table.'

Jane Plenderleith spoke.

'What was missing?'

Poirot turned to her.

'*A sheet of blotting-paper, mademoiselle.* The blotting-book had on top a clean, untouched piece of blotting-paper.'

Jane shrugged her shoulders.

'Really, M. Poirot. People do occasionally tear off a very much used sheet!'

'Yes, but what do they do with it? Throw it into the waste-paper basket, do they not? *But it was not in the waste-paper basket. I looked.*'

Jane Plenderleith seemed impatient.

'Because it had probably been already thrown away the day before. The sheet was clean because Barbara hadn't written any letters that day.'

'That could hardly be the case, mademoiselle. *For Mrs*

Allen was seen going to the post-box that evening. Therefore she must have been writing letters. She could not write downstairs—there were no writing materials. She would be hardly likely to go to *your* room to write. So, then, what had happened to the sheet of paper on which she had blotted her letters? It is true that people sometimes throw things in the fire instead of the waste-paper basket, but there was only a gas fire in the room. *And the fire downstairs had not been alight the previous day, since you told me it was all laid ready when you put a match to it.'*

He paused.

'A curious little problem. I looked everywhere, in the waste-paper baskets, in the dustbin, but I could not find a sheet of used blotting-paper—and that seemed to me very important. It looked as though someone had deliberately taken that sheet of blotting paper away. Why? Because there was writing on it that could easily have been read by holding it up to a mirror.

'But there was a second curious point about the writing-table. Perhaps, Japp, you remember roughly the arrangement of it? Blotter and inkstand in the centre, pen tray to the left, calendar and quill pen to the right. *Eh bien?* You do not see? The quill pen, remember, I examined, it was for show only—it had not been used. Ah! *still* you do not see? I will say it again. Blotter in the centre, pen tray to the left—to the *left*, Japp. But is it not usual to find a pen tray *on the right*, convenient to *the right hand*?

'Ah, now it comes to you, does it not? The pen tray on the *left*—the wrist-watch on the *right* wrist—the

75

blotting-paper removed—and something else brought *into* the room—the ashtray with the cigarette ends!

'That room was fresh and pure smelling, Japp, a room in which the window had been *open*, not closed all night . . . And I made myself a picture.'

He spun round and faced Jane.

'A picture of you, mademoiselle, driving up in your taxi, paying it off, running up the stairs, calling perhaps, "Barbara"—and you open the door and you find your friend there lying dead with the pistol clasped in her hand—the left hand, naturally, *since she is left-handed* and therefore, too, the bullet has entered on the *left side of the head*. There is a note there addressed to you. It tells you what it is that has driven her to take her own life. It was, I fancy, a very moving letter . . . A young, gentle, unhappy woman driven by blackmail to take her life . . .

'I think that, almost at once, the idea flashed into your head. This was a certain man's doing. Let him be punished—fully and adequately punished! You take the pistol, wipe it and place it in the *right* hand. You take the note and you tear off the top sheet of the blotting-paper on which the note has been blotted. You go down, light the fire and put them both on the flames. Then you carry up the ashtray—to further the illusion that two people sat there talking—and you also take up a fragment of enamel cuff link that is on the floor. That is a lucky find and you expect it to clinch matters. Then you close the window and lock the door. There must be no suspicion that you have tampered with the room. The police must see it exactly as it is—so you do not seek help in the mews but ring up the police straightaway.

'And so it goes on. You play your chosen role with judgment and coolness. You refuse at first to say anything but cleverly you suggest doubts of suicide. Later you are quite ready to set us on the trail of Major Eustace . . .

'Yes, mademoiselle, it was clever—a very clever murder—for that is what it is. The attempted murder of Major Eustace.'

Jane Plenderleith sprang to her feet.

'It wasn't murder—it was justice. That man *hounded* poor Barbara to her death! She was so sweet and helpless. You see, poor kid, she got involved with a man in India when she first went out. She was only seventeen and he was a married man years older than her. Then she had a baby. She could have put it in a home but she wouldn't hear of that. She went off to some out of the way spot and came back calling herself Mrs Allen. Later the child died. She came back here and she fell in love with Charles—that pompous, stuffed owl; she adored him—and he took her adoration very complacently. If he had been a different kind of man I'd have advised her to tell him everything. But as it was, I urged her to hold her tongue. After all, nobody knew anything about that business except me.

'And then that devil Eustace turned up! You know the rest. He began to bleed her systematically, but it wasn't till that last evening that she realised that she was exposing Charles too, to the risk of scandal. Once married to Charles, Eustace had got her where he wanted her—married to a rich man with a horror of any scandal! When Eustace had gone with the money she had got for him she sat thinking it over. Then she came up and wrote a letter to me. She said she loved Charles and couldn't live without him, but that for his own sake she mustn't marry him. She was taking the best way out, she said.'

Jane flung her head back.

'Do you wonder I did what I did? And you stand there calling it *murder*!'

'Because it is murder,' Poirot's voice was stern. 'Murder can sometimes seem justified, *but it is murder all the same*. You are truthful and clear-minded—face the truth, mademoiselle! Your friend died, in the last resort, *because she had not the courage to live*. We may sympathize with her. We may pity her. But the fact remains—the act was *hers*—not another.'

He paused.

'And you? That man is now in prison, he will serve a long sentence for other matters. Do you really wish, of your own volition, to destroy the life—the *life*, mind— of *any* human being?'

She stared at him. Her eyes darkened. Suddenly she muttered:

'No. You're right. I don't.'

Then, turning on her heel, she went swiftly from the room. The outer door banged . . .

Japp gave a long—a very prolonged—whistle.

'Well, I'm damned!' he said.

Poirot sat down and smiled at him amiably. It was quite a long time before the silence was broken. Then Japp said:

'Not murder disguised as suicide, but suicide made to look like murder!'

'Yes, and very cleverly done, too. Nothing over-emphasized.'

Japp said suddenly:

'But the attaché-case? Where did that come in?'

'But, my dear, my very dear friend, I have already told you that *it did not come in.*'

'Then why—'

'The golf clubs. The golf clubs, Japp. *They were the golf clubs of a left-handed person.* Jane Plenderleith kept her clubs at Wentworth. Those were Barbara Allen's clubs. No wonder the girl got, as you say, the wind up when we opened that cupboard. Her whole plan might have been ruined. But she is quick, she realized that she had, for one short moment, given herself away. *She* saw that *we* saw. So she does the best thing she can think of on the spur of the moment. She tries to focus our attention on the *wrong object.* She says of the attaché-case "That's mine. I—it came back with me this morning. So there can't be anything there." And, as she hoped, away you go on the false trail. For the same reason, when she sets out the following day to get rid of the golf clubs, she continues to use the attaché-case as a—what is it—kippered herring?'

'Red herring. Do you mean that her real object was—?'

'Consider, my friend. Where is the best place to get rid of a bag of golf clubs? One cannot burn them or put them in a dustbin. If one leaves them somewhere they may be returned to you. Miss Plenderleith took them to a golf course. She leaves them in the clubhouse while she gets a couple of irons from her own bag, and then she goes round without a caddy. Doubtless at judicious intervals she breaks a club in half and throws it into some deep undergrowth, and ends by throwing the empty bag away. If anyone should find a broken golf club here and there it will not create surprise. People have been known to break and throw away *all* their clubs in a mood of intense exasperation over the game! It is, in fact, that kind of game!

'But since she realizes that her actions may still be a matter of interest, she throws that useful red herring—the attaché-case—in a somewhat spectacular manner into the lake—and that, my friend, is the truth of "The Mystery of the Attaché-Case."'

Japp looked at his friend for some moments in silence. Then he rose, clapped him on the shoulder, and burst out laughing.

'Not so bad for an old dog! Upon my word, you take the cake! Come out and have a spot of lunch?'

'With pleasure, my friend, but we will not have the cake. Indeed, an Omelette aux Champignons, Blanquette de Veau, Petits pois à la Française, and—to follow—a Baba au Rhum.'

'Lead me to it,' said Japp.

THE INCREDIBLE THEFT

CHAPTER 1

As the butler handed round the soufflé, Lord Mayfield leaned confidentially towards his neighbour on the right, Lady Julia Carrington. Known as a perfect host, Lord Mayfield took trouble to live up to his reputation. Although unmarried, he was always charming to women.

Lady Julia Carrington was a woman of forty, tall, dark and vivacious. She was very thin, but still beautiful. Her hands and feet in particular were exquisite. Her manner was abrupt and restless, that of a woman who lived on her nerves.

About opposite to her at the round table sat her husband, Air Marshal Sir George Carrington. His career had begun in the Navy, and he still retained the bluff breeziness of the ex-Naval man. He was laughing and chaffing the beautiful Mrs Vanderlyn, who was sitting on the other side of her host.

Mrs Vanderlyn was an extremely good-looking blonde. Her voice held a soupçon of American accent, just enough to be pleasant without undue exaggeration.

On the other side of Sir George Carrington sat Mrs Macatta, M.P. Mrs Macatta was a great authority on

Housing and Infant Welfare. She barked out short sentences rather than spoke them, and was generally of somewhat alarming aspect. It was perhaps natural that the Air Marshal would find his righthand neighbour the pleasanter to talk to.

Mrs Macatta, who always talked shop wherever she was, barked out short spates of information on her special subjects to her left-hand neighbour, young Reggie Carrington.

Reggie Carrington was twenty-one, and completely uninterested in Housing, Infant Welfare, and indeed any political subject. He said at intervals, 'How frightful!' and 'I absolutely agree with you,' and his mind was clearly elsewhere. Mr Carlile, Lord Mayfield's private secretary, sat between young Reggie and his mother. A pale young man with pince-nez and an air of intelligent reserve, he talked little, but was always ready to fling himself into any conversational breach. Noticing that Reggie Carrington was struggling with a yawn, he leaned forward and adroitly asked Mrs Macatta a question about her 'Fitness for Children' scheme.

Round the table, moving silently in the subdued amber light, a butler and two footmen offered dishes and filled up wine-glasses. Lord Mayfield paid a very high salary to his chef, and was noted as a connoisseur of wines.

The table was a round one, but there was no mistaking who was the host. Where Lord Mayfield sat was so very decidedly the head of the table. A big man, square-shouldered, with thick silvery hair, a big straight nose and a slightly prominent chin. It was a face that lent itself easily to caricature. As Sir Charles McLaughlin, Lord Mayfield had combined a political career with being the head of a big engineering firm. He was himself a first-class engineer. His peerage had come a year ago, and at the same time he had been created first Minister of Armaments, a new ministry which had only just come into being.

The dessert had been placed on the table. The port had circulated once. Catching Mrs Vanderlyn's eye, Lady Julia rose. The three women left the room.

The port passed once more, and Lord Mayfield referred lightly to pheasants. The conversation for five minutes or so was sporting. Then Sir George said:

'Expect you'd like to join the others in the drawing-room, Reggie, my boy. Lord Mayfield won't mind.'

The boy took the hint easily enough.

'Thanks, Lord Mayfield, I think I will.'

Mr Carlile murmured:

'If you'll excuse me, Lord Mayfield—certain memoranda and other work to get through . . .'

Lord Mayfield nodded. The two young men left the room. The servants had retired some time before. The Minister for Armaments and the head of the Air Force were alone.

After a minute or two, Carrington said:

'Well—O.K.?'

'Absolutely! There's nothing to touch this new bomber in any country in Europe.'

'Make rings round 'em, eh? That's what I thought.'

'Supremacy of the air,' said Lord Mayfield decisively.

Sir George Carrington gave a deep sigh.

'About time! You know, Charles, we've been through a ticklish spell. Lots of gunpowder everywhere all over Europe. And we weren't ready, damn it! We've had a narrow squeak. And we're not out of the wood yet, however much we hurry on construction.'

Lord Mayfield murmured:

'Nevertheless, George, there are some advantages in starting late. A lot of the European stuff is out of date already—and they're perilously near bankruptcy.'

'I don't believe that means anything,' said Sir George gloomily. 'One's always hearing this nation and that is bankrupt! But they carry on just the same. You know, finance is an absolute mystery to me.'

Lord Mayfield's eyes twinkled a little. Sir George Carrington was always so very much the old fashioned 'bluff, honest old sea dog'. There were people who said that it was a pose he deliberately adopted.

Changing the subject, Carrington said in a slightly over-casual manner:

'Attractive woman, Mrs Vanderlyn—eh?'

Lord Mayfield said:

'Are you wondering what she's doing here?'

His eyes were amused.

Carrington looked a little confused.

'Not at all—not at all.'

'Oh, yes, you were! Don't be an old humbug, George. You were wondering, in a slightly dismayed fashion, whether I was the latest victim!'

Carrington said slowly:

'I'll admit that it *did* seem a trifle odd to me that she should be here—well, this particular weekend.'

Lord Mayfield nodded.

'Where the carcass is, there are the vultures gathered together. We've got a very definite carcass, and Mrs Vanderlyn might be described as Vulture No. 1.'

The Air Marshal said abruptly:

'Know anything about this Vanderlyn woman?'

Lord Mayfield clipped off the end of a cigar, lit it with precision and, throwing his head back, dropped out his words with careful deliberation.

'What do I know about Mrs Vanderlyn? I know that she's an American subject. I know that she's had three husbands, one Italian, one German and one Russian, and that in consequence she has made useful what I think are called "contacts" in three countries. I know that she manages to buy very expensive clothes and live in a very luxurious manner, and that there is some slight uncertainty as to where the income comes from which permits her to do so.'

With a grin, Sir George Carrington murmured:

'Your spies have not been inactive, Charles, I see.'

'I know,' Lord Mayfield continued, 'that in addition to having a seductive type of beauty, Mrs Vanderlyn is also a very good listener, and that she can display a fascinating interest in what we call "shop". That is to say, a man can tell her all about his job and feel that he is being intensely interesting to the lady! Sundry young officers have gone a little too far in their zeal to be interesting, and their careers have suffered in consequence. They have told Mrs Vanderlyn a little more than they should have done. Nearly all the lady's friends are in the Services—but last winter she was hunting in a certain county near one of our largest armament firms, and she formed various friendships not at all sporting in character. To put it briefly, Mrs Vanderlyn is a very useful person to . . .' He described a circle in the air with his cigar. 'Perhaps we had better not say to whom! We will just say to a European power—and perhaps to more than one European power.'

Carrington drew a deep breath.

'You take a great load off my mind, Charles.'

'You thought I had fallen for the siren? My dear George! Mrs Vanderlyn is just a little too obvious in her methods for a wary old bird like me. Besides, she is, as they say, not quite so young as she once was. Your young squadron leaders wouldn't notice that. But I am fifty-six, my boy. In another four years I shall probably be a nasty old man continually haunting the society of unwilling debutantes.'

'I was a fool,' said Carrington apologetically, 'but it seemed a bit odd—'

'It seemed to you odd that she should be here, in a somewhat intimate family party just at the moment when you and I were to hold an unofficial conference over a discovery that will probably revolutionize the whole problem of air defence?'

Sir George Carrington nodded.

Lord Mayfield said, smiling:

'That's exactly it. That's the bait.'

'The bait?'

'You see, George, to use the language of the movies, we've nothing actually "on" the woman. And we want something! She's got away with rather more than she should in the past. But she's been careful—damnably careful. *We* know what she's been up to, but we've got no definite proof of it. We've got to tempt her with something big.'

'Something big being the specification of the new bomber?'

'Exactly. It's got to be something big enough to induce her to take a risk—to come out into the open. And then—*we've got her!*'

Sir George grunted.

'Oh, well,' he said. 'I dare say it's all right. But suppose she won't take the risk?'

'That would be a pity,' said Lord Mayfield. Then he added: 'But I think she will . . .'

He rose.

'Shall we join the ladies in the drawing-room? We mustn't deprive your wife of her bridge.'

Sir George grunted:

'Julia's a damned sight too fond of her bridge. Drops a packet over it. She can't afford to play as high as she does, and I've told her so. The trouble is, Julia's a born gambler.'

Coming round the table to join his host, he said:

'Well, I hope your plan comes off, Charles.'

CHAPTER 2

In the drawing-room conversation had flagged more than once. Mrs Vanderlyn was usually at a disadvantage when left alone with members of her own sex. That charming sympathetic manner of hers, so much appreciated by members of the male sex, did not for some reason or other commend itself to women. Lady Julia was a woman whose manners were either very good or very bad. On this occasion she disliked Mrs Vanderlyn, and was bored by Mrs Macatta, and made no secret of her feelings. Conversation languished, and might have ceased altogether but for the latter.

Mrs Macatta was a woman of great earnestness of purpose. Mrs Vanderlyn she dismissed immediately as a useless and parasitic type. Lady Julia she tried to interest in a forthcoming charity entertainment which she was organizing. Lady Julia answered vaguely, stifled a yawn or two and retired into her own inner preoccupation. Why didn't Charles and George come? How tiresome men were. Her comments became even more perfunctory as she became absorbed in her own thoughts and worries.

The three women were sitting in silence when the men finally entered the room.

Lord Mayfield thought to himself:

'Julia looks ill tonight. What a mass of nerves the woman is.'

Aloud he said:

'What about a rubber—eh?'

Lady Julia brightened at once. Bridge was as the breath of life to her.

Reggie Carrington entered the room at that minute, and a four was arranged. Lady Julia, Mrs Vanderlyn, Sir George and young Reggie sat down to the card-table. Lord Mayfield devoted himself to the task of entertaining Mrs Macatta.

When two rubbers had been played, Sir George looked ostentatiously at the clock on the mantelpiece.

'Hardly worth while beginning another,' he remarked.

His wife looked annoyed.

'It's only a quarter to eleven. A short one.'

'They never are, my dear,' said Sir George good-temperedly. 'Anyway, Charles and I have some work to do.'

Mrs Vanderlyn murmured:

'How important that sounds! I suppose you clever men who are at the top of things never get a real rest.'

'No forty-eight hour week for us,' said Sir George.

Mrs Vanderlyn murmured:

'You know, I feel rather ashamed of myself as a raw American, but I do get so *thrilled* at meeting people who control the destinies of a country. I expect that seems a very crude point of view to you, Sir George.'

'My dear Mrs Vanderlyn, I should never think of you as "crude" or "raw."'

He smiled into her eyes. There was, perhaps, a hint of irony in the voice which she did not miss. Adroitly she turned to Reggie, smiling sweetly into his eyes.

'I'm sorry we're not continuing our partnership. That was a frightfully clever four no-trump call of yours.'

Flushed and pleased, Reggie mumbled:

'Bit of a fluke that it came off.'

'Oh, no, it was really a clever bit of deduction on your part. You'd deduced from the bidding exactly where the cards must be, and you played accordingly. I thought it was brilliant.'

Lady Julia rose abruptly.

'The woman lays it on with a palette-knife,' she thought disgustedly.

Then her eyes softened as they rested on her son. He believed it all. How pathetically young and pleased he looked. How incredibly naïve he was. No wonder he got into scrapes. He was too trusting. The truth of it was he had too sweet a nature. George didn't understand him in the least. Men were so unsympathetic in their judgments. They forgot that they had ever been young themselves. George was much too harsh with Reggie.

Mrs Macatta had risen. Goodnights were said.

The three women went out of the room. Lord Mayfield helped himself to a drink after giving one to Sir George, then he looked up as Mr Carlile appeared at the door.

'Get out the files and all the papers, will you, Carlile? Including the plans and the prints. The Air Marshal and I will be along shortly. We'll just take a turn outside first, eh, George? It's stopped raining.'

Mr Carlile, turning to depart, murmured an apology as he almost collided with Mrs Vanderlyn.

She drifted towards them, murmuring:

'My book, I was reading it before dinner.'

Reggie sprang forward and held up a book.

'Is this it? On the sofa?'

'Oh, yes. Thank you *so* much.'

She smiled sweetly, said goodnight again and went out of the room.

Sir George had opened one of the french windows.

'Beautiful night now,' he announced. 'Good idea of yours to take a turn.'

Reggie said:

'Well, goodnight, sir. I'll be toddling off to bed.'

'Goodnight, my boy,' said Lord Mayfield.

Reggie picked up a detective story which he had begun earlier in the evening and left the room.

Lord Mayfield and Sir George stepped out upon the terrace.

It was a beautiful night, with a clear sky studded with stars.

Sir George drew a deep breath.

'Phew, that woman uses a lot of scent,' he remarked.

Lord Mayfield laughed.

'Anyway, it's not cheap scent. One of the most expensive brands on the market, I should say.'

Sir George gave a grimace.

'I suppose one should be thankful for that.'

'You should, indeed. I think a woman smothered in

cheap scent is one of the greatest abominations known to mankind.'

Sir George glanced up at the sky.

'Extraordinary the way it's cleared. I heard the rain beating down when we were at dinner.'

The two men strolled gently along the terrace.

The terrace ran the whole length of the house. Below it the ground sloped gently away, permitting a magnificent view over the Sussex weald.

Sir George lit a cigar.

'About this metal alloy—' he began.

The talk became technical.

As they approached the far end of the terrace for the fifth time, Lord Mayfield said with a sigh:

'Oh, well, I suppose we'd better get down to it.'

'Yes, good bit of work to get through.'

The two men turned, and Lord Mayfield uttered a surprised ejaculation.

'Hallo! See that?'

'See what?' asked Sir George.

'Thought I saw someone slip across the terrace from my study window.'

'Nonsense, old boy. I didn't see anything.'

'Well, I did—or I thought I did.'

'Your eyes are playing tricks on you. I was looking straight down the terrace, and I'd have seen anything there was to be seen. There's precious little *I* don't see—even if I do have to hold a newspaper at arm's length.'

Lord Mayfield chuckled.

'I can put one over on you there, George. I read easily without glasses.'

'But you can't always distinguish the fellow on the other side of the House. Or is that eyeglass of yours sheer intimidation?'

Laughing, the two men entered Lord Mayfield's study, the french window of which was open.

Mr Carlile was busy arranging some papers in a file by the safe.

He looked up as they entered.

'Ha, Carlile, everything ready?'

'Yes, Lord Mayfield, all the papers are on your desk.'

The desk in question was a big important-looking writing-table of mahogany set across a corner by the window. Lord Mayfield went over to it, and began sorting through the various documents laid out.

'Lovely night now,' said Sir George.

Mr Carlile agreed.

'Yes, indeed. Remarkable the way it's cleared up after the rain.'

Putting away his file, Mr Carlile asked:

'Will you want me any more tonight, Lord Mayfield?'

'No, I don't think so, Carlile. I'll put all these away myself. We shall probably be late. You'd better turn in.'

'Thank you. Goodnight, Lord Mayfield. Goodnight, Sir George.'

'Goodnight, Carlile.'

As the secretary was about to leave the room, Lord Mayfield said sharply:

'Just a minute, Carlile. You've forgotten the most important of the lot.'

'I beg your pardon, Lord Mayfield.'

'The actual plans of the bomber, man.'

The secretary stared.

'They're right on the top, sir.'

'They're nothing of the sort.'

'But I've just put them there.'

'Look for yourself, man.'

With a bewildered expression, the young man came forward and joined Lord Mayfield at the desk.

Somewhat impatiently the Minister indicated the pile of papers. Carlile sorted through them, his expression of bewilderment growing.

'You see, they're not there.'

The secretary stammered:

'But—but it's incredible. I laid them there not three minutes ago.'

Lord Mayfield said good-humouredly:

'You must have made a mistake, they must be still in the safe.'

'I don't see how—I *know* I put them there!'

Lord Mayfield brushed past him to the open safe. Sir George joined them. A very few minutes sufficed to show that the plans of the bomber were not there.

Dazed and unbelieving, the three men returned to the desk and once more turned over the papers.

'My God!' said Mayfield. 'They're gone!'

Mr Carlile cried:

'But it's impossible!'

'Who's been in this room?' snapped out the Minister.

'No one. No one at all.'

'Look here, Carlile, those plans haven't vanished into thin air. Someone has taken them. Has Mrs Vanderlyn been in here?'

'Mrs Vanderlyn? Oh, no, sir.'

'I'll back that,' said Carrington. He sniffed the air! 'You'd soon smell if she had. That scent of hers.'

'Nobody has been in here,' insisted Carlile. 'I can't understand it.'

'Look here, Carlile,' said Lord Mayfield. 'Pull yourself together. We've got to get to the bottom of this. You're absolutely sure the plans were in the safe?'

'Absolutely.'

'You actually saw them? You didn't just assume they were among the others?'

'No, no, Lord Mayfield. I saw them. I put them on top of the others on the desk.'

'And since then, you say, nobody has been in the room. Have you been out of the room?'

'No—at least—yes.'

'Ah!' cried Sir George. 'Now we're getting at it!'

Lord Mayfield said sharply:

'What on earth—' when Carlile interrupted.

'In the normal course of events, Lord Mayfield, I should not, of course, have dreamt of leaving the room when

97

important papers were lying about, but hearing a woman scream—'

'A woman scream?' ejaculated Lord Mayfield in a surprised voice.

'Yes, Lord Mayfield. It startled me more than I can say. I was just laying the papers on the desk when I heard it, and naturally I ran out into the hall.'

'Who screamed?'

'Mrs Vanderlyn's French maid. She was standing half-way up the stairs, looking very white and upset and shaking all over. She said she had seen a ghost.'

'Seen a ghost?'

'Yes, a tall woman dressed all in white who moved without a sound and floated in the air.'

'What a ridiculous story!'

'Yes, Lord Mayfield, that is what I told her. I must say she seemed rather ashamed of herself. She went off upstairs and I came back in here.'

'How long ago was this?'

'Just a minute or two before you and Sir George came in.'

'And you were out of the room—how long?'

The secretary considered.

'Two minutes—at the most three.'

'Long enough,' groaned Lord Mayfield. Suddenly he clutched his friend's arm.

'George, that shadow I saw—slinking away from this window. That was it! As soon as Carlile left the room, he nipped in, seized the plans and made off.'

'Dirty work,' said Sir George.

Then he seized his friend by the arm.

'Look here, Charles, this is the devil of a business. What the hell are we going to do about it?'

CHAPTER 3

'At any rate give it a trial, Charles.'

It was half an hour later. The two men were in Lord Mayfield's study, and Sir George had been expending a considerable amount of persuasion to induce his friend to adopt a certain course.

Lord Mayfield, at first most unwilling, was gradually becoming less averse to the idea.

Sir George went on:

'Don't be so damned pig-headed, Charles.'

Lord Mayfield said slowly:

'Why drag in a wretched foreigner we know nothing about?'

'But I happen to know a lot about him. The man's a marvel.'

'Humph.'

'Look here, Charles. It's a chance! Discretion is the essence of this business. If it leaks out—'

'*When* it leaks out is what you mean!'

'Not necessarily. This man, Hercule Poirot—'

'Will come down here and produce the plans like a conjurer taking rabbits out of his hat, I suppose?'

'He'll get at the truth. And the truth is what we want. Look here, Charles, I take all responsibility on myself.'

Lord Mayfield said slowly:

'Oh, well, have it your own way, but I don't see what the fellow can do . . .'

Sir George picked up the phone.

'I'm going to get through to him—now.'

'He'll be in bed.'

'He can get up. Dash it all, Charles, you can't let that woman get away with it.'

'Mrs Vanderlyn, you mean?'

'Yes. You don't doubt, do you, that she's at the bottom of this?'

'No, I don't. She's turned the tables on me with a vengeance. I don't like admitting, George, that a woman's been too clever for us. It goes against the grain. But it's true. We shan't be able to prove anything against her, and yet we both know that she's been the prime mover in the affair.'

'Women are the devil,' said Carrington with feeling.

'Nothing to connect her with it, damn it all! We may believe that she put the girl up to that screaming trick, and that the man lurking outside was her accomplice, but the devil of it is we can't prove it.'

'Perhaps Hercule Poirot can.'

Suddenly Lord Mayfield laughed.

'By the Lord, George, I thought you were too much of an old John Bull to put your trust in a Frenchman, however clever.'

'He's not even a Frenchman, he's a Belgian,' said Sir George in a rather shamefaced manner.

'Well, have your Belgian down. Let him try his wits on this business. I'll bet he can't make more of it than we can.'

Without replying, Sir George stretched a hand to the telephone.

CHAPTER 4

Blinking a little, Hercule Poirot turned his head from one man to the other. Very delicately he smothered a yawn.

It was half-past two in the morning. He had been roused from sleep and rushed down through the darkness in a big Rolls Royce. Now he had just finished hearing what the two men had to tell him.

'Those are the facts, M. Poirot,' said Lord Mayfield.

He leaned back in his chair, and slowly fixed his monocle in one eye. Through it a shrewd, pale-blue eye watched Poirot attentively. Besides being shrewd the eye was definitely sceptical. Poirot cast a swift glance at Sir George Carrington.

That gentleman was leaning forward with an expression of almost childlike hopefulness on his face.

Poirot said slowly:

'I have the facts, yes. The maid screams, the secretary goes out, the nameless watcher comes in, the plans are there on top of the desk, he snatches them up and goes. The facts—they are all very convenient.'

Something in the way he uttered the last phrase seemed to attract Lord Mayfield's attention. He sat up a little straighter, his monocle dropped. It was as though a new alertness came to him.

'I beg your pardon, M. Poirot?'

'I said, Lord Mayfield, that the facts were all very convenient—for the thief. By the way, you are sure it was a *man* you saw?'

Lord Mayfield shook his head.

'That I couldn't say. It was just a—shadow. In fact, I was almost doubtful if I had seen anyone.'

Poirot transferred his gaze to the Air Marshal.

'And you, Sir George? Could you say if it was a man or a woman?'

'I didn't see anyone myself.'

Poirot nodded thoughtfully. Then he skipped suddenly to his feet and went over to the writing-table.

'I can assure you that the plans are not there,' said Lord Mayfield. 'We have all three been through those papers half a dozen times.'

'All three? You mean, your secretary also?'

'Yes, Carlile.'

Poirot turned suddenly.

'Tell me, Lord Mayfield, which paper was on top when you went over to the desk?'

Mayfield frowned a little in the effort of remembrance.

'Let me see—yes, it was a rough memorandum of some sort of our air defence positions.'

Deftly, Poirot nipped out a paper and brought it over.

'Is this the one, Lord Mayfield?'

Lord Mayfield took it and glanced over it.

'Yes, that's the one.'

Poirot took it over to Carrington.

'Did you notice this paper on the desk?'

Sir George took it, held it away from him, then slipped on his pince-nez.

'Yes, that's right. I looked through them too, with Carlile and Mayfield. This was on top.'

Poirot nodded thoughtfully. He replaced the paper on the desk. Mayfield looked at him in a slightly puzzled manner.

'If there are any other questions—' he began.

'But yes, certainly there is a question. Carlile. Carlile is the question!'

Lord Mayfield's colour rose a little.

'Carlile, M. Poirot, is quite above suspicion! He has been my confidential secretary for nine years. He has access to all my private papers, and I may point out to you that he could have made a copy of the plans and a tracing of the specifications quite easily without anyone being the wiser.'

'I appreciate your point,' said Poirot. 'If he had been guilty there would be no need for him to stage a clumsy robbery.'

'In any case,' said Lord Mayfield, 'I am sure of Carlile. I will guarantee him.'

'Carlile,' said Carrington gruffly, 'is all right.'

Poirot spread out his hands gracefully.

'And this Mrs Vanderlyn—she is all wrong?'

'She's a wrong 'un all right,' said Sir George.

Lord Mayfield said in more measured tones:

'I think, M. Poirot, that there can be no doubt of Mrs Vanderlyn's—well—activities. The Foreign Office can give you more precious data as to that.'

'And the maid, you take it, is in with her mistress?'

'Not a doubt of it,' said Sir George.

'It seems to me a plausible assumption,' said Lord Mayfield more cautiously.

There was a pause. Poirot sighed, and absent-mindedly rearranged one or two articles on a table at his right hand. Then he said:

'I take it that these papers represented money? That is, the stolen papers would be definitely worth a large sum in cash.'

'If presented in a certain quarter—yes.'

'Such as?'

Sir George mentioned the names of two European powers.

Poirot nodded.

'That fact would be known to anyone, I take it?'

'Mrs Vanderlyn would know it all right.'

'I said to *anyone*?'

'I suppose so, yes.'

'Anyone with a minimum of intelligence would appreciate the cash value of the plans?'

'Yes, but M. Poirot—' Lord Mayfield was looking rather uncomfortable.

Poirot held up a hand.

'I do what you call explore all the avenues.'

Suddenly he rose again, stepped nimbly out of the

window and with a flashlight examined the edge of the grass at the farther side of the terrace.

The two men watched him.

He came in again, sat down and said:

'Tell me, Lord Mayfield, this malefactor, this skulker in the shadows, you do not have him pursued?'

Lord Mayfield shrugged his shoulders.

'At the bottom of the garden he could make his way out to a main road. If he had a car waiting there, he would soon be out of reach—'

'But there are the police—the A.A. scouts—'

Sir George interrupted.

'You forget, M. Poirot. *We cannot risk publicity.* If it were to get out that these plans had been stolen, the result would be extremely unfavourable to the Party.'

'Ah, yes,' said Poirot. 'One must remember *La Politique*. The great discretion must be observed. You send instead for me. Ah well, perhaps it is simpler.'

'You are hopeful of success, M. Poirot?' Lord Mayfield sounded a trifle incredulous.

The little man shrugged his shoulders.

'Why not? One has only to reason—to reflect.'

He paused a moment and then said:

'I would like now to speak to Mr Carlile.'

'Certainly.' Lord Mayfield rose. 'I asked him to wait up. He will be somewhere at hand.'

He went out of the room.

Poirot looked at Sir George.

'*Eh bien*,' he said. 'What about this man on the terrace?'

'My dear M. Poirot. Don't ask me! I didn't see him, and I can't describe him.'

Poirot leaned forward.

'So you have already said. But it is a little different from that is it not?'

'What d'you mean?' asked Sir George abruptly.

'How shall I say it? Your disbelief, it is more profound.'

Sir George started to speak, then stopped.

'But yes,' said Poirot encouragingly. 'Tell me. You are both at the end of the terrace. Lord Mayfield sees a shadow slip from the window and across the grass. Why do you not see that shadow?'

Carrington stared at him.

'You've hit it, M. Poirot. I've been worrying about that ever since. You see, I'd swear that no one did leave this window. I thought Mayfield had imagined it—branch of a tree waving—something of that kind. And then when we came in here and found there had been a robbery, it seemed as though Mayfield must have been right and I'd been wrong. And yet—'

Poirot smiled.

'And yet you still in your heart of hearts believe in the evidence (the negative evidence) of your own eyes?'

'You're right, M. Poirot, I do.'

Poirot gave a sudden smile.

'How wise you are.'

Sir George said sharply:

'There were no footprints on the grass edge?'

Poirot nodded.

'Exactly. Lord Mayfield, he fancies he sees a shadow. Then there comes the robbery and he is sure—but sure! It is no longer a fancy—he actually *saw* the man. But that is not so. Me, I do not concern myself much with footprints and such things but for what it is worth we have that negative evidence. *There were no footprints on the grass.* It had rained heavily this evening. If a man had crossed the terrace to the grass this evening his footprints would have shown.'

Sir George said, staring: 'But then—but then—'

'It brings us back to the house. To the people in the house.'

He broke off as the door opened and Lord Mayfield entered with Mr Carlile.

Though still looking very pale and worried, the secretary had regained a certain composure of manner. Adjusting his pince-nez he sat down and looked at Poirot inquiringly.

'How long had you been in this room when you heard the scream, monsieur?'

Carlile considered.

'Between five and ten minutes, I should say.'

'And before that there had been no disturbance of any kind?'

'No.'

'I understand that the house-party had been in one room for the greater part of the evening.'

'Yes, the drawing-room.'

Poirot consulted his notebook.

'Sir George Carrington and his wife. Mrs Macatta.

Mrs Vanderlyn. Mr Reggie Carrington. Lord Mayfield and yourself. Is that right?'

'I myself was not in the drawing-room. I was working here the greater part of the evening.'

Poirot turned to Lord Mayfield.

'Who went up to bed first?'

'Lady Julia Carrington, I think. As a matter of fact, the three ladies went out together.'

'And then?'

'Mr Carlile came in and I told him to get out the papers as Sir George and I would be along in a minute.'

'It was then that you decided to take a turn on the terrace?'

'It was.'

'Was anything said in Mrs Vanderlyn's hearing as to your working in the study?'

'The matter was mentioned, yes.'

'But she was not in the room when you instructed Mr Carlile to get out the papers?'

'No.'

'Excuse me, Lord Mayfield,' said Carlile. 'Just after you had said that, I collided with her in the doorway. She had come back for a book.'

'So you think she might have overheard?'

'I think it quite possible, yes.'

'She came back for a book,' mused Poirot. 'Did you find her her book, Lord Mayfield?'

'Yes, Reggie gave it to her.'

'Ah, yes, it is what you call the old gasp—no, pardon,

the old wheeze—that—to come back for a book. It is often useful!'

'You think it was deliberate?'

Poirot shrugged his shoulders.

'And after that, you two gentlemen go out on the terrace. And Mrs Vanderlyn?'

'She went off with her book.'

'And the young M. Reggie. He went to bed also?'

'Yes.'

'And Mr Carlile he comes here and sometime between five and ten minutes later he heard a scream. Continue, M. Carlile. You heard a scream and you went out into the hall. Ah, perhaps it would be simplest if you reproduced exactly your actions.'

Mr Carlile got up a little awkwardly.

'Here I scream,' said Poirot helpfully. He opened his mouth and emitted a shrill bleat. Lord Mayfield turned his head away to hide a smile and Mr Carlile looked extremely uncomfortable.

'*Allez!* Forward! March!' cried Poirot. 'It is your cue that I give you there.'

Mr Carlile walked stiffly to the door, opened it and went out. Poirot followed him. The other two came behind.

'The door, did you close it after you or leave it open?'

'I can't really remember. I think I must have left it open.'

'No matter. Proceed.'

Still with extreme stiffness, Mr Carlile walked to the bottom of the staircase and stood there looking up.

Poirot said:

'The maid, you say, was on the stairs. Whereabouts?'

'About half-way up.'

'And she was looking upset.'

'Definitely so.'

'*Eh bien*, me, I am the maid.' Poirot ran nimbly up the stairs. 'About here?'

'A step or two higher.'

'Like this?'

Poirot struck an attitude.

'Well—er—not quite like that.'

'How then?'

'Well, she had her hands to her head.'

'Ah, her hands to her *head*. That is very interesting. Like this?' Poirot raised his arms, his hands rested on his head just above each ear.

'Yes that's it.'

'Aha! And tell me, M. Carlile, she was a pretty girl—yes?'

'Really, I didn't notice.'

Carlile's voice was repressive.

'Aha, you did not notice? But you are a young man. Does not a young man notice when a girl is pretty?'

'Really, M. Poirot, I can only repeat that *I* did not do so.'

Carlile cast an agonized glance at his employer. Sir George Carrington gave a sudden chuckle.

'M. Poirot seems determined to make you out a gay dog, Carlile,' he remarked.

Mr Carlile gave him a cold glance.

'Me, I always notice when a girl is pretty,' announced Poirot as he descended the stairs.

The silence with which Mr Carlile greeted this remark was somewhat pointed. Poirot went on:

'And it was then she told this tale of having seen a ghost?'

'Yes.'

'Did you believe the story?'

'Well, hardly, M. Poirot!'

'I do not mean, do you believe in ghosts. I mean, did it strike you that the girl herself really thought she had seen something?'

'Oh, as to that, I couldn't say. She was certainly breathing fast and seemed upset.'

'You did not see or hear anything of her mistress?'

'Yes, as a matter of fact I did. She came out of her room in the gallery above and called, "Leonie."'

'And then?'

'The girl ran up to her and I went back to the study.'

'Whilst you were standing at the foot of the stairs here, could anyone have entered the study by the door you had left open?'

Carlile shook his head.

'Not without passing me. The study door is at the end of the passage, as you see.'

Poirot nodded thoughtfully. Mr Carlile went on in his careful, precise voice.

'I may say that I am very thankful that Lord Mayfield actually saw the thief leaving the window. Otherwise I myself should be in a very unpleasant position.'

'Nonsense, my dear Carlile,' broke in Lord Mayfield impatiently. 'No suspicion could possibly attach to you.'

'It is very kind of you to say so, Lord Mayfield, but facts are facts, and I can quite see that it looks badly for me. In any case I hope that my belongings and myself may be searched.'

'Nonsense, my dear fellow,' said Mayfield.

Poirot murmured:

'You are serious in wishing that?'

'I should infinitely prefer it.'

Poirot looked at him thoughtfully for a minute or two and murmured, 'I see.'

Then he asked:

'Where is Mrs Vanderlyn's room situated in regard to the study?'

'It is directly over it.'

'With a window looking out over the terrace?'

'Yes.'

Again Poirot nodded. Then he said:

'Let us go to the drawing-room.'

Here he wandered round the room, examined the fastenings of the windows, glanced at the scorers on the bridge table and then finally addressed Lord Mayfield.

'This affair,' he said, 'is more complicated than it appears. But one thing is quite certain. The stolen plans have not left this house.'

Lord Mayfield stared at him.

'But, my dear M. Poirot, the man I saw leaving the study—'

'There was no man.'

'But I *saw* him—'

'With the greatest respect, Lord Mayfield, you imagined you saw him. The shadow cast by the branch of a tree deceived you. The fact that a robbery occurred naturally seemed a proof that what you had imagined was true.'

'Really, M. Poirot, the evidence of my own eyes—'

'Back my eyes against yours any day, old boy,' put in Sir George.

'You must permit me, Lord Mayfield, to be very definite on that point. *No one crossed the terrace to the grass.*'

Looking very pale and speaking stiffly, Mr Carlile said:

'In that case, if M. Poirot is correct, suspicion automatically attaches itself to me. I am the only person who could possibly have committed the robbery.'

Lord Mayfield sprang up.

'Nonsense. Whatever M. Poirot thinks about it, I don't agree with him. I am convinced of your innocence, my dear Carlile. In fact, I'm willing to guarantee it.'

Poirot murmured mildly:

'But I have not said that I suspect M. Carlile.'

Carlile answered:

'No, but you've made it perfectly clear that no one else had a chance to commit the robbery.'

'*Du tout! Du tout!*'

'But I have told you nobody passed me in the hall to get to the study door.'

'I agree. But someone might have come in through the study *window.*'

'But that is just what you said did not happen?'

'I said that no one from *outside* could have come and

115

left without leaving marks on the grass. But it could have been managed from *inside* the house. Someone could have gone out from his room by one of these windows, slipped along the terrace, in at the study window, and back again in here.'

Mr Carlile objected:

'But Lord Mayfield and Sir George Carrington were on the terrace.'

'They were on the terrace, yes, but they were *en prom-enade*. Sir George Carrington's eyes may be of the most reliable'—Poirot made a little bow—'but he does not keep them in the back of his head! The study window is at the extreme left of the terrace, the windows of this room come next, but the terrace continues to the right past one, two, three, perhaps four rooms?'

'Dining-room, billiard-room, morning room and library,' said Lord Mayfield.

'And you walked up and down the terrace, how many times?'

'At least five or six.'

'You see, it is easy enough, the thief has only to watch for the right moment!'

Carlile said slowly:

'You mean that when I was in the hall, talking to the French girl, the thief was waiting in the drawing-room?'

'That is my suggestion. It is, of course, only a suggestion.'

'It doesn't sound very probable to me,' said Lord Mayfield. 'Too risky.'

The Air Marshal demurred.

'I don't agree with you, Charles. It's perfectly possible. Wonder I hadn't the wits to think of it for myself.'

'So you see,' said Poirot, 'why I believe that the plans are still in the house. The problem now is to find them!'

Sir George snorted.

'That's simple enough. Search everybody.'

Lord Mayfield made a movement of dissent, but Poirot spoke before he could.

'No, no, it is not so simple as that. The person who took those plans will anticipate that a search will be made and will make quite sure that they are not found amongst his or her belongings. They will have been hidden in neutral ground.'

'Do you suggest that we've got to go playing hide and seek all over the bally house?'

Poirot smiled.

'No, no, we need not be so crude as that. We can arrive at the hiding-place (or alternatively at the identity of the guilty person) by reflection. That will simplify matters. In the morning I would like an interview with every person in the house. It would, I think, be unwise to seek those interviews now.'

Lord Mayfield nodded.

'Cause too much comment,' he said, 'if we dragged everybody out of their beds at three in the morning. In any case you'll have to proceed with a good deal of camouflage, M. Poirot. This matter has got to be kept dark.'

Poirot waved an airy hand.

'Leave it to Hercule Poirot. The lies I invent are always most delicate and most convincing. Tomorrow, then, I conduct my investigations. But tonight, I should like to begin by interviewing you, Sir George and you, Lord Mayfield.'

He bowed to them both.

'You mean—alone?'

'That was my meaning.'

Lord Mayfield raised his eyes slightly, then he said:

'Certainly. I'll leave you alone with Sir George. When you want me, you'll find me in my study. Come, Carlile.'

He and the secretary went out, shutting the door behind them.

Sir George sat down, reaching mechanically for a cigarette. He turned a puzzled face to Poirot.

'You know,' he said slowly. 'I don't quite get this.'

'That is very simply explained,' said Poirot with a smile. 'In two words, to be accurate. Mrs Vanderlyn!'

'Oh,' said Carrington. 'I think I see. Mrs Vanderlyn?'

'Precisely. It might be, you see, that it would not be very delicate to ask Lord Mayfield the question I want to ask. *Why* Mrs Vanderlyn? This lady, she is known to be a suspicious character. Why, then, should she be here? I say to myself there are three explanations. One, that Lord Mayfield has a *penchant* for the lady (and that is why I seek to talk to you alone. I do not wish to embarrass him). Two, that Mrs Vanderlyn is perhaps the dear friend of someone else in the house?'

'You can count me out!' said Sir George with a grin.

'Then, if neither of those cases is true, the question returns in redoubled force. *Why Mrs Vanderlyn?* And it seems to me I perceive a shadowy answer. There was a *reason*. Her presence at this particular juncture was definitely desired by Lord Mayfield for a special reason. Am I right?'

Sir George nodded.

'You're quite right,' he said. 'Mayfield is too old a bird to fall for her wiles. He wanted her here for quite another reason. It was like this.'

He retailed the conversation that had taken place at the dinner-table. Poirot listened attentively.

'Ah,' he said. 'I comprehend now. Nevertheless, it seems that the lady has turned the tables on you both rather neatly!'

Sir George swore freely.

Poirot watched him with some slight amusement, then he said:

'You do not doubt that this theft is her doing—I mean, that she is responsible for it, whether or no she played an active part?'

Sir George stared.

'Of course not! There isn't any doubt of that. Why, who else would have any interest in stealing those plans?'

'Ah!' said Hercule Poirot. He leaned back and looked at the ceiling. 'And yet, Sir George, we agreed, not a quarter of an hour ago, that these papers represented very definitely money. Not perhaps, in quite so obvious a form as banknotes, or gold, or jewellery, but nevertheless they were potential money. If there were anyone here who was hard up—'

The other interrupted him with a snort.

'Who isn't these days? I suppose I can say it without incriminating myself.'

He smiled and Poirot smiled politely back at him and murmured:

'*Mais oui*, you can say what you like, for you, Sir George, have the one unimpeachable alibi in this affair.'

'But I'm damned hard up myself!'

Poirot shook his head sadly.

'Yes, indeed, a man in your position has heavy living expenses. Then you have a young son at a most expensive age—'

Sir George groaned.

'Education's bad enough, then debts on top of it. Mind you, this lad's not a bad lad.'

Poirot listened sympathetically. He heard a lot of the Air Marshal's accumulated grievances. The lack of grit and stamina in the younger generation, the fantastic way in which mothers spoilt their children and always took their side, the curse of gambling once it got hold of a woman, the folly of playing for higher stakes than you could afford. It was couched in general terms, Sir George did not allude directly to either his wife or his son, but his natural transparency made his generalizations very easy to see through.

He broke off suddenly.

'Sorry, mustn't take up your time with something that's

right off the subject, especially at this hour of the night—
or rather, morning.'

He stifled a yawn.

'I suggest, Sir George, that you should go to bed. You
have been most kind and helpful.'

'Right, think I will turn in. You really think there is a
chance of getting the plans back?'

Poirot shrugged his shoulders.

'I mean to try. I do not see why not.'

'Well, I'll be off. Goodnight.'

He left the room.

Poirot remained in his chair staring thoughtfully at the
ceiling, then he took out a little notebook and turning to
a clean page, he wrote:

> *Mrs Vanderlyn?*
> *Lady Julia Carrington?*
> *Mrs Macatta?*
> *Reggie Carrington?*
> *Mr Carlile?*

Underneath he wrote:

> *Mrs Vanderlyn and Mr Reggie Carrington?*
> *Mrs Vanderlyn and Lady Julia?*
> *Mrs Vanderlyn and Mr Carlile?*

He shook his head in a dissatisfied manner, murmuring:
'*C'est plus simple que ça.*'

Agatha Christie

Then he added a few short sentences.

Did Lord Mayfield see a 'shadow'? If not, why did he say he did? Did Sir George see anything? He was positive he had seen nothing AFTER I examined flower-bed. Note: Lord Mayfield is near-sighted, can read without glasses but has to use a monocle to look across a room. Sir George is long-sighted. Therefore, from the far end of the terrace, his sight is more to be depended upon than Lord Mayfield's. Yet Lord Mayfield is very positive that he DID see something and is quite unshaken by his friend's denial.

Can anyone be quite as above suspicion as Mr Carlile appears to be? Lord Mayfield is very emphatic as to his innocence. Too much so. Why? Because he secretly suspects him and is ashamed of his suspicions? Or because he definitely suspects some other person? That is to say, some person OTHER than Mrs Vanderlyn?

He put the notebook away.
Then, getting up, he went along to the study.

CHAPTER 5

Lord Mayfield was seated at his desk when Poirot entered the study. He swung round, laid down his pen, and looked up inquiringly.

'Well, M. Poirot, had your interview with Carrington?'

Poirot smiled and sat down.

'Yes, Lord Mayfield. He cleared up a point that had puzzled me.'

'What was that?'

'The reason for Mrs Vanderlyn's presence here. You comprehend, I thought it possible—'

Mayfield was quick to realize the cause of Poirot's somewhat exaggerated embarrassment.

'You thought I had a weakness for the lady? Not at all! Far from it. Funnily enough, Carrington thought the same.'

'Yes, he has told me of the conversation he held with you on the subject.'

Lord Mayfield looked rather rueful.

'My little scheme didn't come off. Always annoying to have to admit that a woman has got the better of you.'

Agatha Christie

'Ah, but she has not got the better of you *yet*, Lord Mayfield.'

'You think we may yet win? Well, I'm glad to hear you say so. I'd like to think it was true.'

He sighed.

'I feel I've acted like a complete fool—so pleased with my stratagem for entrapping the lady.'

Hercule Poirot said, as he lit one of his tiny cigarettes:

'What *was* your stratagem exactly, Lord Mayfield?'

'Well,' Lord Mayfield hesitated. 'I hadn't exactly got down to details.'

'You didn't discuss it with anyone?'

'No.'

'Not even with Mr Carlile?'

'No.'

Poirot smiled.

'You prefer to play a lone hand, Lord Mayfield.'

'I have usually found it the best way,' said the other a little grimly.

'Yes, you are wise. *Trust no one.* But you *did* mention the matter to Sir George Carrington?'

'Simply because I realized that the dear fellow was seriously perturbed about me.'

Lord Mayfield smiled at the remembrance.

'He is an old friend of yours?'

'Yes. I have known him for over twenty years.'

'And his wife?'

'I have known his wife also, of course.'

'But (pardon me if I am impertinent) you are not on the same terms of intimacy with her?'

'I don't really see what my personal relationships to people has to do with the matter in hand, M. Poirot.'

'But I think, Lord Mayfield, that they may have a good deal to do with it. You agreed, did you not, that my theory of someone in the drawing-room was a possible one?'

'Yes. In fact, I agree with you that that is what must have happened.'

'We will not say "must." That is too self-confident a word. But if that theory of mine is true, who do you think the person in the drawing-room could have been?'

'Obviously Mrs Vanderlyn. She had been back there once for a book. She could have come back for another book, or a handbag, or a dropped handkerchief—one of a dozen feminine excuses. She arranges with her maid to scream and get Carlile away from the study. Then she slips in and out by the windows as you said.'

'You forget it could not have been Mrs Vanderlyn. Carlile heard her call the maid from *upstairs* while he was talking to the girl.'

Lord Mayfield bit his lip.

'True. I forgot that.' He looked throughly annoyed.

'You see,' said Poirot gently. 'We progress. We have first the simple explanation of a thief who comes from *outside* and makes off with the booty. A very convenient theory as I said at the time, too convenient to be readily accepted. We have disposed of that. Then we come to the theory of the foreign agent, Mrs Vanderlyn, and that again seems to fit together beautifully up to a certain point. But now it looks as though that, too, was too easy—too convenient—to be accepted.'

'You'd wash Mrs Vanderlyn out of it altogether?'

'It was not Mrs Vanderlyn in the drawing-room. It may have been an ally of Mrs Vanderlyn's who committed the theft, but it is just possible that it was committed by another person altogether. If so, we have to consider the question of motive.'

'Isn't this rather far-fetched, M. Poirot?'

'I do not think so. Now what motives could there be? There is the motive of money. The papers may have been stolen with the object of turning them into cash. That is the simplest motive to consider. But the motive might possibly be something quite different.'

'Such as—'

Poirot said slowly:

'It might have been done definitely with the idea of damaging someone.'

'Who?'

'Possibly Mr Carlile. He would be the obvious suspect. But there might be more to it than that. The men who control the destiny of a country, Lord Mayfield, are particularly vulnerable to displays of popular feeling.'

'Meaning that the theft was aimed at damaging *me*?'

Poirot nodded.

'I think I am correct in saying, Lord Mayfield, that about five years ago you passed through a somewhat trying time. You were suspected of friendship with a European Power at that time bitterly unpopular with the electorate of this country.'

'Quite true, M. Poirot.'

'A statesman in these days has a difficult task. He has to pursue the policy he deems advantageous to his country, but he has at the same time to recognize the force of popular feeling. Popular feeling is very often sentimental, muddle-headed, and eminently unsound, but it cannot be disregarded for all that.'

'How well you express it! That is exactly the curse of a politician's life. He has to bow to the country's feeling, however dangerous and foolhardy he knows it to be.'

'That was your dilemma, I think. There were rumours that you had concluded an agreement with the country in question. This country and the newspapers were up in arms about it. Fortunately the Prime Minister was able categorically to deny the story, and you repudiated it, though still making no secret of the way your sympathies lay.'

'All this is quite true, M. Poirot, but why rake up past history?'

'Because I consider it possible that an enemy, disappointed in the way you surmounted that crisis, might endeavour to stage a further dilemma. You soon regained public confidence. Those particular circumstances have passed away, you are now, deservedly, one of the most popular figures in political life. You are spoken of freely as the next Prime Minister when Mr Hunberly retires.'

'You think this is an attempt to discredit me? Nonsense!'

'*Tout de même*, Lord Mayfield, it would not look well if it were known that the plans of Britain's new bomber had been stolen during a weekend when a certain very charming lady had been your guest. Little hints in the newspapers as to your relationship with that lady would create a feeling of distrust in you.'

'Such a thing could not really be taken seriously.'

'My dear Lord Mayfield, you know perfectly well it could! It takes so little to undermine public confidence in a man.'

'Yes, that's true,' said Lord Mayfield. He looked suddenly very worried. 'God! how desperately complicated this business is becoming. Do you really think—but it's impossible—impossible.'

'You know of nobody who is—jealous of you?'

'Absurd!'

'At any rate you will admit that my questions about your personal relationships with the members of this house-party are not totally irrelevant.'

'Oh, perhaps—perhaps. You asked me about Julia Carrington. There's really not very much to say. I've never taken to her very much, and I don't think she cares for me. She's one of these restless, nervy women, recklessly extravagant and mad about cards. She's old-fashioned enough, I think, to despise me as being a self-made man.'

Poirot said:

'I looked you up in *Who's Who* before I came down. You were the head of a famous engineering firm and you are yourself a first-class engineer.'

'There's certainly nothing I don't know about the practical side. I've worked my way up from the bottom.'

Lord Mayfield spoke rather grimly.

'Oh la la!' cried Poirot. 'I have been a fool—but a fool!'
The other stared at him.

'I beg your pardon, M. Poirot?'

'It is that a portion of the puzzle has become clear to me. Something I did not see before . . . But it all fits in. Yes—it fits in with beautiful precision.'

Lord Mayfield looked at him in somewhat astonished inquiry.

But with a slight smile Poirot shook his head.

'No, no, not now. I must arrange my ideas a little more clearly.'

He rose.

'Goodnight, Lord Mayfield. I think I know where those plans are.'

Lord Mayfield cried out:

'You know? Then let us get hold of them at once!'

Poirot shook his head.

'No, no, that would not do. Precipitancy would be fatal. But leave it all to Hercule Poirot.'

He went out of the room. Lord Mayfield raised his shoulders in contempt.

'Man's a mountebank,' he muttered. Then, putting away his papers and turning out the lights, he, too, made his way up to bed.

CHAPTER 6

'If there's been a burglary, why the devil doesn't old Mayfield send for the police?' demanded Reggie Carrington.

He pushed his chair slightly back from the breakfast table.

He was the last down. His host, Mrs Macatta and Sir George had finished their breakfasts some time before. His mother and Mrs Vanderlyn were breakfasting in bed.

Sir George, repeating his statement on the lines agreed upon between Lord Mayfield and Hercule Poirot, had a feeling that he was not managing it as well as he might have done.

'To send for a queer foreigner like this seems very odd to me,' said Reggie. 'What has been taken, Father?'

'I don't know exactly, my boy.'

Reggie got up. He looked rather nervy and on edge this morning.

'Nothing—important? No—papers or anything like that?'

'To tell you the truth, Reggie, I can't tell you exactly.'

'Very hush-hush, is it? I see.'

Reggie ran up the stairs, paused for a moment half-way

with a frown on his face, and then continued his ascent and tapped on his mother's door. Her voice bade him enter.

Lady Julia was sitting up in bed, scribbling figures on the back of an envelope.

'Good morning, darling.' She looked up, then said sharply:

'Reggie, is anything the matter?'

'Nothing much, but it seems there was a burglary last night.'

'A burglary? What was taken?'

'Oh, I don't know. It's all very hush hush. There's some odd kind of private-inquiry agent downstairs asking everybody questions.'

'How extraordinary!'

'It's rather unpleasant,' said Reggie slowly, 'staying in a house when that kind of thing happens.'

'What did happen exactly?'

'Don't know. It was some time after we all went to bed. Look out, Mother, you'll have that tray off.'

He rescued the breakfast-tray and carried it to a table by the window.

'Was money taken?'

'I tell you I don't know.'

Lady Julia said slowly:

'I suppose this inquiry man is asking everybody questions?'

'I suppose so.'

'Where they were last night? All that kind of thing?'

'Probably. Well, I can't tell him much. I went straight up to bed and was asleep in next to no time.'

Lady Julia did not answer.

'I say, Mother, I suppose you couldn't let me have a spot of cash. I'm absolutely broke.'

'No, I couldn't,' his mother replied decisively. 'I've got the most frightful overdraft myself. I don't know what your father will say when he hears about it.'

There was a tap at the door and Sir George entered.

'Ah, there you are, Reggie. Will you go down to the library? M. Hercule Poirot wants to see you.'

Poirot had just concluded an interview with the redoubtable Mrs Macatta.

A few brief questions had elicited the information that Mrs Macatta had gone up to bed just before eleven, and had heard or seen nothing helpful.

Poirot slid gently from the topic of the burglary to more personal matters. He himself had a great admiration for Lord Mayfield. As a member of the general public he felt that Lord Mayfield was a truly great man. Of course, Mrs Macatta, being in the know, would have a far better means of estimating that than himself.

'Lord Mayfield has brains,' allowed Mrs Macatta. 'And he has carved his career out entirely for himself. He owes nothing to hereditary influence. He has a certain lack of vision, perhaps. In that I find all men sadly alike. They lack the breadth of a woman's imagination. Woman, M. Poirot, is going to be the great force in government in ten years' time.'

Poirot said that he was sure of it.

He slid to the topic of Mrs Vanderlyn. Was it true, as he had heard hinted, that she and Lord Mayfield were very close friends?

'Not in the least. To tell you the truth I was very surprised to meet her here. Very surprised indeed.'

Poirot invited Mrs Macatta's opinion of Mrs Vanderlyn— and got it.

'One of those absolutely *useless* women, M. Poirot. Women that make one despair of one's own sex! A parasite, first and last a parasite.'

'Men admired her?'

'Men!' Mrs Macatta spoke the word with contempt. 'Men are always taken in by those very obvious good looks. That boy, now, young Reggie Carrington, flushing up every time she spoke to him, absurdly flattered by being taken notice of by her. And the silly way she flattered him too. Praising his bridge—which actually was far from brilliant.'

'He is not a good player?'

'He made all sorts of mistakes last night.'

'Lady Julia is a good player, is she not?'

'Much *too* good in my opinion,' said Mrs Macatta. 'It's almost a profession with her. She plays morning, noon, and night.'

'For high stakes?'

'Yes, indeed, much higher than I would care to play. Indeed I shouldn't consider it *right*.'

'She makes a good deal of money at the game?'

Mrs Macatta gave a loud and virtuous snort.

'She reckons on paying her debts that way. But she's been having a run of bad luck lately, so I've heard. She looked last night as though she had something on her mind. The evils of gambling, M. Poirot, are only slightly less than the evils caused by drink. If I had my way this country should be purified—'

Poirot was forced to listen to a somewhat lengthy discussion on the purification of England's morals. Then he closed the conversation adroitly and sent for Reggie Carrington.

He summed the young man up carefully as he entered the room, the weak mouth camouflaged by the rather charming smile, the indecisive chin, the eyes set far apart, the rather narrow head. He thought that he knew Reggie Carrington's type fairly well.

'Mr Reggie Carrington?'

'Yes. Anything I can do?'

'Just tell me what you can about last night?'

'Well, let me see, we played bridge—in the drawing-room. After that I went up to bed.'

'That was at what time?'

'Just before eleven. I suppose the robbery took place after that?'

'Yes, after that. You did not hear or see anything?'

Reggie shook his head regretfully.

'I'm afraid not. I went straight to bed and I sleep pretty soundly.'

'You went straight up from the drawing-room to your bedroom and remained there until the morning?'

'That's right.'

'Curious,' said Poirot.

Reggie said sharply:

'What do you mean, curious?'

'You did not, for instance, hear a scream?'

'No, I didn't.'

'Ah, very curious.'

'Look here, I don't know what you mean.'

'You are, perhaps, slightly deaf?'

'Certainly not.'

Poirot's lips moved. It was possible that he was repeating the word curious for the third time. Then he said:

'Well, thank you, Mr Carrington, that is all.'

Reggie got up and stood rather irresolutely.

'You know,' he said, 'now you come to mention it, I believe I did hear something of the kind.'

'Ah, you did hear something?'

'Yes, but you see, I was reading a book—a detective story as a matter of fact—and I—well, I didn't really quite take it in.'

'Ah,' said Poirot, 'a most satisfying explanation.'

His face was quite impassive.

Reggie still hesitated, then he turned and walked slowly to the door. There he paused and asked:

'I say, what was stolen?'

'Something of great value, Mr Carrington. That is all I am at liberty to say.'

'Oh,' said Reggie rather blankly.

He went out.

Poirot nodded his head.

'It fits,' he murmured. 'It fits very nicely.'

He touched a bell and inquired courteously if Mrs Vanderlyn was up yet.

CHAPTER 7

Mrs Vanderlyn swept into the room looking very handsome. She was wearing an artfully-cut russet sports-suit that showed up the warm lights of her hair. She swept to a chair and smiled in a dazzling fashion at the little man in front of her.

For a moment something showed through the smile. It might have been triumph, it might almost have been mockery. It was gone almost immediately, but it had been there. Poirot found the suggestion of it interesting.

'Burglars? Last night? But how dreadful! Why no, I never heard a *thing*. What about the police? Can't they *do* anything?'

Again, just for a moment, the mockery showed in her eyes.

Hercule Poirot thought:

'It is very clear that *you* are not afraid of the police, my lady. You know very well that they are not going to be called in.'

And from that followed—what?

He said soberly:

'You comprehend, madame, it is an affair of the most discreet.'

'Why, naturally, M.—Poirot—isn't it?—I shouldn't dream of breathing a word. I'm much too great an admirer of dear Lord Mayfield's to do anything to cause him the least little bit of worry.'

She crossed her knees. A highly-polished slipper of brown leather dangled on the tip of her silk-shod foot.

She smiled, a warm, compelling smile of perfect health and deep satisfaction.

'Do tell me if there's anything at all I can do?'

'I thank you, madame. You played bridge in the drawing-room last night?'

'Yes.'

'I understand that then all the ladies went up to bed?'

'That is right.'

'But someone came back to fetch a book. That was you, was it not, Mrs Vanderlyn?'

'I was the first one to come back—yes.'

'What do you mean—the *first* one?' said Poirot sharply.

'I came back right away,' explained Mrs Vanderlyn. 'Then I went up and rang for my maid. She was a long time in coming. I rang again. Then I went out on the landing. I heard her voice and I called her. After she had brushed my hair I sent her away, she was in a nervous, upset state and tangled the brush in my hair once or twice. It was then, just as I sent her away, that I saw Lady Julia coming up the stairs. She told me she had been down again for a book, too. Curious, wasn't it?'

Mrs Vanderlyn smiled as she finished, a wide, rather

feline smile. Hercule Poirot thought to himself that Mrs Vanderlyn did not like Lady Julia Carrington.

'As you say, madame. Tell me, did you hear your maid scream?'

'Why, yes, I did hear something of that kind.'

'Did you ask her about it?'

'Yes. She told me she thought she had seen a floating figure in white—such nonsense!'

'What was Lady Julia wearing last night?'

'Oh, you think perhaps—Yes, I see. She *was* wearing a white evening-dress. Of course, that explains it. She must have caught sight of her in the darkness just as a white figure. These girls are so superstitious.'

'Your maid has been with you a long time, madame?'

'Oh, no.' Mrs Vanderlyn opened her eyes rather wide. 'Only about five months.'

'I should like to see her presently, if you do not mind, madame.'

Mrs Vanderlyn raised her eyebrows.

'Oh, certainly,' she said rather coldly.

'I should like, you understand, to question her.'

'Oh, yes.'

Again a flicker of amusement.

Poirot rose and bowed.

'Madame,' he said. 'You have my complete admiration.'

Mrs Vanderlyn for once seemed a trifle taken aback.

'Oh, M. Poirot, how nice of you, but why?'

'You are, madame, so perfectly armoured, so completely sure of yourself.'

Mrs Vanderlyn laughed a little uncertainly.

'Now I wonder,' she said, 'if I am to take that as a compliment?'

Poirot said:

'It is, perhaps, a warning—not to treat life with arrogance.'

Mrs Vanderlyn laughed with more assurance. She got up and held out a hand.

'Dear M. Poirot, I do wish you all success. Thank you for all the charming things you have said to me.'

She went out. Poirot murmured to himself:

'You wish me success, do you? Ah, but you are very sure I am not going to meet with success! Yes, you are very sure indeed. That, it annoys me very much.'

With a certain petulance, he pulled the bell and asked that Mademoiselle Leonie might be sent to him.

His eyes roamed over her appreciatively as she stood hesitating in the doorway, demure in her black dress with her neatly-parted black waves of hair and her modestly-dropped eyelids. He nodded slow approval.

'Come in, Mademoiselle Leonie,' he said. 'Do not be afraid.'

She came in and stood demurely before him.

'Do you know,' said Poirot with a sudden change of tone, 'that I find you very good to look at.'

Leonie responded promptly. She flashed him a glance out of the corner of her eyes and murmured softly:

'Monsieur is very kind.'

'Figure to yourself,' said Poirot. 'I demand of M. Carlile

whether you are or not good-looking and he replies that he does not know!'

Leonie cocked her chin up contemptuously.

'That image!'

'That describes him very well.'

'I do not believe he has ever looked at a girl in his life, that one.'

'Probably not. A pity. He has missed a lot. But there are others in this house who are more appreciative, is it not so?'

'Really, I do not know what monsieur means.'

'Oh, yes, Mademoiselle Leonie, you know very well. A pretty history that you recount last night about a ghost that you have seen. As soon as I hear that you are standing there with your hands to your head, I know very well that there is no question of ghosts. If a girl is frightened she clasps her heart, or she raises her hands to her mouth to stifle a cry, but if her hands are on her hair it means something very different. *It means that her hair has been ruffled and that she is hastily patting it into shape again!* Now then, mademoiselle, let us have the truth. Why did you scream on the stairs?'

'But monsieur it is true, I saw a tall figure all in white—'

'Mademoiselle, do not insult my intelligence. That story, it may have been good enough for M. Carlile, but it is not good enough for Hercule Poirot. The truth is that you had just been kissed, is it not so? And I will make a guess that it was M. Reggie Carrington who kissed you.'

Leonie twinkled an unabashed eye at him.

'*Eh bien*,' she demanded, 'after all, what is a kiss?'

'What, indeed?' said Poirot gallantly.

'You see, the young gentleman he came up behind me and caught me round the waist—and so naturally he startled me and I screamed. If I had known—well, then naturally I would not have screamed.'

'Naturally,' agreed Poirot.

'But he came upon me like a cat. Then the study door opened and out came M. le secrétaire and the young gentleman slipped away upstairs and there I was looking like a fool. Naturally I had to say something—especially to——' she broke into French, '*un jeune homme comme ça, tellement comme il faut!*'

'So you invent a ghost?'

'Indeed, monsieur, it was all I could think of. A tall figure all in white, that floated. It is ridiculous but what else could I do?'

'Nothing. So now, all is explained. I had my suspicions from the first.'

Leonie shot him a provocative glance.

'Monsieur is very clever, and very sympathetic.'

'And since I am not going to make you any embarrassments over the affair you will do something for me in return?'

'Most willingly, monsieur.'

'How much do you know of your mistress's affairs?'

The girl shrugged her shoulders.

'Not very much, monsieur. I have my ideas, of course.'

'And those ideas?'

'Well, it does not escape me that the friends of madame are always soldiers or sailors or airmen. And then there are other friends—foreign gentlemen who come to see her very quietly sometimes. Madame is very handsome, though I do not think she will be so much longer. The young men, they find her very attractive. Sometimes I think, they say too much. But it is only my idea, that. Madame does not confide in me.'

'What you would have me to understand is that madame plays a lone hand?'

'That is right, monsieur.'

'In other words, you cannot help me.'

'I fear not, monsieur. I would do if I could.'

'Tell me, your mistress is in a good mood today?'

'Decidedly, monsieur.'

'Something has happened to please her?'

'She has been in good spirits ever since she came here.'

'Well, Leonie, you should know.'

The girl answered confidently:

'Yes, monsieur. I could not be mistaken there. I know all madame's moods. She is in high spirits.'

'Positively triumphant?'

'That is exactly the word, monsieur.'

Poirot nodded gloomily.

'I find that—a little hard to bear. Yet I perceive that it is inevitable. Thank you, mademoiselle, that is all.'

Leonie threw him a coquettish glance.

'Thank you, monsieur. If I meet monsieur on the stairs, be well assured that I shall not scream.'

143

'My child,' said Poirot with dignity. 'I am of advanced years. What have I to do with such frivolities?'

But with a little twitter of laughter, Leonie took herself off.

Poirot paced slowly up and down the room. His face became grave and anxious.

'And now,' he said at last, 'for Lady Julia. What will she say, I wonder?'

Lady Julia came into the room with a quiet air of assurance. She bent her head graciously, accepted the chair that Poirot drew forward and spoke in a low, well-bred voice.

'Lord Mayfield says that you wish to ask me some questions.'

'Yes, madame. It is about last night.'

'About last night, yes?'

'What happened after you had finished your game of bridge?'

'My husband thought it was too late to begin another. I went up to bed.'

'And then?'

'I went to sleep.'

'That is all?'

'Yes. I'm afraid I can't tell you anything of much interest. When did this'—she hesitated—'burglary occur?'

'Very soon after you went upstairs.'

'I see. And what exactly was taken?'

'Some private papers, madame.'

'Important papers?'

'Very important.'

She frowned a little and then said:

'They were—valuable?'

'Yes, madame, they were worth a good deal of money.'

'I see.'

There was a pause, and then Poirot said:

'What about your book, madame?'

'My book?' She raised bewildered eyes to him.

'Yes, I understand Mrs Vanderlyn to say that some time after you three ladies had retired you went down again to fetch a book.'

'Yes, of course, so I did.'

'So that, as a matter of fact, you did *not* go straight to bed when you went upstairs? You returned to the drawing-room?'

'Yes, that is true. I had forgotten.'

'While you were in the drawing-room, did you hear someone scream?'

'No—yes—I don't think so.'

'Surely, madame. You could not have failed to hear it in the drawing-room.'

Lady Julia flung her head back and said firmly:

'I heard nothing.'

Poirot raised his eyebrows, but did not reply.

The silence grew uncomfortable. Lady Julia asked abruptly:

'What is being done?'

'Being done? I do not understand you, madame.'

'I mean about the robbery. Surely the police must be doing something.'

Poirot shook his head.

'The police have not been called in. I am in charge.'

She stared at him, her restless haggard face sharpened and tense. Her eyes, dark and searching, sought to pierce his impassivity.

They fell at last—defeated.

'You cannot tell me what is being done?'

'I can only assure you, madame, that I am leaving no stone unturned.'

'To catch the thief—or to—recover the papers?'

'The recovery of the papers is the main thing, madame.'

Her manner changed. It became bored, listless.

'Yes,' she said indifferently. 'I suppose it is.'

There was another pause.

'Is there anything else, M. Poirot?'

'No, madame. I will not detain you further.'

'Thank you.'

He opened the door for her. She passed out without glancing at him.

Poirot went back to the fireplace and carefully rearranged the ornaments on the mantelpiece. He was still at it when Lord Mayfield came in through the window.

'Well?' said the latter.

'Very well, I think. Events are shaping themselves as they should.'

Lord Mayfield said, staring at him:

'You are pleased.'

'No, I am not pleased. But I am content.'

'Really, M. Poirot, I cannot make you out.'

'I am not such a charlatan as you think.'

'I never said—'

'No, but you *thought*! No matter. I am not offended. It is sometimes necessary for me to adopt a certain pose.'

Lord Mayfield looked at him doubtfully with a certain amount of distrust. Hercule Poirot was a man he did not understand. He wanted to despise him, but something warned him that this ridiculous little man was not so futile as he appeared. Charles McLaughlin had always been able to recognize capability when he saw it.

'Well,' he said, 'we are in your hands. What do you advise next?'

'Can you get rid of your guests?'

'I think it might be arranged . . . I could explain that I have to go to London over this affair. They will then probably offer to leave.'

'Very good. Try and arrange it like that.'

Lord Mayfield hesitated.

'You don't think—?'

'I am quite sure that that would be the wise course to take.'

Lord Mayfield shrugged his shoulders.

'Well, if you say so.'

He went out.

CHAPTER 8

The guests left after lunch. Mrs Vanderlyn and Mrs Macatta went by train, the Carringtons had their car. Poirot was standing in the hall as Mrs Vanderlyn bade her host a charming farewell.

'So terribly sorry for you having this bother and anxiety. I do hope it will turn out all right for you. I shan't breathe a word of anything.'

She pressed his hand and went out to where the Rolls was waiting to take her to the station. Mrs Macatta was already inside. Her adieu had been curt and unsympathetic.

Suddenly Leonie, who had been getting in front with the chauffeur, came running back into the hall.

'The dressing-case of madame, it is not in the car,' she exclaimed.

There was a hurried search. At last Lord Mayfield discovered it where it had been put down in the shadow of an old oak chest. Leonie uttered a glad little cry as she seized the elegant affair of green morocco, and hurried out with it.

Then Mrs Vanderlyn leaned out of the car.

'Lord Mayfield, Lord Mayfield.' She handed him a letter.

'Would you mind putting this in your post-bag? If I keep it meaning to post it in town, I'm sure to forget. Letters just stay in my bag for days.'

Sir George Carrington was fidgeting with his watch, opening and shutting it. He was a maniac for punctuality.

'They're cutting it fine,' he murmured. 'Very fine. Unless they're careful, they'll miss the train—'

His wife said irritably:

'Oh, don't fuss, George. After all, it's their train, not ours!'

He looked at her reproachfully.

The Rolls drove off.

Reggie drew up at the front door in the Carringtons' Morris.

'All ready, Father,' he said.

The servants began bringing out the Carringtons' luggage. Reggie supervised its disposal in the dickey.

Poirot moved out of the front door, watching the proceedings.

Suddenly he felt a hand on his arm. Lady Julia's voice spoke in an agitated whisper.

'M. Poirot. I must speak to you—at once.'

He yielded to her insistent hand. She drew him into a small morning-room and closed the door. She came close to him.

'Is it true what you said—that the discovery of the papers is what matters most to Lord Mayfield?'

Poirot looked at her curiously.

'It is quite true, madame.'

'If—if those papers were returned to you, would you undertake that they should be given back to Lord Mayfield, and no questions asked?'

'I am not sure that I understand you.'

'You must! I am sure that you do! I am suggesting that the—the thief should remain anonymous if the papers are returned.'

Poirot asked:

'How soon would that be, madame?'

'Definitely within twelve hours.'

'You can promise that?'

'I can promise it.'

As he did not answer, she repeated urgently:

'Will you guarantee that there will be no publicity?'

He answered then—very gravely:

'Yes, madame, I will guarantee that.'

'Then everything can be arranged.'

She passed abruptly from the room. A moment later Poirot heard the car drive away.

He crossed the hall and went along the passage to the study. Lord Mayfield was there. He looked up as Poirot entered.

'Well?' he said.

Poirot spread out his hands.

'The case is ended, Lord Mayfield.'

'What?'

Poirot repeated word for word the scene between himself and Lady Julia.

Lord Mayfield looked at him with a stupefied expression.

'But what does it mean? I don't understand.'

'It is very clear, is it not? Lady Julia knows who stole the plans.'

'You don't mean she took them herself?'

'Certainly not. Lady Julia may be a gambler. She is not a thief. But if she offers to return the plans, it means that they were taken by her husband or her son. Now Sir George Carrington was out on the terrace with you. That leaves us the son. I think I can reconstruct the happenings of last night fairly accurately. Lady Julia went to her son's room last night and found it empty. She came downstairs to look for him, but did not find him. This morning she hears of the theft, and she also hears that her son declares that he went straight to his room *and never left it*. That, she knows, is not true. And she knows something else about her son. She knows that he is weak, that he is desperately hard-up for money. She has observed his infatuation for Mrs Vanderlyn. The whole thing is clear to her. Mrs Vanderlyn has persuaded Reggie to steal the plans. But she determines to play her part also. She will tackle Reggie, get hold of the papers and return them.'

'But the whole thing is quite impossible,' cried Lord Mayfield.

'Yes, it is impossible, but Lady Julia does not know that. She does not know what I, Hercule Poirot, know, that young Reggie Carrington was not stealing papers last night, but instead was philandering with Mrs Vanderlyn's French maid.'

'The whole thing is a mare's nest!'

'Exactly.'

'And the case is not ended at all!'

'Yes, it is ended. *I, Hercule Poirot, know the truth.* You do not believe me? You did not believe me yesterday when I said I knew where the plans were. But I did know. They were very close at hand.'

'Where?'

'They were in your pocket, my lord.'

There was a pause, then Lord Mayfield said:

'Do you really know what you are saying, M. Poirot?'

'Yes, I know. I know that I am speaking to a very clever man. From the first it worried me that you, who were admittedly short-sighted, should be so positive about the figure you had seen leaving the window. You wanted that solution—the convenient solution—to be accepted. Why? Later, one by one, I eliminated everyone else. Mrs Vanderlyn was upstairs, Sir George was with you on the terrace, Reggie Carrington was with the French girl on the stairs, Mrs Macatta was blamelessly in her bedroom. (It is next to the house-keeper's room, and Mrs Macatta snores!) Lady Julia, it is true, was in the drawing-room; but Lady Julia clearly believed her son guilty. So there remained only two possibilities. Either Carlile did not put the papers on the desk but into his own pocket (and that is not reasonable, because, as you pointed out, he could have taken a tracing of them), or else—or else the plans were there when you walked over to the desk, and the only place they could have gone was into *your* pocket. In that case everything was clear. Your insistence on the figure you had seen, your insistence on Carlile's innocence, your disinclination to have me summoned.

'One thing did puzzle me—the motive. You were, I was convinced, an honest man, a man of integrity. That showed in your anxiety that no innocent person should be suspected. It was also obvious that the theft of the plans might easily affect your career unfavourably. Why, then, this wholly unreasonable theft? And at last the answer came to me. The crisis in your career, some years ago, the assurances given to the world by the Prime Minister that you had had no negotiations with the power in question. Suppose that that was not strictly true, that there remained some record— a letter, perhaps—showing that in actual fact you *had* done what you had publicly denied. Such a denial was necessary in the interests of public policy. But it is doubtful if the man in the street would see it that way. It might mean that at the moment when supreme power might be given into your hands, some stupid echo from the past would undo everything.

'I suspect that that letter has been preserved in the hands of a certain government, that that government offered to trade with you—the letter in exchange for the plans of the new bomber. Some men would have refused. You—did not! You agreed. Mrs Vanderlyn was the agent in the matter. She came here by arrangement to make the exchange. You gave yourself away when you admitted that you had formed no definite stratagem for entrapping her. That admission made your reason for inviting her here incredibly weak.

'You arranged the robbery. Pretended to see the thief on the terrace—thereby clearing Carlile of suspicion. Even if he had not left the room, the desk was so near the window that a thief might have taken the plans while Carlile was busy at the safe with his back turned. You walked over to the desk, took the plans and kept them on your own person until the moment when, by prearranged plan, you slipped them into Mrs Vanderlyn's dressing-case. In return she handed you the fatal letter disguised as an unposted letter of her own.'

Poirot stopped.

Lord Mayfield said:

'Your knowledge is very complete, M. Poirot. You must think me an unutterable skunk.'

Poirot made a quick gesture.

'No, no, Lord Mayfield. I think, as I said, that you are a very clever man. It came to me suddenly as we talked here last night. You are a first-class engineer. There will be, I think, some subtle alterations in the specifications of that bomber, alterations done so skilfully that it will be difficult to grasp why the machine is not the success it ought to be. A certain foreign power will find the type a failure . . . It will be a disappointment to them, I am sure . . .'

Again there was a silence—then Lord Mayfield said:

'You are much too clever, M. Poirot. I will only ask you to believe one thing. I have faith in myself. I believe that I am the man to guide England through the days of crisis that I see coming. If I did not honestly believe that I am needed by my country to steer the ship of state, I would not have done what I have done—made the best of both worlds—saved myself from disaster by a clever trick.'

'My lord,' said Poirot, 'if you could not make the best of both worlds, you could not be a politician!'

DEAD MAN'S MIRROR

CHAPTER 1

The flat was a modern one. The furnishings of the room were modern, too. The armchairs were squarely built, the upright chairs were angular. A modern writing-table was set squarely in front of the window, and at it sat a small, elderly man. His head was practically the only thing in the room that was not square. It was egg-shaped.

M. Hercule Poirot was reading a letter:

Station: Whimperley.   *Hamborough Close,*
Telegrams: *Hamborough St Mary*
  Hamborough St. John.   *Westshire.*
                               September 24th, 1936.

M. Hercule Poirot.
Dear Sir,—A matter has arisen which requires handling with great delicacy and discretion. I have heard good accounts of you, and have decided to entrust the matter to you. I have reason to believe that I am the victim of fraud, but for family reasons I do not wish to call in the police. I am taking certain measures of my own to deal with the business, but you must be prepared to come

*down here immediately on receipt of a telegram. I should
be obliged if you will not answer this letter.*

Yours faithfully,

Gervase Chevenix-Gore.

The eyebrows of M. Hercule Poirot climbed slowly up
his forehead until they nearly disappeared into his hair.

'And who, then,' he demanded of space, 'is this Gervase
Chevenix-Gore?'

He crossed to a bookcase and took out a large, fat book.
He found what he wanted easily enough.

*Chevenix-Gore, Sir Gervase Francis Xavier, 10th Bt. cr.
1694; formerly Captain 17th Lancers; b. 18th May,
1878; e.s. of Sir Guy Chevenix-Gore, 9th Bt., and Lady
Claudia Bretherton, 2nd. d. of 8th Earl of Wallingford. S.
father, 1911; m. 1912, Vanda Elizabeth, e.d. of Colonel
Frederick Arbuthnot, q.v.; educ. Eton. Served European
War, 1914–18. Recreations: travelling, big-game hunting.
Address: Hamborough St Mary, Westshire, and 218
Lowndes Square, S.W.1. Clubs: Cavalry. Travellers.*

Poirot shook his head in a slightly dissatisfied manner.
For a moment or two he remained lost in thought, then
he went to the desk, pulled open a drawer and took out
a little pile of invitation cards.

His face brightened.

'*A la bonne heure!* Exactly my affair! He will certainly
be there.'

A duchess greeted M. Hercule Poirot in fulsome tones.

'So you could manage to come after all, M. Poirot! Why, that's splendid.'

'The pleasure is mine, madame,' murmured Poirot, bowing.

He escaped from several important and splendid beings—a famous diplomat, an equally famous actress and a well-known sporting peer—and found at last the person he had come to seek, that invariably 'also present' guest, Mr Satterthwaite.

Mr Satterthwaite twittered amiably.

'The dear duchess—I always enjoy her parties . . . Such a *personality*, if you know what I mean. I saw a lot of her in Corsica some years ago . . .'

Mr Satterthwaite's conversation was apt to be unduly burdened by mentions of his titled acquaintances. It is possible that he *may* sometimes have found pleasure in the company of Messrs. Jones, Brown or Robinson, but, if so, he did not mention the fact. And yet, to describe Mr Satterthwaite as a mere snob and leave it at that would have been to do him an injustice. He was a keen observer of human nature, and if it is true that the looker-on knows most of the game, Mr Satterthwaite knew a good deal.

'You know, my dear fellow, it is really ages since I saw you. I always feel myself privileged to have seen you work at close quarters in the Crow's Nest business. I feel since then that I am in the know, so to speak. I saw Lady Mary only last week, by the way. A charming creature—pot-pourri and lavender!'

After passing lightly on one or two scandals of the moment—the indiscretions of an earl's daughter, and the lamentable conduct of a viscount—Poirot succeeded in introducing the name of Gervase Chevenix-Gore.

Mr Satterthwaite responded immediately.

'Ah, now, there *is* a character, if you like! The Last of the Baronets—that's his nickname.'

'*Pardon*, I do not quite comprehend.'

Mr Satterthwaite unbent indulgently to the lower comprehension of a foreigner.

'It's a joke, you know—a *joke*. Naturally, he's not *really* the last baronet in England—but he *does* represent the end of an era. The Bold Bad Baronet—the mad harum-scarum baronet so popular in the novels of the last century—the kind of fellow who laid impossible wagers and won 'em.'

He went on to expound what he meant in more detail. In younger years, Gervase Chevenix-Gore had sailed round the world in a windjammer. He had been on an expedition to the Pole. He had challenged a racing peer to a duel. For a wager he had ridden his favourite mare up the staircase of a ducal house. He had once leapt from a box to the stage and carried off a well-known actress in the middle of her role.

The anecdotes of him were innumerable.

'It's an old family,' went on Mr Satterthwaite. 'Sir Guy de Chevenix went on the first crusade. Now, alas, the line looks like coming to an end. Old Gervase is the last Chevenix-Gore.'

'The estate, it is impoverished?'

'Not a bit of it. Gervase is fabulously wealthy. Owns valuable house property—coalfields—and in addition he staked out a claim to some mine in Peru or somewhere in South America, when he was a young man, which has yielded him a fortune. An amazing man. Always lucky in everything he's undertaken.'

'He is now an elderly man, of course?'

'Yes, poor old Gervase.' Mr Satterthwaite sighed, shook his head. 'Most people would describe him to you as mad as a hatter. It's true, in a way. He *is* mad—not in the sense of being certifiable or having delusions—but mad in the sense of being abnormal. He's always been a man of great originality of character.'

'And originality becomes eccentricity as the years go by?' suggested Poirot.

'Very true. That's exactly what's happened to poor old Gervase.'

'He has perhaps, a swollen idea of his own importance?'

'Absolutely. I should imagine that, in Gervase's mind, the world has always been divided into two parts—there are the Chevenix-Gores, and the other people!'

'An exaggerated sense of family!'

'Yes. The Chevenix-Gores are all arrogant as the devil—a law unto themselves. Gervase, being the last of them, has got it badly. He is—well, really, you know, to hear him talk, you might imagine him to be—er, the Almighty!'

Poirot nodded his head slowly and thoughtfully.

'Yes, I imagined that. I have had, you see, a letter from

him. It was an unusual letter. It did not demand. It summoned!'

'A royal command,' said Mr Satterthwaite, tittering a little.

'Precisely. It did not seem to occur to this Sir Gervase that I, Hercule Poirot, am a man of importance, a man of infinite affairs! That it was extremely unlikely that I should be able to fling everything aside and come hastening like an obedient dog—like a mere nobody, gratified to receive a commission!'

Mr Satterthwaite bit his lip in an effort to suppress a smile. It may have occurred to him that where egoism was concerned, there was not much to choose between Hercule Poirot and Gervase Chevenix-Gore.

He murmured:

'Of course, if the cause of the summons was urgent—?'

'It was not!' Poirot's hands rose in the air in an emphatic gesture. 'I was to hold myself at his disposition, that was all, *in case* he should require me! *Enfin, je vous demande!*'

Again the hands rose eloquently, expressing better than words could do M. Hercule Poirot's sense of utter outrage.

'I take it,' said Mr Satterthwaite, 'that you refused?'

'I have not yet had the opportunity,' said Poirot slowly.

'But you will refuse?'

A new expression passed over the little man's face. His brow furrowed itself perplexedly.

He said:

'How can I express myself? To refuse—yes, that was my

first instinct. But I do not know . . . One has, sometimes, a feeling. Faintly, I seem to smell the fish . . .'

Mr Satterthwaite received this last statement without any sign of amusement.

'Oh?' he said. 'That is interesting . . .'

'It seems to me,' went on Hercule Poirot, 'that a man such as you have described might be very vulnerable—'

'Vulnerable?' queried Mr Satterthwaite. For the moment he was surprised. The word was not one that he would naturally have associated with Gervase Chevenix-Gore. But he was a man of perception, quick in observation. He said slowly:

'I think I see what you mean.'

'Such a one is encased, is he not, in an armour—such an armour! The armour of the crusaders was nothing to it—an armour of arrogance, of pride, of complete self-esteem. This armour, it is in some ways a protection, the arrows, the everyday arrows of life glance off it. But there is this danger; *Sometimes a man in armour might not even know he was being attacked*. He will be slow to see, slow to hear—slower still to feel.'

He paused, then asked with a change of manner:

'Of what does the family of this Sir Gervase consist?'

'There's Vanda—his wife. She was an Arbuthnot—very handsome girl. She's still quite a handsome woman. Frightfully vague, though. Devoted to Gervase. She's got a leaning towards the occult, I believe. Wears amulets and scarabs and gives out that she's the reincarnation of an Egyptian Queen . . . Then there's Ruth—she's their adopted daughter. They've no children of their own. Very attractive girl in the modern style. That's all the family. Except, of course, for Hugo Trent. He's Gervase's nephew. Pamela Chevenix-Gore married Reggie Trent and Hugo was their only child. He's an orphan. He can't inherit the title, of course, but I imagine he'll come in for most of Gervase's money in the end. Good-looking lad, he's in the Blues.'

Poirot nodded his head thoughtfully. Then he asked:

'It is a grief to Sir Gervase, yes, that he has no son to inherit his name?'

'I should imagine that it cuts pretty deep.'

'The family name, it is a passion with him?'

'Yes.'

Mr Satterthwaite was silent a moment or two. He was very intrigued. Finally he ventured:

'You see a definite reason for going down to Hamborough Close?'

Slowly, Poirot shook his head.

'No,' he said. 'As far as I can see, there is no reason at all. But, all the same, I fancy I shall go.'

CHAPTER 2

Hercule Poirot sat in the corner of a first-class carriage speeding through the English countryside.

Meditatively he took from his pocket a neatly-folded telegram, which he opened and re-read:

Take four-thirty from St Pancras instruct guard have express stopped at Whimperley.
                                    Chevenix-Gore.

He folded up the telegram again and put it back in his pocket.

The guard on the train had been obsequious. The gentleman was going to Hamborough Close? Oh, yes, Sir Gervase Chevenix-Gore's guests always had the express stopped at Whimperley. 'A special kind of prerogative, I think it is, sir.'

Since then the guard had paid two visits to the carriage—the first in order to assure the traveller that everything would be done to keep the carriage for himself, the second to announce that the express was running ten minutes late.

The train was due to arrive at 7.50, but it was exactly two

minutes past eight when Hercule Poirot descended on to the platform of the little country station and pressed the expected half-crown into the attentive guard's hand.

There was a whistle from the engine, and the Northern Express began to move once more. A tall chauffeur in dark green uniform stepped up to Poirot.

'Mr Poirot? For Hamborough Close?'

He picked up the detective's neat valise and led the way out of the station. A big Rolls was waiting. The chauffeur held the door open for Poirot to get in, arranged a sumptuous fur rug over his knees, and they drove off.

After some ten minutes of cross-country driving, round sharp corners and down country lanes, the car turned in at a wide gateway flanked with huge stone griffons.

They drove through a park and up to the house. The door of it was opened as they drew up, and a butler of imposing proportions showed himself upon the front step.

'Mr Poirot? This way, sir.'

He led the way along the hall and threw open a door half-way along it on the right.

'Mr Hercule Poirot,' he announced.

The room contained a number of people in evening dress, and as Poirot walked in his quick eyes perceived at once that his appearance was not expected. The eyes of all present rested on him in unfeigned surprise.

Then a tall woman, whose dark hair was threaded with grey, made an uncertain advance towards him.

Poirot bowed over her hand.

'My apologies, madame,' he said. 'I fear that my train was late.'

'Not at all,' said Lady Chevenix-Gore vaguely. Her eyes still stared at him in a puzzled fashion. 'Not at all, Mr—er—I didn't quite hear—'

'Hercule Poirot.'

He said the name clearly and distinctly.

Somewhere behind him he heard a sudden sharp intake of breath.

At the same time he realized that clearly his host could not be in the room. He murmured gently:

'You knew I was coming, madame?'

'Oh—oh, yes . . .' Her manner was not convincing. 'I think—I mean I suppose so, but I am so terribly impractical, M. Poirot. I forget everything.' Her tone held a melancholy pleasure in the fact. 'I am told things. I appear to take them in—but they just pass through my brain and are gone! Vanished! As though they had never been.'

Then, with a slight air of performing a duty long overdue, she glanced round her vaguely and murmured:

'I expect you know everybody.'

Though this was patently not the case, the phrase was clearly a well-worn formula by means of which Lady Chevenix-Gore spared herself the trouble of introduction and the strain of remembering people's right names.

Making a supreme effort to meet the difficulties of this particular case, she added:

'My daughter—Ruth.'

The girl who stood before him was also tall and dark, but

she was of a very different type. Instead of the flattish, inde-terminate features of Lady Chevenix-Gore, she had a well-chiselled nose, slightly aquiline, and a clear, sharp line of jaw. Her black hair swept back from her face into a mass of little tight curls. Her colouring was of carnation clearness and brilliance, and owed little to make-up. She was, so Hercule Poirot thought, one of the loveliest girls he had seen.

He recognized, too, that she had brains as well as beauty, and guessed at certain qualities of pride and temper. Her voice, when she spoke, came with a slight drawl that struck him as deliberately put on.

'How exciting,' she said, 'to entertain M. Hercule Poirot! The old man arranged a little surprise for us, I suppose.'

'So you did not know I was coming, mademoiselle?' he said quickly.

'I hadn't an idea of it. As it is, I must postpone getting my autograph book until after dinner.'

The notes of a gong sounded from the hall, then the butler opened the door and announced:

'Dinner is served.'

And then, almost before the last word, 'served', had been uttered, something very curious happened. The pontificial domestic figure became, just for one moment, a highly-astonished human being . . .

The metamorphosis was so quick and the mask of the well-trained servant was back again so soon, that anyone who had not happened to be looking would not have noticed the change. Poirot, however, *had* happened to be looking. He wondered.

The butler hesitated in the doorway. Though his face was again correctly expressionless, an air of tension hung about his figure.

Lady Chevenix-Gore said uncertainly:

'Oh, dear—this is most extraordinary. Really, I—one hardly knows what to do.'

Ruth said to Poirot:

'This singular consternation, M. Poirot, is occasioned by the fact that my father, for the first time for at least twenty years, is late for dinner.'

'It is most extraordinary—' wailed Lady Chevenix-Gore. 'Gervase never—'

An elderly man of upright soldierly carriage came to her side. He laughed genially.

'Good old Gervase! Late at last! Upon my word, we'll rag him over this. Elusive collar-stud, d'you think? Or is Gervase immune from our common weaknesses?'

Lady Chevenix-Gore said in a low, puzzled voice:

'But Gervase is *never* late.'

It was almost ludicrous, the consternation caused by this simple *contretemps*. And yet, to Hercule Poirot, it was *not* ludicrous . . . Behind the consternation he felt uneasiness—perhaps even apprehension. And he, too, found it strange that Gervase Chevenix-Gore should not appear to greet the guest he had summoned in such a mysterious manner.

In the meantime, it was clear that nobody knew quite what to do. An unprecedented situation had arisen with which nobody knew how to deal.

Lady Chevenix-Gore at last took the initiative, if initiative it can be called. Certainly her manner was vague in the extreme.

'Snell,' she said, 'is your master—?'

She did not finish the sentence, merely looked at the butler expectantly.

Snell, who was clearly used to his mistress's methods of seeking information, replied promptly to the unspecified question:

'Sir Gervase came downstairs at five minutes to eight, m'lady, and went straight to the study.'

'Oh, I see—' Her mouth remained open, her eyes seemed far away. 'You don't think—I mean—he heard the gong?'

'I think he must have done so, m'lady, the gong being immediately outside the study door. I did not, of course, know that Sir Gervase was still in the study, otherwise I should have announced to him that dinner was ready. Shall I do so now, m'lady?'

Lady Chevenix-Gore seized on the suggestion with manifest relief.

'Oh, thank you, Snell. Yes, please do. Yes, certainly.'

She said, as the butler left the room:

'Snell is such a treasure. I rely on him absolutely. I really don't know what I should *do* without Snell.'

Somebody murmured a sympathetic assent, but nobody spoke. Hercule Poirot, watching that room full of people with suddenly sharpened attention, had an idea that one and all were in a state of tension. His eyes ran quickly over them, tabulating them roughly. Two elderly men, the soldierly one who had spoken just now, and a thin, spare, grey-haired man with closely pinched legal lips. Two youngish men—very different in type from each other. One with a moustache and an air of modest arrogance, he guessed to be possibly Sir Gervase's nephew, the one in the Blues. The other, with sleek brushed-back hair and a rather obvious style of good looks, he put down as of a definitely inferior social class. There was a small middle-aged woman with pince-nez and intelligent eyes, and there was a girl with flaming red hair.

Snell appeared at the door. His manner was perfect, but once again the veneer of the impersonal butler showed signs of the perturbed human being beneath the surface.

'Excuse me, m'lady, the study door is locked.'

'Locked?'

It was a man's voice—young, alert, with a ring of excitement in it. It was the good-looking young man with the slicked-back hair who had spoken. He went on, hurrying forward:

'Shall I go and see—?'

But very quietly Hercule Poirot took command. He did it so naturally that no one thought it odd that this stranger, who had just arrived, should suddenly assume charge of the situation.

'Come,' he said. 'Let us go to the study.'

He continued, speaking to Snell:

'Lead the way, if you please.'

Snell obeyed. Poirot followed close behind him, and, like a flock of sheep, everyone else followed.

Snell led the way through the big hall, past the great

branching curve of the staircase, past an enormous grandfather clock and a recess in which stood a gong, along a narrow passage which ended in a door.

Here Poirot passed Snell and gently tried the handle. It turned, but the door did not open. Poirot rapped gently with his knuckles on the panel of the door. He rapped louder and louder. Then, suddenly desisting, he dropped to his knees and applied his eye to the keyhole.

Slowly he rose to his feet and looked round. His face was stern.

'Gentlemen!' he said. 'This door must be broken open immediately!'

Under his direction the two young men, who were both tall and powerfully built, attacked the door. It was no easy matter. The doors of Hamborough Close were solidly built.

At last, however, the lock gave, and the door swung inwards with a noise of splintering, rending wood.

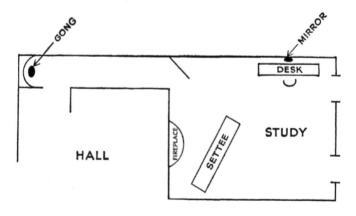

And then, for a moment, everyone stood still, huddled in the doorway looking at the scene inside. The lights were on. Along the left-hand wall was a big writing-table, a massive affair of solid mahogany. Sitting, not at the table, but sideways to it, so that his back was directly towards them, was a big man slouched down in a chair. His head and the upper part of his body hung down over the right side of the chair, and his right hand and arm hung limply down. Just below it on the carpet was a small, gleaming pistol . . .

There was no need of speculation. The picture was clear. Sir Gervase Chevenix-Gore had shot himself.

CHAPTER 3

For a moment or two the group in the doorway stood motionless, staring at the scene. Then Poirot strode forward.

At the same moment Hugo Trent said crisply:

'My God, the Old Man's shot himself!'

And there was a long, shuddering moan from Lady Chevenix-Gore.

'Oh, Gervase—Gervase!'

Over his shoulder Poirot said sharply:

'Take Lady Chevenix-Gore away. She can do nothing here.'

The elderly soldierly man obeyed. He said:

'Come, Vanda. Come, my dear. You can do nothing. It's all over. Ruth, come and look after your mother.'

But Ruth Chevenix-Gore had pressed into the room and stood close by Poirot's side as he bent over the dreadful sprawled figure in the chair—the figure of a man of Herculean build with a Viking beard.

She said in a low, tense voice, curiously restrained and muffled:

'You're quite sure he's—dead?'

Poirot looked up.

The girl's face was alive with some emotion—an emotion sternly checked and repressed—that he did not quite understand. It was not grief—it seemed more like a kind of half-fearful excitement.

The little woman in the pince-nez murmured:

'Your mother, my dear—don't you think—?'

In a high, hysterical voice the girl with the red hair cried out:

'Then it *wasn't* a car or a champagne cork! It was a *shot* we heard . . .'

Poirot turned and faced them all.

'Somebody must communicate with the police—'

Ruth Chevenix-Gore cried out violently:

'No!'

The elderly man with the legal face said:

'Unavoidable, I am afraid. Will you see to that, Burrows? Hugo—'

Poirot said:

'You are Mr Hugo Trent?' to the tall young man with the moustache. 'It would be well, I think, if everyone except you and I were to leave this room.'

Again his authority was not questioned. The lawyer shepherded the others away. Poirot and Hugo Trent were left alone.

The latter said, staring:

'Look here—who *are* you? I mean, I haven't the foggiest idea. What are you doing here?'

Poirot took a card-case from his pocket and selected a card.

Hugo Trent said, staring at it:

'Private detective—eh? Of course, I've heard of you . . . But I still don't see what you are doing *here*.'

'You did not know that your uncle—he was your uncle, was he not—?'

Hugo's eyes dropped for a fleeting moment to the dead man.

'The Old Man? Yes, he was my uncle all right.'

'You did not know that he had sent for me?'

Hugo shook his head. He said slowly:

'I'd no idea of it.'

There was an emotion in his voice that was rather hard to classify. His face looked wooden and stupid—the kind of expression, Poirot thought, that made a useful mask in times of stress.

Poirot said quietly:

'We are in Westshire, are we not? I know your Chief Constable, Major Riddle, very well.'

Hugo said:

'Riddle lives about half a mile away. He'll probably come over himself.'

'That,' said Poirot, 'will be very convenient.'

He began prowling gently round the room. He twitched aside the window curtain and examined the french windows, trying them gently. They were closed.

On the wall behind the desk there hung a round mirror. The mirror was shivered. Poirot bent down and picked up a small object.

'What's that?' asked Hugo Trent.

'The bullet.'

'It passed straight through his head and struck the mirror?'

'It seems so.'

Poirot replaced the bullet meticulously where he had found it. He came up to the desk. Some papers were arranged neatly stacked in heaps. On the blotting-pad itself there was a loose sheet of paper with the word *SORRY* printed across it in large, shaky handwriting.

Hugo said: 'He must have written that just before he—did it.'

Poirot nodded thoughtfully.

He looked again at the smashed mirror, then at the dead man. His brow creased itself a little as though in perplexity. He went over to the door, where it hung crookedly with its splintered lock. There was no key in the door, as he knew—otherwise he would not have been able to see through the keyhole. There was no sign of it on the floor. Poirot leaned over the dead man and ran his fingers over him.

'Yes,' he said. 'The key is in his pocket.'

Hugo drew out a cigarette-case and lighted a cigarette. He spoke rather hoarsely.

'It seems all quite clear,' he said. 'My uncle shut himself up in here, scrawled that message on a piece of paper, and then shot himself.'

Poirot nodded meditatively. Hugo went on:

'But I don't understand why he sent for you. What was it all about?'

'That is rather more difficult to explain. While we are waiting, Mr Trent, for the authorities to take charge, perhaps you will tell me exactly who all the people are whom I saw tonight when I arrived?'

'Who they are?' Hugo spoke almost absently. 'Oh, yes, of course. Sorry. Shall we sit down?' He indicated a settee in the farthest corner of the room from the body. He went on, speaking jerkily: 'Well, there's Vanda—my aunt, you know. And Ruth, my cousin. But you know them. Then the other girl is Susan Cardwell. She's just staying here. And there's Colonel Bury. He's an old friend of the family. And Mr Forbes. He's an old friend, too, beside being the family lawyer and all that. Both the old boys had a passion for Vanda when she was young, and they still hang round in a faithful, devoted sort of way. Ridiculous, but rather touching. Then there's Godfrey Burrows, the Old Man's—I mean my uncle's—secretary, and Miss Lingard, who's here to help him write a history of the Chevenix-Gores. She mugs up historical stuff for writers. That's the lot, I think.'

Poirot nodded. Then he said:

'And I understand you actually heard the shot that killed your uncle?'

'Yes, we did. Thought it was a champagne cork—at least, I did. Susan and Miss Lingard thought it was a car back-firing outside—the road runs quite near, you know.'

'When was this?'

'Oh, about ten past eight. Snell had just sounded the first gong.'

'And where were you when you heard it?'

'In the hall. We—we were laughing about it—arguing, you know, as to where the sound came from. I said it came from the dining-room, and Susan said it came from the direction of the drawing-room, and Miss Lingard said it sounded like upstairs, and Snell said it came from the road outside, only it came through the upstairs windows. And Susan said, 'Any more theories?' And I laughed and said there was always murder! Seems pretty rotten to think of it now.'

His face twitched nervously.

'It did not occur to anyone that Sir Gervase might have shot himself?'

'No, of course not.'

'You have, in fact, no idea why he should have shot himself?'

Hugo said slowly:

'Oh, well, I shouldn't say that—'

'You *have* an idea?'

'Yes—well—it's difficult to explain. Naturally I didn't expect him to commit suicide, but all the same I'm not frightfully surprised. The truth of it is that my uncle was as mad as a hatter, M. Poirot. Everyone knew that.'

'That strikes you as a sufficient explanation?'

'Well, people do shoot themselves when they're a bit barmy.'

'An explanation of an admirable simplicity.'

Hugo stared.

Poirot got up again and wandered aimlessly round the room. It was comfortably furnished, mainly in a rather heavy

Victorian style. There were massive bookcases, huge arm-chairs, and some upright chairs of genuine Chippendale. There were not many ornaments, but some bronzes on the mantel-piece attracted Poirot's attention and apparently stirred his admiration. He picked them up one by one, carefully examining them before replacing them with care. From the one on the extreme left he detached something with a fingernail.

'What's that?' asked Hugo without much interest.

'Nothing very much. A tiny sliver of looking-glass.'

Hugo said:

'Funny the way that mirror was smashed by the shot. A broken mirror means bad luck. Poor old Gervase . . . I suppose his luck had held a bit too long.'

'Your uncle was a lucky man?'

Hugo gave a short laugh.

'Why, his luck was proverbial! Everything he touched turned to gold! If he backed an outsider, it romped home! If he invested in a doubtful mine, they struck a vein of ore at once! He's had the most amazing escapes from the tightest of tight places. His life's been saved by a kind of miracle more than once. He was rather a fine old boy, in his way, you know. He'd certainly "been places and seen things"— more than most of his generation.'

Poirot murmured in a conversational tone:

'You were attached to your uncle, Mr Trent?'

Hugo Trent seemed a little startled by the question.

'Oh—er—yes, of course,' he said rather vaguely. 'You know, he was a bit difficult at times. Frightful strain to live with, and all that. Fortunately I didn't have to see much of him.'

'*He* was fond of *you*?'

'Not so that you'd notice it! As a matter of fact, he rather resented my existence, so to speak.'

'How was that, Mr Trent?'

'Well, you see, he had no son of his own—and he was pretty sore about it. He was mad about family and all that sort of thing. I believe it cut him to the quick to know that when he died the Chevenix-Gores would cease to exist. They've been going ever since the Norman Conquest, you know. The Old Man was the last of them. I suppose it *was* rather rotten from his point of view.'

'You yourself do not share that sentiment?'

Hugo shrugged his shoulders.

'All that sort of thing seems to me rather out of date.'

'What will happen to the estate?'

'Don't really know. I might get it. Or he may have left it to Ruth. Probably Vanda has it for her lifetime.'

'Your uncle did not definitely declare his intentions?'

'Well, he had his pet idea.'

'And what was that?'

'His idea was that Ruth and I should make a match of it.'

'That would doubtless have been very suitable.'

'Eminently suitable. But Ruth—well, Ruth has very decided views of her own about life. Mind you, she's an extremely attractive young woman, and she knows it. She's in no hurry to marry and settle down.'

Poirot leaned forward.

'But you yourself would have been willing, M. Trent?'

Hugo said in a bored tone of voice:

'I really can't see it makes a ha'p'orth of difference who you marry nowadays. Divorce is so easy. If you're not hitting it off, nothing is easier than to cut the tangle and start again.'

The door opened and Forbes entered with a tall, spruce-looking man.

The latter nodded to Trent.

'Hallo, Hugo. I'm extremely sorry about this. Very rough on all of you.'

Hercule Poirot came forward.

'How do you do, Major Riddle? You remember me?'

'Yes, indeed.' The chief constable shook hands. 'So *you're* down here?'

There was a meditative note in his voice. He glanced curiously at Hercule Poirot.

CHAPTER 4

'Well?' said Major Riddle.

It was twenty minutes later. The chief constable's interrogative 'Well?' was addressed to the police surgeon, a lank elderly man with grizzled hair.

The latter shrugged his shoulders.

'He's been dead over half an hour—but not more than an hour. You don't want technicalities, I know, so I'll spare you them. The man was shot through the head, the pistol being held a few inches from the right temple. Bullet passed right through the brain and out again.'

'Perfectly compatible with suicide?'

'Oh, perfectly. The body then slumped down in the chair, and the pistol dropped from his hand.'

'You've got the bullet?'

'Yes.' The doctor held it up.

'Good,' said Major Riddle. 'We'll keep it for comparison with the pistol. Glad it's a clear case and no difficulties.'

Hercule Poirot asked gently:

'You are sure there *are* no difficulties, Doctor?'

The doctor replied slowly:

'Well, I suppose you might call one thing a little odd.

When he shot himself he must have been leaning slightly over to the right. Otherwise the bullet would have hit the wall *below* the mirror, instead of plumb in the middle.'

'An uncomfortable position in which to commit suicide,' said Poirot.

The doctor shrugged his shoulders.

'Oh, well—comfort—if you're going to end it all—' He left the sentence unfinished.

Major Riddle said:

'The body can be moved now?'

'Oh, yes. I've done with it until the P.-M.'

'What about you, Inspector?' Major Riddle spoke to a tall impassive-faced man in plain clothes.

'O.K., sir. We've got all we want. Only the deceased's fingerprints on the pistol.'

'Then you can get on with it.'

The mortal remains of Gervase Chevenix-Gore were removed. The chief constable and Poirot were left together.

'Well,' said Riddle, 'everything seems quite clear and aboveboard. Door locked, window fastened, key of door in dead man's pocket. Everything according to Cocker—but for one circumstance.'

'And what is that, my friend?' inquired Poirot.

'*You*!' said Riddle bluntly. 'What are *you* doing down here?'

By way of reply, Poirot handed to him the letter he had received from the dead man a week ago, and the telegram which had finally brought him there.

'Humph,' said the chief constable. 'Interesting. We'll have

to get to the bottom of this. I should say it had a direct bearing upon his suicide.'

'I agree.'

'We must check up on who is in the house.'

'I can tell you their names. I have just been making inquiries of Mr Trent.'

He repeated the list of names.

'Perhaps you, Major Riddle, know something about these people?'

'I know something of them, naturally. Lady Chevenix-Gore is quite as mad in her own way as old Sir Gervase. They were devoted to each other—and both quite mad. She's the vaguest creature that ever lived, with an occasional uncanny shrewdness that strikes the nail on the head in the most surprising fashion. People laugh at her a good deal. I think she knows it, but she doesn't care. She's absolutely no sense of humour.'

'Miss Chevenix-Gore is only their adopted daughter, I understand?'

'Yes.'

'A very handsome young lady.'

'She's a devilishly attractive girl. Has played havoc with most of the young fellows round here. Leads them all on and then turns round and laughs at them. Good seat on a horse, and wonderful hands.'

'That, for the moment, does not concern us.'

'Er—no, perhaps not . . . Well, about the other people. I know old Bury, of course. He's here most of the time. Almost a tame cat about the house. Kind of A.D.C. to

Lady Chevenix-Gore. He's a very old friend. They've known him all their lives. I think he and Sir Gervase were both interested in some company of which Bury was a director.'

'Oswald Forbes, do you know anything of him?'

'I rather believe I've met him once.'

'Miss Lingard?'

'Never heard of her.'

'Miss Susan Cardwell?'

'Rather a good-looking girl with red hair? I've seen her about with Ruth Chevenix-Gore the last few days.'

'Mr Burrows?'

'Yes, I know him. Chevenix-Gore's secretary. Between you and me, I don't take to him much. He's good-looking, and knows it. Not quite out of the top drawer.'

'Had he been with Sir Gervase long?'

'About two years, I fancy.'

'And there is no one else—?'

Poirot broke off.

A tall, fair-haired man in a lounge suit came hurrying in. He was out of breath and looked disturbed.

'Good evening, Major Riddle. I heard a rumour that Sir Gervase had shot himself, and I hurried up here. Snell tells me it's true. It's incredible! I can't believe it!'

'It's true enough, Lake. Let me introduce you. This is Captain Lake, Sir Gervase's agent for the estate. M. Hercule Poirot, of whom you may have heard.'

Lake's face lit up with what seemed a kind of delighted incredulity.

'M. Hercule Poirot? I'm most awfully pleased to meet

you. At least—' He broke off, the quick charming smile vanished—he looked disturbed and upset. 'There isn't anything—fishy—about this suicide, is there, sir?'

'Why should there be anything "fishy," as you call it?' asked the chief constable sharply.

'I mean, because M. Poirot is here. Oh, and because the whole business seems so incredible!'

'No, no,' said Poirot quickly. 'I am not here on account of the death of Sir Gervase. I was already in the house—as a guest.'

'Oh, I see. Funny, he never told me you were coming when I was going over accounts with him this afternoon.'

Poirot said quietly:

'You have twice used the word "incredible," Captain Lake. Are you, then, so surprised to hear of Sir Gervase commiting suicide?'

'Indeed I am. Of course, he was mad as a hatter; everyone would agree about that. But all the same, I simply can't imagine his thinking the world would be able to get on without him.'

'Yes,' said Poirot. 'It is a point, that.' And he looked with appreciation at the frank, intelligent countenance of the young man.

Major Riddle cleared his throat.

'Since you are here, Captain Lake, perhaps you will sit down and answer a few questions.'

'Certainly, sir.'

Lake took a chair opposite the other two.

'When did you last see Sir Gervase?'

'This afternoon, just before three o'clock. There were some accounts to be checked, and the question of a new tenant for one of the farms.'

'How long were you with him?'

'Perhaps half an hour.'

'Think carefully, and tell me whether you noticed anything unusual in his manner.'

The young man considered.

'No, I hardly think so. He was, perhaps, a trifle excited—but that wasn't unusual with him.'

'He was not depressed in any way?'

'Oh, no, he seemed in good spirits. He was enjoying himself very much just now, writing up a history of the family.'

'How long had he been doing this?'

'He began it about six months ago.'

'Is that when Miss Lingard came here?'

'No. She arrived about two months ago when he had discovered that he could not manage the necessary research work by himself.'

'And you consider he was enjoying himself?'

'Oh, simply enormously! He really didn't think that anything else mattered in the world except his family.'

There was a momentary bitterness in the young man's tone.

'Then, as far as you know, Sir Gervase had no worries of any kind?'

There was a slight—a very slight—pause before Captain Lake answered.

'No.'

Poirot suddenly interposed a question:

'Sir Gervase was not, you think, worried about his daughter in any way?'

'His daughter?'

'That is what I said.'

'Not as far as I know,' said the young man stiffly.

Poirot said nothing further. Major Riddle said:

'Well, thank you, Lake. Perhaps you'd stay around in case I might want to ask you anything.'

'Certainly, sir.' He rose. 'Anything I can do?'

'Yes, you might send the butler here. And perhaps you'd find out for me how Lady Chevenix-Gore is, and if I could have a few words with her presently, or if she's too upset.'

The young man nodded and left the room with a quick, decisive step.

'An attractive personality,' said Hercule Poirot.

'Yes, nice fellow, and good at his job. Everyone likes him.'

CHAPTER 5

'Sit down, Snell,' said Major Riddle in a friendly tone. 'I've a good many questions to ask you, and I expect this has been a shock to you.'

'Oh, it has indeed, sir. Thank you, sir.' Snell sat down with such a discreet air that it was practically the same as though he had remained on his feet.

'Been here a good long time, haven't you?'

'Sixteen years, sir, ever since Sir Gervase—er—settled down, so to speak.'

'Ah, yes, of course, your master was a great traveller in his day.'

'Yes, sir. He went on an expedition to the Pole and many other interesting places.'

'Now, Snell, can you tell me when you last saw your master this evening?'

'I was in the dining-room, sir, seeing that the table arrangements were all complete. The door into the hall was open, and I saw Sir Gervase come down the stairs, cross the hall and go along the passage to the study.'

'That was at what time?'

'Just before eight o'clock. It might have been as much as five minutes before eight.'

'And that was the last you saw of him?'

'Yes, sir.'

'Did you hear a shot?'

'Oh, yes, indeed, sir; but of course I had no idea at the time—how should I have had?'

'What did you think it was?'

'I thought it was a car, sir. The road runs quite near the park wall. Or it might have been a shot in the woods—a poacher, perhaps. I never dreamed—'

Major Riddle cut him short.

'What time was that?'

'It was exactly eight minutes past eight, sir.'

The chief constable said sharply:

'How is it you can fix the time to a minute?'

'That's easy, sir. I had just sounded the first going.'

'The first gong?'

'Yes, sir. By Sir Gervase's orders, a gong was always to be sounded seven minutes before the actual dinner gong. Very particular he was, sir, that everyone should be assembled ready in the drawing-room when the second gong went. As soon as I had sounded the second gong, I went to the drawing-room and announced dinner, and everyone went in.'

'I begin to understand,' said Hercule Poirot, 'why you looked so surprised when you announced dinner this evening. It was usual for Sir Gervase to be in the drawing-room?'

'I'd never known him not be there before, sir. It was quite a shock. I little thought—'

Again Major Riddle interrupted adroitly:

'And were the others also usually there?'

Snell coughed.

'Anyone who was late for dinner, sir, was never asked to the house again.'

'H'm, very drastic.'

'Sir Gervase, sir, employed a chef who was formerly with the Emperor of Moravia. He used to say, sir, that dinner was as important as a religious ritual.'

'And what about his own family?'

'Lady Chevenix-Gore was always very particular not to upset him, sir, and even Miss Ruth dared not be late for dinner.'

'Interesting,' murmured Hercule Poirot.

'I see,' said Riddle. 'So, dinner being at a quarter past eight, you sounded the first gong at eight minutes past as usual?'

'That is so, sir—but it wasn't as usual. Dinner was usually at eight. Sir Gervase gave orders that dinner was to be a quarter of an hour later this evening, as he was expecting a gentleman by the late train.'

Snell made a little bow towards Poirot as he spoke.

'When your master went to the study, did he look upset or worried in any way?'

'I could not say, sir. It was too far for me to judge of his expression. I just noticed him, that was all.'

'Was he left alone when he went to the study?'

'Yes, sir.'

'Did anyone go to the study after that?'

'I could not say, sir. I went to the butler's pantry after that, and was there until I sounded the first gong at eight minutes past eight.'

'That was when you heard the shot?'

'Yes, sir.'

Poirot gently interposed a question.

'There were others, I think, who also heard the shot?'

'Yes, sir. Mr Hugo and Miss Cardwell. And Miss Lingard.'

'These people were also in the hall?'

'Miss Lingard came out from the drawing-room, and Miss Cardwell and Mr Hugo were just coming down the stairs.'

Poirot asked:

'Was there any conversation about the matter?'

'Well, sir, Mr Hugo asked if there was champagne for dinner. I told him that sherry, hock and burgundy were being served.'

'He thought it was a champagne cork?'

'Yes, sir.'

'But nobody took it seriously?'

'Oh, no, sir. They all went into the drawing-room talking and laughing.'

'Where were the other members of the household?'

'I could not say, sir.'

Major Riddle said:

'Do you know anything about this pistol?' He held it out as he spoke.

'Oh, yes, sir. That belonged to Sir Gervase. He always kept it in the drawer of his desk in here.'

'Was it usually loaded?'

'I couldn't say, sir.'

Major Riddle laid down the pistol and cleared his throat.

'Now, Snell, I'm going to ask you a rather important question. I hope you will answer it as truthfully as you can. *Do you know of any reason which might lead your master to commit suicide?*'

'No, sir. I know of nothing.'

'Sir Gervase had not been odd in his manner of late? Not depressed? Or worried?'

Snell coughed apologetically.

'You'll excuse my saying it, sir, but Sir Gervase was always what might have seemed to strangers a little odd in his manner. He was a highly original gentleman, sir.'

'Yes, yes, I am quite aware of that.'

'Outsiders, sir, did not always Understand Sir Gervase.'

Snell gave the phrase a definite value of capital letter.

'I know. I know. But there was nothing that *you* would have called unusual?'

The butler hesitated.

'I think, sir, that Sir Gervase was worried about something,' he said at last.

'Worried and depressed?'

'I shouldn't say depressed, sir. But worried, yes.'

'Have you any idea of the cause of that worry?'

'No, sir.'

'Was it connected with any particular person, for instance?'

'I could not say at all, sir. In any case, it is only an impression of mine.'

Poirot spoke again.

'You were surprised at his suicide?'

'Very surprised, sir. It has been a terrible shock to me. I never dreamed of such a thing.'

Poirot nodded thoughtfully.

Riddle glanced at him, then he said:

'Well, Snell, I think that is all we want to ask you. You are quite sure that there is nothing else you can tell us—no unusual incident, for instance, that has happened in the last few days?'

The butler, rising to his feet, shook his head.

'There is nothing, sir, nothing whatever.'

'Then you can go.'

'Thank you, sir.'

Moving towards the doorway, Snell drew back and stood aside. Lady Chevenix-Gore floated into the room.

She was wearing an oriental-looking garment of purple and orange silk wound tightly round her body. Her face was serene and her manner collected and calm.

'Lady Chevenix-Gore.' Major Riddle sprang to his feet.

She said:

'They told me you would like to talk to me, so I came.'

'Shall we go into another room? This must be painful for you in the extreme.'

Lady Chevenix-Gore shook her head and sat down on one of the Chippendale chairs. She murmured:

'Oh, no, what does it matter?'

'It is very good of you, Lady Chevenix-Gore, to put your feelings aside. I know what a frightful shock this must have been and—'

She interrupted him.

'It was rather a shock at first,' she admitted. Her tone was easy and conversational. 'But there is no such thing as Death, really, you know, only Change.' She added: 'As a matter of fact, Gervase is standing just behind your left shoulder now. I can see him distinctly.'

Major Riddle's left shoulder twitched slightly. He looked at Lady Chevenix-Gore rather doubtfully.

She smiled at him, a vague, happy smile.

'You don't believe, of course! So few people will. To me, the spirit world is quite as real as this one. But please ask me anything you like, and don't worry about distressing me. I'm not in the least distressed. Everything, you see, is Fate. One cannot escape one's Karma. It all fits in—the mirror—everything.'

'The mirror, madame?' asked Poirot.

She nodded her head towards it vaguely.

'Yes. It's splintered, you see. A symbol! You know Tennyson's poem? I used to read it as a girl—though, of course, I didn't realise then the esoteric side of it. "*The mirror cracked from side to side. 'The curse is come upon me!' cried the Lady of Shalott.*" That's what happened to Gervase. The Curse came upon him suddenly. I think, you know, most very old families have a curse . . . the mirror cracked. He knew that he was doomed! *The Curse had come!*'

'But, madame, it was not a curse that cracked the mirror—it was a bullet!'

Lady Chevenix-Gore said, still in the same sweet vague manner:

'It's all the same thing, really . . . It was Fate.'

'But your husband shot himself.'

Lady Chevenix-Gore smiled indulgently.

'He shouldn't have done that, of course. But Gervase was always impatient. He could never wait. His hour had come—he went forward to meet it. It's all so simple, really.'

Major Riddle, clearing his throat in exasperation, said sharply:

'Then you weren't surprised at your husband's taking his own life? Had you been expecting such a thing to happen?'

'Oh, no.' Her eyes opened wide. 'One can't always foresee the future. Gervase, of course, was a very strange man, a very unusual man. He was quite unlike anyone else. He was one of the Great Ones born again. I've known that for some time. I think he knew it himself. He found it very hard to conform to the silly little standards of the everyday world.' She added, looking over Major Riddle's shoulder, 'He's smiling now. He's thinking how foolish we all are. So we are really. Just like children. Pretending that life is real and that it matters . . . Life is only one of the Great Illusions.'

Feeling that he was fighting a losing battle, Major Riddle asked desperately:

'You can't help us at all as to *why* your husband should have taken his life?'

She shrugged her thin shoulders.

'Forces move us—they move us . . . You cannot understand. You move only on the material plane.'

Poirot coughed.

'Talking of the material plane, have you any idea, madame, as to how your husband has left his money?'

'Money?' she stared at him. 'I never think of money.'

Her tone was disdainful.

Poirot switched to another point.

'At what time did you come downstairs to dinner tonight?'

'Time? What is Time? Infinite, that is the answer. Time is infinite.'

Poirot murmured:

'But your husband, madame, was rather particular about time—especially, so I have been told, as regards the dinner hour.'

'Dear Gervase,' she smiled indulgently. 'He was very foolish about that. But it made him happy. So we were never late.'

'Were you in the drawing-room, madame, when the first gong went?'

'No, I was in my room then.'

'Do you remember who was in the drawing-room when you did come down?'

'Nearly everybody, I think,' said Lady Chevenix-Gore vaguely. 'Does it matter?'

'Possibly not,' admitted Poirot. 'Then there is something else. Did your husband ever tell you that he suspected he was being robbed?'

Lady Chevenix-Gore did not seem much interested in the question.

'Robbed? No, I don't think so.'

'Robbed, swindled—victimized in some way—?'

'No—no—I don't think so . . . Gervase would have been very angry if anybody had dared to do anything like that.'

'At any rate he said nothing about it to you?'

'No—no.' Lady Chevenix-Goreshook her head, still without much real interest. 'I should have remembered . . .'

'When did you last see your husband alive?'

'He looked in, as usual, on his way downstairs before dinner. My maid was there. He just said he was going down.'

'What has he talked about most in the last few weeks?'

'Oh, the family history. He was getting on so well with it. He found that funny old thing, Miss Lingard, quite invaluable. She looked up things for him in the British Museum—all that sort of thing. She worked with Lord Mulcaster on his book, you know. And she was tactful—I mean, she didn't look up the wrong things. After all, there are ancestors one doesn't want raked up. Gervase was very sensitive. She helped me, too. She got a lot of information for me about Hatshepsut. I am a reincarnation of Hatshepsut, you know.'

Lady Chevenix-Gore made this announcement in a calm voice.

'Before that,' she went on, 'I was a Priestess in Atlantis.'

Major Riddle shifted a little in his chair.

'Er—er—very interesting,' he said. 'Well, really, Lady Chevenix-Gore, I think that will be all. Very kind of you.'

Lady Chevenix-Gore rose, clasping her oriental robes about her.

'Goodnight,' she said. And then, her eyes shifting to a point behind Major Riddle. 'Goodnight, Gervase dear. I wish you could come, but I know you have to stay here.' She added in an explanatory fashion, 'You have to stay in the place where you've passed over for at least twenty-four hours. It's some time before you can move about freely and communicate.'

She trailed out of the room.

Major Riddle wiped his brow.

'Phew,' he murmured. 'She's a great deal madder than I ever thought. Does she really believe all that nonsense?'

Poirot shook his head thoughtfully.

'It is possible that she finds it helpful,' he said. 'She needs, at this moment, to create for herself a world of illusion so that she can escape the stark reality of her husband's death.'

'She seems almost certifiable to me,' said Major Riddle. 'A long farrago of nonsense without one word of sense in it.'

'No, no, my friend. The interesting thing is, as Mr Hugo Trent casually remarked to me, that amidst all the vapouring there is an occasional shrewd thrust. She showed it by her remark about Miss Lingard's tact in not stressing undesirable ancestors. Believe me, Lady Chevenix-Gore is no fool.'

He got up and paced up and down the room.

'There are things in this affair that I do not like. No, I do not like them at all.'

Riddle looked at him curiously.

'You mean the motive for his suicide?'

'Suicide—suicide! It is all wrong, I tell you. *It is wrong psychologically*. How did Chevenix-Gore think of himself? As a Colossus, as an immensely important person, as the centre of the universe! Does such a man destroy himself? Surely not. He is far more likely to destroy someone else— some miserable crawling ant of a human being who had dared to cause him annoyance . . . Such an act he might regard as necessary—as sanctified! But self-destruction? The destruction of such a Self?'

'It's all very well, Poirot. But the evidence is clear enough. Door locked, key in his own pocket. Window closed and fastened. I know these things happen in books—but I've never come across them in real life. Anything else?'

'But yes, there is something else.' Poirot sat down in the chair. 'Here I am. I am Chevenix-Gore. I am sitting at my desk. I am determined to kill myself—because, let us say, I have made a discovery concerning some terrific dishonour to the family name. It is not very convincing, that, but it must suffice.

'*Eh bien*, what do I do? I scrawl on a piece of paper the word SORRY. Yes, that is quite possible. Then I open a drawer of the desk, take out the pistol which I keep there, load it, if it is not loaded, and then—do I proceed to shoot myself? No, I first turn my chair round—so, and I lean over a little to the right—so—and then I put the pistol to my temple and fire!'

Poirot sprang up from his chair, and wheeling round, demanded:

203

'I ask you, does that make sense? *Why* turn the chair round? If, for instance, there had been a picture on the wall there, then, yes, there might be an explanation. Some portrait which a dying man might wish to be the last thing on earth his eyes would see, but a window-curtain—*ah non*, that does not make sense.'

'He might have wished to look out of the window. Last view out over the estate.'

'My dear friend, you do not suggest that with any conviction. In fact, you know it is nonsense. At eight minutes past eight it was dark, and in any case the curtains are drawn. No, there must be some other explanation . . .'

'There's only one as far as I can see. Gervase Chevenix-Gore was mad.'

Poirot shook his head in a dissatisfied manner.

Major Riddle rose.

'Come,' he said. 'Let us go and interview the rest of the party. We may get at something that way.'

CHAPTER 6

After the difficulties of getting a direct statement from Lady Chevenix-Gore, Major Riddle found considerable relief in dealing with a shrewd lawyer like Forbes.

Mr Forbes was extremely guarded and cautious in his statements, but his replies were all directly to the point.

He admitted that Sir Gervase's suicide had been a great shock to him. He should never have considered Sir Gervase the kind of man who would take his own life. He knew nothing of any cause for such an act.

'Sir Gervase was not only my client, but was a very old friend. I have known him since boyhood. I should say that he had always enjoyed life.'

'In the circumstances, Mr Forbes, I must ask you to speak quite candidly. You did not know of any secret anxiety or sorrow in Sir Gervase's life?'

'No. He had minor worries, like most men, but there was nothing of a serious nature.'

'No illness? No trouble between him and his wife?'

'No. Sir Gervase and Lady Chevenix-Gore were devoted to each other.'

Major Riddle said cautiously:

'Lady Chevenix-Gore appears to hold somewhat curious views.'

Mr Forbes smiled—an indulgent, manly smile.

'Ladies,' he said, 'must be allowed their fancies.'

The chief constable went on:

'You managed all Sir Gervase's legal affairs?'

'Yes, my firm, Forbes, Ogilvie and Spence, have acted for the Chevenix-Gore family for well over a hundred years.'

'Were there any—scandals in the Chevenix-Gore family?'

Mr Forbes's eyebrows rose.

'Really, I fail to understand you?'

'M. Poirot, will you show Mr Forbes the letter you showed me?'

In silence Poirot rose and handed the letter to Mr Forbes with a little bow.

Mr Forbes read it and his eyebrows rose still more.

'A most remarkable letter,' he said. 'I appreciate your question now. No, so far as my knowledge went, there was nothing to justify the writing of such a letter.'

'Sir Gervase said nothing of this matter to you?'

'Nothing at all. I must say I find it very curious that he should not have done so.'

'He was accustomed to confide in you?'

'I think he relied on my judgment.'

'And you have no idea as to what this letter refers?'

'I should not like to make any rash speculations.'

Major Riddle appreciated the subtlety of this reply.

'Now, Mr Forbes, perhaps you can tell us how Sir Gervase has left his property.'

'Certainly. I see no objection to such a course. To his wife, Sir Gervase left an annual income of six thousand pounds chargeable on the estate, and the choice of the Dower House or the town house in Lowndes Square, whichever she should prefer. There were, of course, several legacies and bequests, but nothing of an outstanding nature. The residue of his property was left to his adopted daughter, Ruth, on condition that, if she married, her husband should take the name of Chevenix-Gore.'

'Was nothing left to his nephew, Mr Hugo Trent?'

'Yes. A legacy of five thousand pounds.'

'And I take it that Sir Gervase was a rich man?'

'He was extremely wealthy. He had a vast private fortune apart from the estate. Of course, he was not quite so well-off as in the past. Practically all invested incomes have felt the strain. Also, Sir Gervase had dropped a good deal of money over a certain company—the Paragon Synthetic Rubber Substitute in which Colonel Bury persuaded him to invest a good deal of money.'

'Not very wise advice?'

Mr Forbes sighed.

'Retired soldiers are the worst sufferers when they engage in financial operations. I have found that their credulity far exceeds that of widows—and that is saying a good deal.'

'But these unfortunate investments did not seriously affect Sir Gervase's income?'

'Oh, no, not seriously. He was still an extremely rich man.'

'When was this will made?'

'Two years ago.'

Poirot murmured:

'This arrangement, was it not possibly a little unfair to Mr Hugo Trent, Sir Gervase's nephew? He is, after all, Sir Gervase's nearest blood relation.'

Mr Forbes shrugged his shoulders.

'One has to take a certain amount of family history into account.'

'Such as—?'

Mr Forbes seemed slightly unwilling to proceed.

Major Riddle said:

'You mustn't think we're unduly concerned with raking up old scandals or anything of that sort. But this letter of Sir Gervase's to M. Poirot has got to be explained.'

'There is certainly nothing scandalous in the explanation of Sir Gervase's attitude to his nephew,' said Mr Forbes quickly. 'It was simply that Sir Gervase always took his position as head of the family very seriously. He had a younger brother and sister. The brother, Anthony Chevenix-Gore, was killed in the war. The sister, Pamela, married, and Sir Gervase disapproved of the marriage. That is to say, he considered that she ought to obtain his consent and approval before marrying. He thought that Captain Trent's family was not of sufficient prominence to be allied with a Chevenix-Gore. His sister was merely amused by his attitude. As a result, Sir Gervase has always been inclined to dislike his nephew. I think that dislike may have influenced him in deciding to adopt a child.'

'There was no hope of his having children of his own?'

'No. There was a still-born child about a year after his marriage. The doctors told Lady Chevenix-Gore that she would never be able to have another child. About two years later he adopted Ruth.'

'And who *was* Mademoiselle Ruth? How did they come to settle upon her?'

'She was, I believe, the child of a distant connection.'

'That I had guessed,' said Poirot. He looked up at the wall which was hung with family portraits. 'One can see that she was of the same blood—the nose, the line of the chin. It repeats itself on these walls many times.'

'She inherits the temper too,' said Mr Forbes dryly.

'So I should imagine. How did she and her adopted father get on?'

'Much as you might imagine. There was a fierce clash of wills more than once. But in spite of these quarrels I believe there was also an underlying harmony.'

'Nevertheless, she caused him a good deal of anxiety?'

'Incessant anxiety. But I can assure you not to the point of causing him to take his own life.'

'Ah, that, no,' agreed Poirot. 'One does not blow one's brains out because one has a headstrong daughter! And so mademoiselle inherits! Sir Gervase, he never thought of altering his will?'

'Ahem!' Mr Forbes coughed to hide a little discomposure. 'As a matter of fact, I took instructions from Sir Gervase on my arrival here (two days ago, that is to say) as to the drafting of a new will.'

'What's this?' Major Riddle hitched his chair a little closer. 'You didn't tell us this.'

Mr Forbes said quickly:

'You merely asked me what the terms of Sir Gervase's will were. I gave you the information for which you asked. The new will was not even properly drawn up—much less signed.'

'What were its provisions? They may be some guide to Sir Gervase's state of mind.'

'In the main, they were the same as before, but Miss Chevenix-Gore was only to inherit on condition that she married Mr Hugo Trent.'

'Aha,' said Poirot. 'But there is a very decided difference there.'

'I did not approve of the clause,' said Mr Forbes. 'And I felt bound to point out that it was quite possible it might be contested successfully. The Court does not look upon such conditional bequests with approval. Sir Gervase, however, was quite decided.'

'And if Miss Chevenix-Gore (or, incidentally, Mr Trent) refused to comply?'

'If Mr Trent was not willing to marry Miss Chevenix-Gore, then the money went to her unconditionally. But if *he* was willing and *she* refused, then the money went to him instead.'

'Odd business,' said Major Riddle.

Poirot leaned forward. He tapped the lawyer on the knee.

'But what is behind it? What was in the mind of

Sir Gervase when he made that stipulation? There must have been something very definite . . . There must, I think, have been the image of another man . . . a man of whom he disapproved. I think, Mr Forbes, that *you* must know who that man was?'

'Really, M. Poirot, I have no information.'

'But you could make a guess.'

'I never guess,' said Mr Forbes, and his tone was scandalized.

Removing his pince-nez, he wiped them with a silk handkerchief and inquired:

'Is there anything else that you desire to know?'

'At the moment, no,' said Poirot. 'Not, that is, as far as I am concerned.'

Mr Forbes looked as though, in his opinion, that was not very far, and bent his attention on the chief constable.

'Thank you, Mr Forbes. I think that's all. I should like, if I may, to speak to Miss Chevenix-Gore.'

'Certainly. I think she is upstairs with Lady Chevenix-Gore.'

'Oh, well, perhaps I'll have a word with—what's his name?—Burrows, first, and the family-history woman.'

'They're both in the library. I will tell them.'

CHAPTER 7

'Hard work, that,' said Major Riddle, as the lawyer left the room. 'Extracting information from these old-fashioned legal wallahs takes a bit of doing. The whole business seems to me to centre about the girl.'

'It would seem so—yes.'

'Ah, here comes Burrows.'

Godfrey Burrows came in with a pleasant eagerness to be of use. His smile was discreetly tempered with gloom and showed only a fraction too much teeth. It seemed more mechanical than spontaneous.

'Now, Mr Burrows, we want to ask you a few questions.'

'Certainly, Major Riddle. Anything you like.'

'Well, first and foremost, to put it quite simply, have you any ideas of your own about Sir Gervase's suicide?'

'Absolutely none. It was the greatest shock to me.'

'You heard the shot?'

'No; I must have been in the library at the time, as far as I can make out. I came down rather early and went to the library to look up a reference I wanted. The library's right the other side of the house from the study, so I shouldn't hear anything.'

'Was anyone with you in the library?' asked Poirot.

'No one at all.'

'You've no idea where the other members of the household were at that time?'

'Mostly upstairs dressing, I should imagine.'

'When did you come to the drawing-room?'

'Just before M. Poirot arrived. Everybody was there then—except Sir Gervase, of course.'

'Did it strike you as strange that he wasn't there?'

'Yes, it did, as a matter of fact. As a rule he was always in the drawing-room before the first gong sounded.'

'Have you noticed any difference in Sir Gervase's manner lately? Has he been worried? Or anxious? Depressed?'

Godfrey Burrows considered.

'No—I don't think so. A little—well, preoccupied, perhaps.'

'But he did not appear to be worried about any one definite matter?'

'Oh, no.'

'No—financial worries of any kind?'

'He was rather perturbed about the affairs of one particular company—the Paragon Synthetic Rubber Company to be exact.'

'What did he actually say about it?'

Again Godfrey Burrows' mechanical smile flashed out, and again it seemed slightly unreal.

'Well—as a matter of fact—what he said was, "Old Bury's either a fool or a knave. A fool, I suppose. I must go easy with him for Vanda's sake."'

'And why did he say that—*for Vanda's sake?*' inquired Poirot.

'Well, you see, Lady Chevenix-Gore was very fond of Colonel Bury, and he worshipped her. Followed her about like a dog.'

'Sir Gervase was not—jealous at all?'

'Jealous?' Burrows stared and then laughed. 'Sir Gervase jealous? He wouldn't know how to set about it. Why, it would never have entered his head that anyone could ever prefer another man to him. Such a thing couldn't be, you understand.'

Poirot said gently:

'You did not, I think, like Sir Gervase Chevenix-Gore very much?'

Burrows flushed.

'Oh, yes, I did. At least—well, all that sort of thing strikes one as rather ridiculous nowadays.'

'All what sort of thing?' asked Poirot.

'Well, the feudal motif, if you like. This worship of ancestry and personal arrogance. Sir Gervase was a very able man in many ways, and had led an interesting life, but he would have been more interesting if he hadn't been so entirely wrapped up in himself and his own egoism.'

'Did his daughter agree with you there?'

Burrows flushed again—this time a deep purple.

He said:

'I should imagine Miss Chevenix-Gore is quite one of the moderns! Naturally, I shouldn't discuss her father with her.'

'But the moderns *do* discuss their fathers a good deal!' said Poirot. 'It is entirely in the modern spirit to criticize your parents!'

Burrows shrugged his shoulders.

Major Riddle asked:

'And there was nothing else—no other financial anxiety? Sir Gervase never spoke of having been *victimized*?'

'Victimized?' Burrows sounded very astonished. 'Oh, no.'

'And you yourself were on quite good terms with him?'

'Certainly I was. Why not?'

'I am asking you, Mr Burrows.'

The young man looked sulky.

'We were on the best of terms.'

'Did you know that Sir Gervase had written to M. Poirot asking him to come down here?'

'No.'

'Did Sir Gervase usually write his own letters?'

'No, he nearly always dictated them to me.'

'But he did not do so in this case?'

'No.'

'Why was that, do you think?'

'I can't imagine.'

'You can suggest no reason why he should have written this particular letter himself?'

'No, I can't.'

'Ah!' said Major Riddle, adding smoothly, 'Rather curious. When did you last see Sir Gervase?'

'Just before I went to dress for dinner. I took him some letters to sign.'

'What was his manner then?'

'Quite normal. In fact I should say he was feeling rather pleased with himself about something.'

Poirot stirred a little in his chair.

'Ah?' he said. 'So that was your impression, was it? That he was pleased about something. And yet, not so very long afterwards, he shoots himself. It is odd, that!'

Godfrey Burrows shrugged his shoulders.

'I'm only telling you my impressions.'

'Yes, yes, they are very valuable. After all, you are probably one of the last people who saw Sir Gervase alive.'

'Snell was the last person to see him.'

'To see him, yes, but not to speak to him.'

Burrows did not reply.

Major Riddle said:

'What time was it when you went up to dress for dinner?'

'About five minutes past seven.'

'What did Sir Gervase do?'

'I left him in the study.'

'How long did he usually take to change?'

'He usually gave himself a full three-quarters of an hour.'

'Then, if dinner was at a quarter-past eight, he would probably have gone up at half-past seven at the latest?'

'Very likely.'

'You yourself went to change early?'

'Yes, I thought I would change and then go to the library and look up the references I wanted.'

Poirot nodded thoughtfully. Major Riddle said:

'Well, I think that's all for the moment. Will you send Miss What's-her-name along?'

Little Miss Lingard tripped in almost immediately. She was wearing several chains which tinkled a little as she sat down and looked inquiringly from one to the other of the two men.

'This is all very—er—sad, Miss Lingard,' began Major Riddle.

'Very sad indeed,' said Miss Lingard decorously.

'You came to this house—when?'

'About two months ago. Sir Gervase wrote to a friend of his in the Museum—Colonel Fotheringay it was—and Colonel Fotheringay recommended me. I have done a good deal of historical research work.'

'Did you find Sir Gervase difficult to work for?'

'Oh, not really. One had to humour him a little, of course. But then I always find one has to do that with men.'

With an uneasy feeling that Miss Lingard was probably humouring him at this moment, Major Riddle went on:

'Your work here was to help Sir Gervase with the book he was writing?'

'Yes.'

'What did it involve?'

For a moment, Miss Lingard looked quite human. Her eyes twinkled as she replied:

'Well, actually, you know, it involved writing the book! I looked up all the information and made notes, and arranged the material. And then, later, I revised what Sir Gervase had written.'

'You must have had to exercise a good deal of tact, mademoiselle,' said Poirot.

'Tact and firmness. One needs them both,' said Miss Lingard.

'Sir Gervase did not resent your—er—firmness?'

'Oh not at all. Of course I put it to him that he mustn't be bothered with all the petty detail.'

'Oh, yes, I see.'

'It was quite simple, really,' said Miss Lingard. 'Sir Gervase was perfectly easy to manage if one took him the right way.'

'Now, Miss Lingard, I wonder if you know anything that can throw light on this tragedy?'

Miss Lingard shook her head.

'I'm afraid I don't. You see, naturally he wouldn't confide in me at all. I was practically a stranger. In any case I think he was far too proud to speak to anyone of family troubles.'

'But you think it *was* family troubles that caused him to take his life?'

Miss Lingard looked rather surprised.

'But of course! Is there any other suggestion?'

'You feel sure that there were family troubles worrying him?'

'I know that he was in great distress of mind.'

'Oh, you know that?'

'Why, of course.'

'Tell me, mademoiselle, did he speak to you of the matter?'

'Not explicitly.'

'What did he say?'

'Let me see. I found that he didn't seem to be taking in what I was saying—'

'One moment. *Pardon*. When was this?'

'This afternoon. We usually worked from three to five.'

'Pray go on.'

'As I say, Sir Gervase seemed to be finding it hard to concentrate—in fact, he said as much, adding that he had several grave matters preying on his mind. And he said— let me see—something like this—(of course, I can't be sure of the exact words): "*It's a terrible thing, Miss Lingard, when a family has been one of the proudest in the land, that dishonour should be brought on it.*"'

'And what did you say to that?'

'Oh, just something soothing. I think I said that every generation had its weaklings—that that was one of the penalties of greatness—but that their failings were seldom remembered by posterity.'

'And did that have the soothing effect you hoped?'

'More or less. We got back to Sir Roger Chevenix-Gore. I had found a most interesting mention of him in a contemporary manuscript. But Sir Gervase's attention wandered again. In the end he said he would not do any more work that afternoon. He said he had had a shock.'

'A shock?'

'That is what he said. Of course, I didn't ask any questions. I just said, "I am sorry to hear it, Sir Gervase." And then he asked me to tell Snell that M. Poirot would be arriving and to put off dinner until eight-fifteen, and send the car to meet the seven-fifty train.'

'Did he usually ask you to make these arrangements?'

'Well—no—that was really Mr Burrows's business. I did nothing but my own literary work. I wasn't a secretary in any sense of the word.'

Poirot asked:

'Do you think Sir Gervase had a definite reason for asking you to make these arrangements, instead of asking Mr Burrows to do so?'

Miss Lingard considered.

'Well, he may have had . . . I did not think of it at the time. I thought it was just a matter of convenience. Still, it's true now I come to think of it, that he *did* ask me not to tell anyone that M. Poirot was coming. It was to be a surprise, he said.'

'Ah! he said that, did he? Very curious, very interesting. And *did* you tell anyone?'

'Certainly not, M. Poirot. I told Snell about dinner and to send the chauffeur to meet the seven-fifty as a gentleman was arriving by it.'

'Did Sir Gervase say anything else that may have had a bearing on the situation?'

Miss Lingard thought.

'No—I don't think so—he was very much strung-up—I do remember that just as I was leaving the room, he said, "*Not that it's any good his coming now. It's too late.*"'

'And you have no idea at all what he meant by that?'

'N—no.'

Just the faintest suspicion of indecision about the simple
negative. Poirot repeated with a frown:

'"*Too late.*" That is what he said, is it? "*Too late.*"'

Major Riddle said:

'You can give us no idea, Miss Lingard, as to the nature
of the circumstance that so distressed Sir Gervase?'

Miss Lingard said slowly:

'I have an idea that it was in some way connected with
Mr Hugo Trent.'

'With Hugo Trent? Why do you think that?'

'Well, it was nothing definite, but yesterday afternoon
we were just touching on Sir Hugo de Chevenix (who, I'm
afraid, didn't bear too good a character in the Wars of the
Roses), and Sir Gervase said, "My sister *would* choose the
family name of Hugo for her son! It's always been an
unsatisfactory name in our family. She might have known
no Hugo would turn out well."'

'What you tell us there is suggestive,' said Poirot. 'Yes,
it suggests a new idea to me.'

'Sir Gervase said nothing more definite than that?' asked
Major Riddle.

Miss Lingard shook her head.

'No, and of course it wouldn't have done for me to say
anything. Sir Gervase was really just talking to himself. He
wasn't really speaking to me.'

'Quite so.'

Poirot said:

'Mademoiselle, you, a stranger, have been here for two
months. It would be, I think, very valuable if you were to

tell us quite frankly your impressions of the family and household.'

Miss Lingard took off her pince-nez and blinked reflectively.

'Well, at first, quite frankly, I felt as though I'd walked straight into a madhouse! What with Lady Chevenix-Gore continually seeing things that weren't there, and Sir Gervase behaving like—like a king—and dramatizing himself in the most extraordinary way—well, I really did think they were the queerest people I had ever come across. Of course, Miss Chevenix-Gore was perfectly normal, and I soon found that Lady Chevenix-Gore was really an extremely kind, nice woman. Nobody could be kinder and nicer to me than she has been. Sir Gervase—well, I really think he *was* mad. His egomania—isn't that what you call it?—was getting worse and worse every day.'

'And the others?'

'Mr Burrows had rather a difficult time with Sir Gervase, I should imagine. I think he was glad that our work on the book gave him a little more breathing space. Colonel Bury was always charming. He was devoted to Lady Chevenix-Gore and he managed Sir Gervase quite well. Mr Trent, Mr Forbes and Miss Cardwell have only been here a few days, so of course I don't know much about them.'

'Thank you, mademoiselle. And what about Captain Lake, the agent?'

'Oh, he's very nice. Everybody liked him.'

'Including Sir Gervase?'

'Oh, yes. I've heard him say Lake was much the best

agent he'd had. Of course, Captain Lake had his difficulties with Sir Gervase, too—but he managed pretty well on the whole. It wasn't easy.'

Poirot nodded thoughtfully. He murmured, 'There was something—something—that I had in mind to ask you—some little thing . . . What was it now?'

Miss Lingard turned a patient face towards him.

Poirot shook his head vexedly.

'Tchah! It is on the tip of my tongue.'

Major Riddle waited a minute or two, then as Poirot continued to frown perplexedly, he took up the interrogation once more.

'When was the last time you saw Sir Gervase?'

'At tea-time, in this room.'

'What was his manner then? Normal?'

'As normal as it ever was.'

'Was there any sense of strain among the party?'

'No, I think everybody seemed quite ordinary.'

'Where did Sir Gervase go after tea?'

'He took Mr Burrows with him into the study, as usual.'

'That was the last time you saw him?'

'Yes. I went to the small morning-room where I worked, and typed a chapter of the book from the notes I had gone over with Sir Gervase, until seven o'clock, when I went upstairs to rest and dress for dinner.'

'You actually heard the shot, I understand?'

'Yes, I was in this room. I heard what sounded like a shot and I went out into the hall. Mr Trent was there, and Miss Cardwell. Mr Trent asked Snell if there was champagne for dinner, and made rather a joke of it. It never entered our heads to take the matter seriously, I'm afraid. We felt sure it must have been a car back-firing.'

Poirot said:

'Did you hear Mr Trent say, "*There's always murder*"?'

'I believe he did say something like that—joking, of course.'

'What happened next?'

'We all came in here.'

'Can you remember the order in which the others came down to dinner?'

'Miss Chevenix-Gore was the first, I think, and then Mr Forbes. Then Colonel Bury and Lady Chevenix-Gore together, and Mr Burrows immediately after them. I think that was the order, but I can't be quite sure because they more or less came in all together.'

'Gathered by the sound of the first gong?'

'Yes. Everyone always hustled when they heard that gong. Sir Gervase was a terrible stickler for punctuality in the evening.'

'What time did he himself usually come down?'

'He was nearly always in the room before the first gong went.'

'Did it surprise you that he was not down on this occasion?'

'Very much.'

'Ah, I have it!' cried Poirot.

As the other two looked inquiringly at him he went on:

'I have remembered what I wanted to ask. This evening,

mademoiselle, as we all went along to the study on Snell's reporting it to be locked, you stooped and picked something up.'

'I did?' Miss Lingard seemed very surprised.

'Yes, just as we turned into the straight passage to the study. Something small and bright.'

'How extraordinary—I don't remember. Wait a minute—yes, I do. Only I wasn't thinking. Let me see—it must be in here.'

Opening her black satin bag, she poured the contents on a table.

Poirot and Major Riddle surveyed the collection with interest. There were two handkerchiefs, a powder-compact, a small bunch of keys, a spectacle-case and one other object on which Poirot pounced eagerly.

'A bullet, by jove!' said Major Riddle.

The thing was indeed shaped like a bullet, but it proved to be a small pencil.

'That's what I picked up,' said Miss Lingard. 'I'd forgotten all about it.'

'Do you know who this belongs to, Miss Lingard?'

'Oh, yes, it's Colonel Bury's. He had it made out of a bullet that hit him—or rather, didn't hit him, if you know what I mean—in the South African War.'

'Do you know when he had it last?'

'Well, he had it this afternoon when they were playing bridge, because I noticed him writing with it on the score when I came in to tea.'

'Who was playing bridge?'

'Colonel Bury, Lady Chevenix-Gore, Mr Trent and Miss Cardwell.'

'I think,' said Poirot gently, 'we will keep this and return it to the colonel ourselves.'

'Oh, please do. I am so forgetful, I might not remember to do so.'

'Perhaps, mademoiselle, you would be so good as to ask Colonel Bury to come here now?'

'Certainly. I will go and find him at once.'

She hurried away. Poirot got up and began walking aimlessly round the room.

'We begin,' he said, 'to reconstruct the afternoon. It is interesting. At half-past two Sir Gervase goes over accounts with Captain Lake. *He is slightly preoccupied.* At three, he discusses the book he is writing with Miss Lingard. *He is in great distress of mind.* Miss Lingard associates that distress of mind with Hugo Trent on the strength of a chance remark. At teatime *his behaviour is normal.* After tea, Godfrey Burrows tells us *he was in good spirits over something.* At five minutes to eight he comes downstairs, goes to his study, scrawls "*Sorry*" on a sheet of paper, and shoots himself!'

Riddle said slowly:

'I see what you mean. It isn't consistent.'

'Strange alterations of moods in Sir Gervase Chevenix-Gore! He is preoccupied—he is seriously upset—he is normal—he is in high spirits! There is something very curious here! And then that phrase he used, "*Too late.*" That I should get here "Too late." Well, it is true that. I *did* get here too late—*to see him alive.*'

'I see. You really think—?'

'I shall never know now why Sir Gervase sent for me! That is certain!'

Poirot was still wandering round the room. He straightened one or two objects on the mantelpiece; he examined a card-table that stood against a wall, he opened the drawer of it and took out the bridge-markers. Then he wandered over to the writing-table and peered into the wastepaper basket. There was nothing in it but a paper bag. Poirot took it out, smelt it, murmured 'Oranges' and flattened it out, reading the name on it. 'Carpenter and Sons, Fruiterers, Hamborough St Mary.' He was just folding it neatly into squares when Colonel Bury entered the room.

CHAPTER 8

The Colonel dropped into a chair, shook his head, sighed and said:

'Terrible business, this, Riddle. Lady Chevenix-Gore is being wonderful—wonderful. Grand woman! Full of courage!'

Coming softly back to his chair, Poirot said:

'You have known her very many years, I think?'

'Yes, indeed, I was at her coming-out dance. Wore rosebuds in her hair, I remember. And a white, fluffy dress . . . Wasn't anyone to touch her in the room!'

His voice was full of enthusiasm. Poirot held out the pencil to him.

'This is yours, I think?'

'Eh? What? Oh, thank you, had it this afternoon when we were playing bridge. Amazing, you know, I held a hundred honours in spades three times running. Never done such a thing before.'

'You were playing bridge before tea, I understand?' said Poirot. 'What was Sir Gervase's frame of mind when he came in to tea?'

'Usual—quite usual. Never dreamed he was thinking of

making away with himself. Perhaps he was a little more excitable than usual, now I come to think of it.'

'When was the last time you saw him?'

'Why, then! Tea-time. Never saw the poor chap alive again.'

'You didn't go to the study at all after tea?'

'No, never saw him again.'

'What time did you come down to dinner?'

'After the first gong went.'

'You and Lady Chevenix-Gore came down together?'

'No, we—er—met in the hall. I think she'd been into the dining-room to see to the flowers—something like that.'

Major Riddle said:

'I hope you won't mind, Colonel Bury, if I ask you a somewhat personal question. Was there any trouble between you and Sir Gervase over the question of the Paragon Synthetic Rubber Company?'

Colonel Bury's face became suddenly purple. He spluttered a little.

'Not at all. Not at all. Old Gervase was an unreasonable sort of fellow. You've got to remember that. He always expected everything he touched to turn out trumps! Didn't seem to realize that the whole world was going through a period of crisis. All stocks and shares bound to be affected.'

'So there *was* a certain amount of trouble between you?'

'No trouble. Just damned unreasonable of Gervase!'

'He blamed you for certain losses he had sustained?'

'Gervase wasn't normal! Vanda knew that. But she could always handle him. I was content to leave it all in her hands.'

Poirot coughed and Major Riddle, after glancing at him, changed the subject.

'You are a very old friend of the family, I know, Colonel Bury. Had you any knowledge as to how Sir Gervase had left his money?'

'Well, I should imagine the bulk of it would go to Ruth. That's what I gathered from what Gervase let fall.'

'You don't think that was at all unfair on Hugo Trent?'

'Gervase didn't like Hugo. Never could stick him.'

'But he had a great sense of family. Miss Chevenix-Gore was, after all, only his adopted daughter.'

Colonel Bury hesitated, then after humming and hawing a moment, he said:

'Look here, I think I'd better tell you something. Strict confidence, and all that.'

'Of course—of course.'

'Ruth's illegitimate, but she's a Chevenix-Gore all right. Daughter of Gervase's brother, Anthony, who was killed in the war. Seemed he'd had an affair with a typist. When he was killed, the girl wrote to Vanda. Vanda went to see her—girl was expecting a baby. Vanda took it up with Gervase, she'd just been told that she herself could never have another child. Result was they took over the child when it was born, adopted it legally. The mother renounced all rights in it. They've brought Ruth up as their own daughter and to all intents and purposes, she *is* their own daughter, and you've only got to look at her to realise she's a Chevenix-Gore all right!'

'Aha,' said Poirot. 'I see. That makes Sir Gervase's attitude very much clearer. But if he did not like Mr Hugo Trent, why was he so anxious to arrange a marriage between him and Mademoiselle Ruth?'

'To regularize the family position. It pleased his sense of fitness.'

'Even though he did not like or trust the young man?'

Colonel Bury snorted.

'You don't understand old Gervase. He couldn't regard people as human beings. He arranged alliances as though the parties were royal personages! He considered it fitting that Ruth and Hugo should marry, Hugo taking the name of Chevenix-Gore. What Hugo and Ruth thought about it didn't matter.'

'And was Mademoiselle Ruth willing to fall in with this arrangement?'

Colonel Bury chuckled.

'Not she! She's a tartar!'

'Did you know that shortly before his death Sir Gervase was drafting a new will by which Miss Chevenix-Gore would inherit only on condition that she should marry Mr Trent?'

Colonel Bury whistled.

'Then he really *had* got the wind-up about her and Burrows—'

As soon as he had spoken, he bit the words off, but it was too late. Poirot had pounced upon the admission.

'There was something between Mademoiselle Ruth and young Monsieur Burrows?'

'Probably nothing in it—nothing in it at all.'

Major Riddle coughed and said:

'I think, Colonel Bury, that you must tell us all you know. It might have a direct bearing on Sir Gervase's state of mind.'

'I suppose it might,' said Colonel Bury, doubtfully. 'Well, the truth of it is, young Burrows is not a bad-looking chap—at least, women seem to think so. He and Ruth seem to have got as thick as thieves just lately, and Gervase didn't like it—didn't like it at all. Didn't like to sack Burrows for fear of precipitating matters. He knows what Ruth's like. She won't be dictated to in any way. So I suppose he hit on this scheme. Ruth's not the sort of girl to sacrifice everything for love. She's fond of the fleshpots and she likes money.'

'Do you yourself approve of Mr Burrows?'

The colonel delivered himself of the opinion that Godfrey Burrows was slightly hairy at the heel, a pronouncement which baffled Poirot completely, but made Major Riddle smile into his moustache.

A few more questions were asked and answered, and then Colonel Bury departed.

Riddle glanced over at Poirot who was sitting absorbed in thought.

'What do you make of it all, M. Poirot?'

The little man raised his hands.

'I seem to see a pattern—a purposeful design.'

Riddle said, 'It's difficult.'

'Yes, it is difficult. But more and more one phrase, lightly uttered, strikes me as significant.'

'What was that?'

'That laughing sentence spoken by Hugo Trent: "*There's always murder*" . . .'

Riddle said sharply:

'Yes, I can see that you've been leaning that way all along.'

'Do you not agree, my friend, that the more we learn, the less and less motive we find for suicide? But for murder, we begin to have a surprising collection of motives!'

'Still, you've got to remember the facts—door locked, key in dead man's pocket. Oh, I know there are ways and means. Bent pins, strings—all sorts of devices. It would, I suppose, be *possible* . . . But do those things really work? That's what I very much doubt.'

'At all events, let us examine the position from the point of view of murder, not of suicide.'

'Oh, all right. As *you* are on the scene, it probably *would* be murder!'

For a moment Poirot smiled.

'I hardly like that remark.'

Then he became grave once more.

'Yes, let us examine the case from the standpoint of murder. The shot is heard, four people are in the hall, Miss Lingard, Hugo Trent, Miss Cardwell and Snell. Where are all the others?'

'Burrows was in the library, according to his own story.

No one to check that statement. The others were presumably in their rooms, but who is to know if they were really there? Everybody seems to have come down separately. Even Lady Chevenix-Gore and Bury only met in the hall. Lady Chevenix-Gore came from the dining-room. Where did Bury come from? Isn't it possible that he came, not from upstairs, but *from the study*? There's that pencil.'

'Yes, the pencil is interesting. He showed no emotion when I produced it, but that might be because he did not know where I found it and was unaware himself of having dropped it. Let us see, who else was playing bridge when the pencil was in use? Hugo Trent and Miss Cardwell. They're out of it. Miss Lingard and the butler can vouch for their alibis. The fourth was Lady Chevenix-Gore.'

'You can't seriously suspect her.'

'Why not, my friend? I tell you, me, I can suspect everybody! Supposing that, in spite of her apparent devotion to her husband, it is the faithful Bury she really loves?'

'H'm,' said Riddle. 'In a way it has been a kind of *ménage à trois* for years.'

'And there is some trouble about this company between Sir Gervase and Colonel Bury.'

'It's true that Sir Gervase might have been meaning to turn really nasty. We don't know the ins-and-outs of it. It might fit in with that summons to you. Say Sir Gervase suspects that Bury has deliberately fleeced him, but he doesn't want publicity because of a suspicion that his wife may be mixed up in it. Yes, that's possible. That gives either of those two a possible motive. And it *is* a bit odd really that Lady

Chevenix-Gore should take her husband's death so calmly. All this spirit business may be acting!'

'Then there is the other complication,' said Poirot. 'Miss Chevenix-Gore and Burrows. It is very much to their interest that Sir Gervase should not sign the new will. As it is, she gets everything on condition that her husband takes the family name—'

'Yes, and Burrows's account of Sir Gervase's attitude this evening is a bit fishy. High spirits, pleased about something! That doesn't fit with anything else we've been told.'

'There is, too, Mr Forbes. Most correct, most severe, of an old and well-established firm. But lawyers, even the most respectable, have been known to embezzle their client's money when they themselves are in a hole.'

'You're getting a bit too sensational, I think, Poirot.'

'You think what I suggest is too like the pictures? But life, Major Riddle, is often amazingly like the pictures.'

'It has been, so far, in Westshire,' said the chief constable. 'We'd better finish interviewing the rest of them, don't you think? It's getting late. We haven't seen Ruth Chevenix-Gore yet, and she's probably the most important of the lot.'

'I agree. There is Miss Cardwell, too. Perhaps we might see her first, since that will not take long, and interview Miss Chevenix-Gore last.

'Quite a good idea.'

CHAPTER 9

That evening Poirot had only given Susan Cardwell a fleeting glance. He examined her now more attentively. An intelligent face, he thought, not strictly good-looking, but possessing an attraction that a merely pretty girl might envy. Her hair was magnificent, her face skilfully made-up. Her eyes, he thought, were watchful.

After a few preliminary questions, Major Riddle said:

'I don't know how close a friend you are of the family, Miss Cardwell?'

'I don't know them at all. Hugo arranged that I should be asked down here.'

'You are, then, a friend of Hugo Trent's?'

'Yes, that's my position. Hugo's girl-friend.' Susan Cardwell smiled as she drawled out the words.

'You have known him a long time?'

'Oh, no, just a month or so.'

She paused and then added:

'I'm by way of being engaged to him.'

'And he brought you down here to introduce you to his people?'

'Oh, dear no, nothing like that. We were keeping it very

hush-hush. I just came down to spy out the land. Hugo told me the place was just like a madhouse. I thought I'd better come and see for myself. Hugo, poor sweet, is a perfect pet, but he's got absolutely no brains. The position, you see, was rather critical. Neither Hugo nor I have any money, and old Sir Gervase, who was Hugo's main hope, had set his heart on Hugo making a match of it with Ruth. Hugo's a bit weak, you know. He might agree to this marriage and count on being able to get out of it later.'

'That idea did not commend itself to you, mademoiselle?' inquired Poirot gently.

'Definitely not. Ruth might have gone all peculiar and refused to divorce him or something. I put my foot down. No trotting off to St Paul's, Knightsbridge, until I could be there dithering with a sheaf of lilies.'

'So you came down to study the situation for yourself?'

'Yes.'

'*Eh bien!*' said Poirot.

'Well, of course, Hugo was right! The whole family were bughouse! Except Ruth, who seems perfectly sensible. She'd got her own boy-friend and wasn't any keener on the marriage idea than I was.'

'You refer to M. Burrows?'

'Burrows? Of course not. Ruth wouldn't fall for a bogus person like that.'

'Then who was the object of her affection?'

Susan Cardwell paused, stretched for a cigarette, lit it, and remarked:

'You'd better ask her that. After all, it isn't my business.'

Major Riddle asked:

'When was the last time you saw Sir Gervase?'

'At tea.'

'Did his manner strike you as peculiar in any way?'

The girl shrugged her shoulders.

'Not more than usual.'

'What did you do after tea?'

'Played billiards with Hugo.'

'You didn't see Sir Gervase again?'

'No.'

'What about the shot?'

'That was rather odd. You see, I thought the first gong had gone, so I hurried up with my dressing, came dashing out of my room, heard, as I thought, the second gong and fairly raced down the stairs. I'd been one minute late for dinner the first night I was here and Hugo told me it had about wrecked our chances with the old man, so I fairly hared down. Hugo was just ahead of me and then there was a queer kind of pop-bang and Hugo said it was a champagne cork, but Snell said "No" to that and, anyway, I didn't think it had come from the dining-room. Miss Lingard thought it came from upstairs, but anyway we agreed it was a back-fire and we trooped into the drawing-room and forgot about it.'

'It did not occur to you for one moment that Sir Gervase might have shot himself?' asked Poirot.

'I ask you, should I be likely to think of such a thing? The Old Man seemed to enjoy himself throwing his weight about. I never imagined he'd do such a thing. I can't think why he did it. I suppose just because he was nuts.'

'An unfortunate occurrence.'

'Very—for Hugo and me. I gather he's left Hugo nothing at all, or practically nothing.'

'Who told you that?'

'Hugo got it out of old Forbes.'

'Well, Miss Cardwell—' Major Riddle paused a moment, 'I think that's all. Do you think Miss Chevenix-Gore is feeling well enough to come down and talk to us?'

'Oh, I should think so. I'll tell her.'

Poirot intervened.

'A little moment, mademoiselle. Have you seen this before?'

He held out the bullet pencil.

'Oh, yes, we had it at bridge this afternoon. Belongs to old Colonel Bury, I think.'

'Did he take it when the rubber was over?'

'I haven't the faintest idea.'

'Thank you, mademoiselle. That is all.'

'Right, I'll tell Ruth.'

Ruth Chevenix-Gore came into the room like a queen. Her colour was vivid, her head held high. But her eyes, like the eyes of Susan Cardwell, were watchful. She wore the same frock she had had on when Poirot arrived. It was a pale shade of apricot. On her shoulder was pinned a deep, salmon-pink rose. It had been fresh and blooming an hour earlier, now it drooped.

'Well?' said Ruth.

'I'm extremely sorry to bother you,' began Major Riddle. She interrupted him.

'Of course you have to bother me. You have to bother

everyone. I can save you time, though. I haven't the faintest idea why the Old Man killed himself. All I can tell you is that it wasn't a bit like him.'

'Did you notice anything amiss in his manner today? Was he depressed, or unduly excited—was there anything at all abnormal?'

'I don't think so. I wasn't noticing—'

'When did you see him last?'

'Tea-time.'

Poirot spoke:

'You did not go to the study—later?'

'No. The last I saw of him was in this room. Sitting there.'

She indicated a chair.

'I see. Do you know this pencil, mademoiselle?'

'It's Colonel Bury's.'

'Have you seen it lately?'

'I don't really remember.'

'Do you know anything of a—disagreement between Sir Gervase and Colonel Bury?'

'Over the Paragon Rubber Company, you mean?'

'Yes.'

'I should think so. The Old Man was rabid about it!'

'He considered, perhaps, that he had been swindled?'

Ruth shrugged her shoulders.

'He didn't understand the first thing about finance.'

Poirot said:

'May I ask you a question, mademoiselle—a somewhat impertinent question?'

'Certainly, if you like.'

'It is this—are you sorry that your—father is dead?'

She stared at him.

'Of course I'm sorry. I don't indulge in sob-stuff. But I shall miss him . . . I was fond of the Old Man. That's what we called him, Hugo and I, always. The "Old Man"—you know—something of the primitive—anthropoid-ape-original-Patriarch-of-the-tribe business. It sounds disrespectful, but there's really a lot of affection behind it. Of course, he was really the most complete, muddle-headed old ass that ever lived!'

'You interest me, mademoiselle.'

'The Old Man had the brains of a louse! Sorry to have to say it, but it's true. He was incapable of any kind of headwork. Mind you, he was a character. Fantastically brave and all that! Could go careering off to the Pole, or fighting duels. I always think that he blustered such a lot because he really knew that his brains weren't up to much. Anyone could have got the better of him.'

Poirot took the letter from his pocket.

'Read this, mademoiselle.'

She read it through and handed it back to him.

'So that's what brought you here!'

'Does it suggest anything to you, that letter?'

She shook her head.

'No. It's probably quite true. Anyone could have robbed the poor old pet. John says the last agent before him swindled him right and left. You see, the Old Man was so grand and so pompous that he never really condescended to look into details! He was an invitation to crooks.'

'You paint a different picture of him, mademoiselle, from the accepted one.'

'Oh, well—he put up a pretty good camouflage. Vanda (my mother) backed him for all she was worth. He was so happy stalking round pretending he was God Almighty. That's why, in a way, I'm glad he's dead. It's the best thing for him.'

'I do not quite follow you, mademoiselle.'

Ruth said broodingly:

'It was growing on him. One of these days he would have had to be locked up . . . People were beginning to talk as it was.'

'Did you know, mademoiselle, that he was contemplating a will whereby you could only inherit his money if you married Mr Trent?'

She cried:

'How absurd! Anyway, I'm sure that could be set aside by law . . . I'm sure you can't dictate to people about whom they shall marry.'

'If he had actually signed such a will, would you have complied with its provisions, mademoiselle?'

She stared.

'I—I—'

She broke off. For two or three minutes she sat irresolute, looking down at her dangling slipper. A little piece of earth detached itself from the heel and fell on the carpet.

Suddenly Ruth Chevenix-Gore said:

'Wait!'

She got up and ran out of the room. She returned almost immediately with Captain Lake by her side.

'It's got to come out,' she said rather breathlessly. 'You might as well know now. John and I were married in London three weeks ago.'

CHAPTER 10

Of the two of them, Captain Lake looked far the more embarrassed.

'This is a great surprise, Miss Chevenix-Gore—Mrs Lake, I should say,' said Major Riddle. 'Did no one know of this marriage of yours?'

'No, we kept it quite dark. John didn't like that part of it much.'

Lake said, stammering a little:

'I—I know that it seems rather a rotten way to set about things. I ought to have gone straight to Sir Gervase—'

Ruth interrupted:

'And told him you wanted to marry his daughter, and have been kicked out on your head and he'd probably have disinherited me, raised hell generally in the house, and we could have told each other how beautifully we'd behaved! Believe me, my way was better! If a thing's done, it's done. There would still have been a row—but he'd have come round.'

Lake still looked unhappy. Poirot asked:

'When did you intend to break the news to Sir Gervase?'

Ruth answered:

'I was preparing the ground. He'd been rather suspicious about me and John, so I pretended to turn my attentions to Godfrey. Naturally, he was ready to go quite off the deep-end about that. I figured it out that the news I was married to John would come almost as a relief!'

'Did anybody at all know of this marriage?'

'Yes, I told Vanda in the end. I wanted to get her on my side.'

'And you succeeded in doing so?'

'Yes. You see, she wasn't very keen about my marrying Hugo—because he was a cousin, I think. She seemed to think the family was so batty already that we'd probably have completely batty children. That was probably rather absurd, because I'm only adopted, you know. I believe I'm some quite distant cousin's child.'

'You are sure Sir Gervase had no suspicion of the truth?'

'Oh, no.'

Poirot said:

'Is that true, Captain Lake? In your interview with Sir Gervase this afternoon, are you quite sure the matter was not mentioned?'

'No, sir. It was not.'

'Because, you see, Captain Lake, there is certain evidence to show that Sir Gervase was in a highly-excitable condition after the time he spent with you, and that he spoke once or twice of family dishonour.'

'The matter was not mentioned,' Lake repeated. His face had gone very white.

'Was that the last time you saw Sir Gervase?'

'Yes, I have already told you so.'

'Where were you at eight minutes past eight this evening?'

'Where was I? In my house. At the end of the village, about half a mile away.'

'You did not come up to Hamborough Close round about that time?'

'No.'

Poirot turned to the girl.

'Where were you, mademoiselle, when your father shot himself?'

'In the garden.'

'In the garden? You heard the shot?'

'Oh, yes. But I didn't think about it particularly. I thought it was someone out shooting rabbits, although now I remember I did think it sounded quite close at hand.'

'You returned to the house—which way?'

'I came in through this window.'

Ruth indicated with a turn of her head the window behind her.

'Was anyone in here?'

'No. But Hugo and Susan and Miss Lingard came in from the hall almost immediately. They were talking about shooting and murders and things.'

'I see,' said Poirot. 'Yes, I think I see now . . .'

Major Riddle said rather doubtfully:

'Well—er—thank you. I think that's all for the moment.'

Ruth and her husband turned and left the room.

'What the devil——' began Major Riddle, and ended

rather hopelessly: 'It gets more and more difficult to keep track of this business.'

Poirot nodded. He had picked up the little piece of earth that had fallen from Ruth's shoe and was holding it thoughtfully in his hand.

'It is like the mirror smashed on the wall,' he said. 'The dead man's mirror. Every new fact we come across shows us some different angle of the dead man. He is reflected from every conceivable point of view. We shall have soon a complete picture . . .'

He rose and put the little piece of earth tidily in the waste-paper basket.

'I will tell you one thing, my friend. The clue to the whole mystery is the mirror. Go into the study and look for yourself, if you do not believe me.'

Major Riddle, said decisively:

'If it's murder, it's up to you to prove it. If you ask me, I say it's definitely suicide. Did you notice what the girl said about a former agent having swindled old Gervase? I bet Lake told that tale for his own purposes. He was probably helping himself a bit, Sir Gervase suspected it, and sent for you because he didn't know how far things had gone between Lake and Ruth. Then this afternoon Lake told him they were married. That broke Gervase up. It was "too late" now for anything to be done. He determined to get out of it all. In fact his brain, never very well balanced at the best of times, gave way. In my opinion that's what happened. What have you got to say against it?'

Poirot stood still in the middle of the room.

'What have I to say? This: I have nothing to say against your theory—but it does not go far enough. There are certain things it does not take into account.'

'Such as?'

'The discrepancies in Sir Gervase's moods today, the finding of Colonel Bury's pencil, the evidence of Miss Cardwell (which is very important), the evidence of Miss Lingard as to the order in which people came down to dinner, the position of Sir Gervase's chair when he was found, the paper bag which had held oranges and, finally, the all-important clue of the broken mirror.'

Major Riddle stared.

'Are you going to tell me that that rigmarole makes *sense*?' he asked.

Hercule Poirot replied softly:

'I hope to make it do so—by tomorrow.'

CHAPTER 11

It was just after dawn when Hercule Poirot awoke on the following morning. He had been given a bedroom on the east side of the house.

Getting out of bed, he drew aside the window-blind and satisfied himself that the sun had risen, and that it was a fine morning.

He began to dress with his usual meticulous care. Having finished his toilet, he wrapped himself up in a thick overcoat and wound a muffler round his neck.

Then he tiptoed out of his room and through the silent house down to the drawing-room. He opened the french windows noiselessly and passed out into the garden.

The sun was just showing now. The air was misty, with the mist of a fine morning. Hercule Poirot followed the terraced walk round the side of the house till he came to the windows of Sir Gervase's study. Here he stopped and surveyed the scene.

Immediately outside the windows was a strip of grass that ran parallel with the house. In front of that was a wide herbaceous border. The michaelmas daisies still made a fine show. In front of the border was the flagged walk where Poirot was standing. A strip of grass ran from the grass walk behind the border to the terrace. Poirot examined it carefully, then shook his head. He turned his attention to the border on either side of it.

Very slowly he nodded his head. In the right-hand bed, distinct in the soft mould, there were footprints.

As he stared down at them, frowning, a sound caught his ears and he lifted his head sharply.

Above him a window had been pushed up. He saw a red head of hair. Framed in an aureole of golden red he saw the intelligent face of Susan Cardwell.

'What on earth are you doing at this hour, M. Poirot? A spot of sleuthing?'

Poirot bowed with the utmost correctitude.

'Good morning, mademoiselle. Yes, it is as you say. You now behold a detective—a great detective, I may say—in the act of detecting!'

The remark was a little flamboyant. Susan put her head on one side.

'I must remember this in my memoirs,' she remarked. 'Shall I come down and help?'

'I should be enchanted.'

'I thought you were a burglar at first. Which way did you get out?'

'Through the drawing-room window.'

'Just a minute and I'll be with you.'

She was as good as her word. To all appearances Poirot was exactly in the same position as when she had first seen him.

'You are awake very early, mademoiselle?'

'I haven't been to sleep really properly. I was just getting that desperate feeling that one does get at five in the morning.'

'It's not quite so early as that!'

'It feels like it! Now then, my super-sleuth, what are we looking at?'

'But observe, mademoiselle, footprints.'

'So they are.'

'Four of them,' continued Poirot. 'See, I will point them out to you. Two going towards the window, two coming from it.'

'Whose are they? The gardener's?'

'Mademoiselle, mademoiselle! Those footmarks are made by the small dainty high-heeled shoes of a woman. See, convince yourself. Step, I beg of you, in the earth here beside them.'

Susan hesitated a minute, then placed a foot gingerly on to the mould in the place indicated by Poirot. She was wearing small high-heeled slippers of dark brown leather.

'You see, yours are nearly the same size. Nearly, but not quite. These others are made by a rather longer foot than yours. Perhaps Miss Chevenix-Gore's—or Miss Lingard's—or even Lady Chevenix-Gore's.'

'Not Lady Chevenix-Gore—she's got tiny feet. People did in those days—manage to have small feet, I mean. And Miss Lingard wears queer flat-heeled things.'

'Then they are the marks of Miss Chevenix-Gore. Ah,

yes, I remember she mentioned having been out in the garden yesterday evening.'

He led the way back round the house.

'Are we still sleuthing?' asked Susan.

'But certainly. We will go now to Sir Gervase's study.'

He led the way. Susan Cardwell followed him.

The door still hung in a melancholy fashion. Inside, the room was as it had been last night. Poirot pulled the curtains and admitted the daylight.

He stood looking out at the border a minute or two, then he said:

'You have not, I presume, mademoiselle, much acquaintance with burglars?'

Susan Cardwell shook her red head regretfully.

'I'm afraid not, M. Poirot.'

'The chief constable, he, too, has not had the advantages of a friendly relationship with them. His connection with the criminal clases has always been strictly official. With me that is not so. I had a very pleasant chat with a burglar once. He told me an interesting thing about french windows—a trick that could sometimes be employed if the fastening was sufficiently loose.'

He turned the handle of the left-hand window as he spoke, the middle shaft came up out of the hole in the ground, and Poirot was able to pull the two doors of the window towards him. Having opened them wide, he closed them again—closed them without turning the handle, so as not to send the shaft down into its socket. He let go of the handle, waited a moment, then struck a quick, jarring blow high up on the centre of the shaft. The jar of the blow sent the shaft down into the socket in the ground—the handle turned of its own accord.

'You see, mademoiselle?'

'I think I do.'

Susan had gone rather pale.

'The window is now closed. It is impossible to *enter* a room when the window is closed, but it *is* possible to *leave* a room, pull the doors to from outside, then hit it as I did, and the bolt goes down into the ground, turning the handle. The window then is firmly closed, and anyone looking at it would say it had been closed from the *inside*.'

'Is that'—Susan's voice shook a little—'is that what happened last night?'

'I think so, yes, mademoiselle.'

Susan said violently:

'I don't believe a word of it.'

Poirot did not answer. He walked over to the mantelpiece. He wheeled sharply round.

'Mademoiselle, I have need of you as a witness. I have already one witness, Mr Trent. He saw me find this tiny sliver of looking-glass last night. I spoke of it to him. I left it where it was for the police. I even told the chief constable that a valuable clue was the broken mirror. But he did not avail himself of my hint. Now you are a witness that I place this sliver of looking-glass (to which, remember, I have already called Mr Trent's attention) into a little envelope— so.' He suited the action to the word. 'And I write on it—so—and seal it up. You are a witness, mademoiselle?'

'Yes—but—but I don't know what it means.'

Poirot walked over to the other side of the room. He stood in front of the desk and stared at the shattered mirror on the wall in front of him.

'I will tell you what it means, mademoiselle. If you had been standing here last night, looking into this mirror, you could have seen in it *murder being committed* . . .'

CHAPTER 12

For once in her life Ruth Chevenix-Gore—now Ruth Lake—came down to breakfast in good time. Hercule Poirot was in the hall and drew her aside before she went into the dining-room.

'I have a question to ask you, madame.'

'Yes?'

'You were in the garden last night. Did you at any time step in the flower-bed outside Sir Gervase's study window?'

Ruth stared at him.

'Yes, twice.'

'Ah! *Twice*. How twice?'

'The first time I was picking michaelmas daisies. That was about seven o'clock.'

'Was it not rather an odd time of day to pick flowers?'

'Yes, it was, as a matter of fact. I'd done the flowers yesterday morning, but Vanda said after tea that the flowers on the dinner-table weren't good enough. I had thought they would be all right, so I hadn't done them fresh.'

'But your mother requested you to do them? Is that right?'

'Yes. So I went out just before seven. I took them from that part of the border because hardly anyone goes round there, and so it didn't matter spoiling the effect.'

'Yes, yes, but the *second* time. You went there a *second* time, you said?'

'That was just before dinner. I had dropped a spot of brilliantine on my dress—just by the shoulder. I didn't want to bother to change, and none of my artificial flowers went with the yellow of that dress. I remembered I'd seen a late rose when I was picking the michaelmas daisies, so I hurried out and got it and pinned it on my shoulder.'

Poirot nodded his head slowly.

'Yes, I remember that you wore a rose last night. What time was it, madame, when you picked that rose?'

'I don't really know.'

'But it is *essential*, madame. Consider—reflect.'

Ruth frowned. She looked swiftly at Poirot and then away again.

'I can't say exactly,' she said at last. 'It must have been— oh, of course—it must have been about five minutes past eight. It was when I was on my way back round the house that I heard the gong go, and then that funny bang. I was hurrying because I thought it was the second gong and not the first.'

'Ah, so you thought that—and did you not try the study window when you stood there in the flower-bed?'

'As a matter of fact, I did. I thought it might be open, and it would be quicker to come in that way. But it was fastened.'

'So everything is explained. I congratulate you, madame.'

She stared at him.

'What do you mean?'

'That you have an explanation for everything, for the mould on your shoes, for your footprints in the flower-bed, for your fingerprints on the outside of the window. It is very convenient that.'

Before Ruth could answer, Miss Lingard came hurrying down the stairs. There was a queer purple flush on her cheeks, and she looked a little startled at seeing Poirot and Ruth standing together.

'I beg your pardon,' she said. 'Is anything the matter?'

Ruth said angrily:

'I think M. Poirot has gone mad!'

She swept by them and into the dining-room. Miss Lingard turned an astonished face on Poirot.

He shook his head.

'After breakfast,' he said. 'I will explain. I should like everyone to assemble in Sir Gervase's study at ten o'clock.'

He repeated this request on entering the dining-room.

Susan Cardwell gave him a quick glance, then transferred her gaze to Ruth. When Hugo said:

'Eh? What's the idea?' she gave him a sharp nudge in the side, and he shut up obediently.

When he had finished his breakfast, Poirot rose and walked to the door. He turned and drew out a large old-fashioned watch.

'It is five minutes to ten. In five minutes—in the study.'

*

Poirot looked round him. A circle of interested faces stared back at him. Everyone was there, he noted, with one exception, and at that very moment the exception swept into the room. Lady Chevenix-Gore came in with a soft, gliding step. She looked haggard and ill.

Poirot drew forward a big chair for her, and she sat down.

She looked up at the broken mirror, shivered, and pulled her chair a little way round.

'Gervase is still here,' she remarked in a matter-of-fact tone. 'Poor Gervase . . . He will soon be free now.'

Poirot cleared his throat and announced:

'I have asked you all to come here so that you may hear the true facts of Sir Gervase's suicide.'

'It was Fate,' said Lady Chevenix-Gore. 'Gervase was strong, but his Fate was stronger.'

Colonel Bury moved forward a little.

'Vanda—my dear.'

She smiled up at him, then put up her hand. He took it in his. She said softly: 'You are such a comfort, Ned.'

Ruth said sharply:

'Are we to understand, M. Poirot, that you have definitely ascertained the cause of my father's suicide?'

Poirot shook his head.

'No, madame.'

'Then what is all this rigmarole about?'

Poirot said quietly:

'I do not know the cause of Sir Gervase Chevenix-Gore's suicide, *because Sir Gervase Chevenix-Gore did not commit suicide*. He did not kill himself. *He was killed . . .'*

'Killed?' Several voices echoed the word. Startled faces were turned in Poirot's direction. Lady Chevenix-Gore looked up, said, 'Killed? Oh, no!' and gently shook her head.

'Killed, did you say?' It was Hugo who spoke now. 'Impossible. There was no one in the room when we broke in. The window was fastened. The door was locked on the inside, and the key was in my uncle's pocket. How could he have been killed?'

'Nevertheless, he was killed.'

'And the murderer escaped through the keyhole, I suppose?' said Colonel Bury sceptically. 'Or flew up the chimney?'

'The murderer,' said Poirot, 'went out through the window. I will show you how.'

He repeated his manoeuvres with the window.

'You see?' he said. 'That was how it was done! From the first I could not consider it likely that Sir Gervase had committed suicide. He had pronounced egomania, and such a man does not kill himself.

'And there were other things! Apparently, just before his death, Sir Gervase had sat down at his desk, scrawled the word *SORRY* on a sheet of note-paper and had then shot himself. But before this last action he had, for some reason or other altered the position of his chair, turning it so that it was sideways to the desk. Why? There must be some reason. I began to see light when I found, sticking to the base of a heavy bronze statuette, a tiny sliver of looking-glass . . .

'I asked myself, how does a sliver of broken looking-glass come to be there?—and an answer suggested itself to me. The mirror had been broken, not by a bullet, *but by being struck with the heavy bronze figure.* That mirror had been broken *deliberately*.

'But why? I returned to the desk and looked down at the chair. Yes, I saw now. It was all wrong. No suicide would turn his chair round, lean over the edge of it, and then shoot himself. The whole thing was arranged. The suicide was a fake!

'And now I come to something very important. The evidence of Miss Cardwell. Miss Cardwell said that she hurried downstairs last night because she thought that the *second* gong had sounded. That is to say, she thought that she had already heard the *first* gong.

'Now observe, *if* Sir Gervase was sitting at his desk in the normal fashion when he was shot, where would the bullet go? Travelling in a straight line, it would pass through the door, if the door were open, and finally *hit the gong*!

'You see now the importance of Miss Cardwell's statement? No one else heard the first gong, but, then, her room is situated immediately above this one, and she was in the best position for hearing it. It would consist of only one single note, remember.

'There could be no question of Sir Gervase's shooting himself. A dead man cannot get up, shut the door, lock it and arrange himself in a convenient position! Somebody else was concerned, and therefore it was not suicide, but murder. Someone whose presence was easily accepted by Sir Gervase, stood by his side talking to him. Sir Gervase was busy writing, perhaps. The murderer brings the pistol up to the right side of his head and fires. The deed is done! Then quick, to work! The murderer slips on gloves. The door is locked, the key put in Sir Gervase's pocket. But supposing that one loud note of the gong has been heard? Then it will be realized that the door was *open*, not *shut*, when the shot was fired. So the chair is turned, the body rearranged, the dead man's fingers pressed on the pistol, the mirror deliberately smashed. Then the murderer goes out through the window, jars it shut, steps, not on the grass, but in the flower-bed where footprints can be smoothed out afterwards; then round the side of the house and into the drawing-room.'

He paused and said:

'*There was only one person who was out in the garden when the shot was fired.* That same person left her footprints in the flower-bed and her fingerprints on the outside of the window.'

He came towards Ruth.

'And there was a motive, wasn't there? Your father had learnt of your secret marriage. He was preparing to disinherit you.'

'It's a lie!' Ruth's voice came scornful and clear. 'There's not a word of truth in your story. It's a lie from start to finish!'

'The proofs against you are very strong, madame. A jury *may* believe you. It may *not*!'

'She won't have to face a jury.'

The others turned—startled. Miss Lingard was on her feet. Her face altered. She was trembling all over.

'*I* shot him. I admit it! I had my reason. I—I've been waiting for some time. M. Poirot is quite right. I followed him in here. I had taken the pistol out of the drawer earlier. I stood beside him talking about the book—and I shot him. That was just after eight. The bullet struck the gong. I never dreamt it would pass right through his head like that. There wasn't time to go out and look for it. I locked the door and put the key in his pocket. Then I swung the chair round, smashed the mirror, and, after scrawling 'Sorry' on a piece of paper, I went out through the window and shut it the way M. Poirot showed you. I stepped in the flower-bed, but I smoothed out the footprints with a little rake I had put there ready. Then I went round to the drawing-room. I had left the window open. I didn't know Ruth had gone out through it. She must have come round the front of the house while I went round the back. I had to put the rake away, you see, in a shed. I waited in the drawing-room till I heard someone coming downstairs and Snell going to the gong, and then—'

She looked at Poirot.

'You don't know what I did then?'

'Oh yes, I do. I found the bag in the wastepaper basket. It was very clever, that idea of yours. You did what children love to do. You blew up the bag and then hit it. It made a satisfactory big bang. You threw the bag into the waste-paper basket and rushed out into the hall. You had established the time of the suicide—and an alibi for yourself. But there was still one thing that worried you. You had not had time to pick up the bullet. It must be somewhere near the gong. It was essential that the bullet should be found in the study somewhere near the mirror. I didn't know when you had the idea of taking Colonel Bury's pencil—'

'It was just then,' said Miss Lingard. 'When we all came in from the hall. I was surprised to see Ruth in the room. I realized she must have come from the garden through the window. Then I noticed Colonel Bury's pencil lying on the bridge table. I slipped it into my bag. If, later, anyone saw me pick up the bullet, I could pretend it was the pencil. As a matter of fact, I didn't think anyone saw me pick up the bullet. I dropped it by the mirror while you were looking at the body. When you tackled me on the subject, I was very glad I had thought of the pencil.'

'Yes, that was clever. It confused me completely.'

'I was afraid someone must hear the real shot, but I knew everyone was dressing for dinner, and would be shut away in their rooms. The servants were in their quarters. Miss Cardwell was the only one at all likely to hear it, and she would probably think it was a backfire. What she did hear was the gong. I thought—I thought everything had gone without a hitch . . .'

Mr Forbes said slowly in his precise tones:

'This is a most extraordinary story. There seems no motive—'

Miss Lingard said clearly: 'There *was* a motive . . .'

She added fiercely:

'Go on, ring up the police! What are you waiting for?'

Poirot said gently:

'Will you all please leave the room? Mr Forbes, ring up Major Riddle. I will stay here till he comes.'

Slowly, one by one, the family filed out of the room. Puzzled, uncomprehending, shocked, they cast abashed glances at the trim, upright figure with its neatly-parted grey hair.

Ruth was the last to go. She stood, hesitating in the doorway.

'I don't understand.' She spoke angrily, defiantly, accusing Poirot. 'Just now, you thought *I* had done it.'

'No, no,' Poirot shook his head. 'No, I never thought that.'

Ruth went out slowly.

Poirot was left with the little middle-aged prim woman who had just confessed to a cleverly-planned and cold-blooded murder.

'No,' said Miss Lingard. 'You didn't think she had done it. You accused *her* to make *me* speak. That's right, isn't it?'

Poirot bowed his head.

'While we're waiting,' said Miss Lingard in a conversational tone, 'you might tell me what made you suspect *me*.'

'Several things. To begin with, your account of Sir Gervase.

A proud man like Sir Gervase would never speak disparagingly of his nephew to an outsider, especially someone in your position. You wanted to strengthen the theory of suicide. You also went out of your way to suggest that the cause of the suicide was some dishonourable trouble connected with Hugo Trent. That, again, was a thing Sir Gervase would never have admitted to a stranger. Then there was the object you picked up in the hall, and the very significant fact that you did not mention that Ruth, when she entered the drawing-room, did so *from the garden*. And then I found the paper bag—a most unlikely object to find in the waste-paper basket in the drawing-room of a house like Hamborough Close! You were the only person who had been in the drawing-room when the "shot" was heard. The paper bag trick was one that would suggest itself to a woman—an ingenious homemade device. So everything fitted in. The endeavour to throw suspicion on Hugo, and to keep it away from Ruth. The mechanism of crime—and its motive.'

The little grey-haired woman stirred.

'You know the motive?'

'I think so. Ruth's happiness—that was the motive! I fancy that you had seen her with John Lake—you knew how it was with them. And then with your easy access to Sir Gervase's papers, you came across the draft of his new will—Ruth disinherited unless she married Hugo Trent. That decided you to take the law into your own hands, using the fact that Sir Gervase had previously written to me. You probably saw a copy of that letter. What muddled feeling of suspicion and fear had caused him to write originally, I do not know. He must have suspected either Burrows or Lake of systematically robbing him. His uncertainty regarding Ruth's feelings made him seek a private investigation. You used that fact and deliberately set the stage for suicide, backing it up by your account of his being very distressed over something connected with Hugo Trent. You sent a telegram to me and reported Sir Gervase as having said I should arrive "too late."'

Miss Lingard said fiercely:

'Gervase Chevenix-Gore was a bully, a snob and a windbag! I wasn't going to have him ruin Ruth's happiness.'

Poirot said gently:

'Ruth is your daughter?'

'Yes—she is my daughter—I've often—thought about her. When I heard Sir Gervase Chevenix-Gore wanted someone to help him with a family history, I jumped at the chance. I was curious to see my—my girl. I knew Lady Chevenix-Gore wouldn't recognize me. It was years ago—I was young and pretty then, and I changed my name after that time. Besides Lady Chevenix-Gore is too vague to know anything definitely. I liked her, but I hated the Chevenix-Gore family. They treated me like dirt. And here was Gervase going to ruin Ruth's life with pride and snobbery. But I determined that she should be happy. And she *will* be happy—*if she never knows about me!*'

It was a plea—not a question.

Poirot bent his head gently.

'No one shall know from me.'

Miss Lingard said quietly:

'Thank you.'

Later, when the police had come and gone, Poirot found Ruth Lake with her husband in the garden.

She said challengingly:

'Did you really think that I had done it, M. Poirot?'

'I knew, madame, that you could *not* have done it—because of the michaelmas daisies.'

'The michaelmas daisies? I don't understand.'

'Madame, there were four footprints and four footprints *only* in the border. But if you had been picking flowers there would have been many more. That meant that between your first visit and your second, *someone had smoothed all those footsteps away*. That could only have been done by the guilty person, and since your footprints had *not* been removed, you were *not* the guilty person. You were automatically cleared.'

Ruth's face lightened.

'Oh, I see. You know—I suppose it's dreadful, but I feel rather sorry for that poor woman. After all, she did confess rather than let me be arrested—or at any rate, that is what she thought. That was—rather noble in a way. I hate to think of her going through a trial for murder.'

Poirot said gently:

'Do not distress yourself. It will not come to that.

The doctor, he tells me that she has serious heart trouble. She will not live many weeks.'

'I'm glad of that.' Ruth picked an autumn crocus and pressed it idly against her cheek.

'Poor woman. I wonder why she did it . . .'

TRIANGLE AT RHODES

CHAPTER 1

Hercule Poirot sat on the white sand and looked out across the sparkling blue water. He was carefully dressed in a dandified fashion in white flannels and a large panama hat protected his head. He belonged to the old-fashioned generation which believed in covering itself carefully from the sun. Miss Pamela Lyall, who sat beside him and talked ceaselessly, represented the modern school of thought in that she was wearing the barest minimum of clothing on her sun-browned person.

Occasionally her flow of conversation stopped whilst she reanointed herself from a bottle of oily fluid which stood beside her.

On the farther side of Miss Pamela Lyall her great friend, Miss Sarah Blake, lay face downwards on a gaudily-striped towel. Miss Blake's tanning was as perfect as possible and her friend cast dissatisfied glances at her more than once.

'I'm so patchy still,' she murmured regretfully. 'M. Poirot—*would* you mind? Just below the right shoulder-blade—I can't reach to rub it in properly.'

M. Poirot obliged and then wiped his oily hand carefully

on his handkerchief. Miss Lyall, whose principal interests in life were the observation of people round her and the sound of her own voice, continued to talk.

'I was right about that woman—the one in the *Chanel* model—it *is* Valentine Dacres—Chantry, I mean. I thought it was. I recognized her at once. She's really rather marvellous, isn't she? I mean I can understand how people go quite crazy about her. She just obviously *expects* them to! That's half the battle. Those other people who came last night are called Gold. He's terribly good-looking.'

'Honeymooners?' murmured Sarah in a stifled voice.

Miss Lyall shook her head in an experienced manner.

'Oh, no—her clothes aren't *new* enough. You can always tell brides! Don't you think it's the most fascinating thing in the world to watch people, M. Poirot, and see what you can find out about them by just looking?'

'Not just looking, darling,' said Sarah sweetly. 'You ask a lot of questions, too.'

'I haven't even spoken to the Golds yet,' said Miss Lyall with dignity. 'And anyway I don't see why one shouldn't be interested in one's fellow-creatures? Human nature is simply fascinating. Don't you think so, M. Poirot?'

This time she paused long enough to allow her companion to reply.

Without taking his eyes off the blue water, M. Poirot replied:

'*Ça dépend.*'

Pamela was shocked.

'Oh, M. Poirot! I don't think *anything's* so interesting—so *incalculable* as a human being!'

'Incalculable? That, no.'

'Oh, but they *are*. Just as you think you've got them beautifully taped—they do something completely unexpected.'

Hercule Poirot shook his head.

'No, no, that is not true. It is most rare that anyone does an action that is not *dans son caractère*. It is in the end monotonous.'

'I don't agree with you at all!' said Miss Pamela Lyall.

She was silent for quite a minute and a half before returning to the attack.

'As soon as I see people I begin wondering about them—what they're like—what relations they are to each other—what they're thinking and feeling. It's—oh, it's quite thrilling.'

'Hardly that,' said Hercule Poirot. 'Nature repeats herself more than one would imagine. The sea,' he added thoughtfully, 'has infinitely more variety.'

Sarah turned her head sideways and asked:

'You think that human beings tend to reproduce certain patterns? Stereotyped patterns?'

'*Précisément*,' said Poirot, and traced a design in the sand with his finger.

'What's that you're drawing?' asked Pamela curiously.

'A triangle,' said Poirot.

But Pamela's attention had been diverted elsewhere.

'Here are the Chantrys,' she said.

A woman was coming down the beach—a tall woman, very conscious of herself and her body. She gave a half-nod and smile and sat down a little distance away on the beach. The scarlet and gold silk wrap slipped down from her shoulders. She was wearing a white bathing-dress.

Pamela sighed.

'Hasn't she got a lovely figure?'

But Poirot was looking at her face—the face of a woman of thirty-nine who had been famous since sixteen for her beauty.

He knew, as everyone knew, all about Valentine Chantry. She had been famous for many things—for her caprices, for her wealth, for her enormous sapphire-blue eyes, for her matrimonial ventures and adventures. She had had five husbands and innumerable lovers. She had in turn been the wife of an Italian count, of an American steel magnate, of a tennis professional, of a racing motorist. Of these four the American had died, but the others had been shed negligently in the divorce court. Six months ago she had married a fifth time—a commander in the navy.

He it was who came striding down the beach behind her. Silent, dark—with a pugnacious jaw and a sullen manner. A touch of the primeval ape about him.

She said:

'Tony darling—my cigarette case . . .'

He had it ready for her—lighted her cigarette—helped her to slip the straps of the white bathing-dress from her shoulders. She lay, arms outstretched in the sun. He sat by her like some wild beast that guards its prey.

Pamela said, her voice just lowered sufficiently:

'You know they interest me *frightfully* . . . He's such a brute! So silent and—sort of *glowering.* I suppose a woman of her kind likes that. It must be like controlling a tiger! I wonder how long it will last. She gets tired of them very soon, I believe—especially nowadays. All the same, if she tried to get rid of him, I think he might be dangerous.'

Another couple came down the beach—rather shyly. They were the newcomers of the night before. Mr and Mrs Douglas Gold as Miss Lyall knew from her inspection of the hotel visitors' book. She knew, too, for such were the Italian regulations—their Christian names and their ages as set down from their passports.

Mr Douglas Cameron Gold was thirty-one and Mrs Marjorie Emma Gold was thirty-five.

Miss Lyall's hobby in life, as has been said, was the study of human beings. Unlike most English people, she was capable of speaking to strangers on sight instead of allowing four days to a week to elapse before making the first cautious advance as is the customary British habit. She, therefore, noting the slight hesitancy and shyness of Mrs Gold's advance, called out:

'Good morning, isn't it a lovely day?'

Mrs Gold was a small woman—rather like a mouse. She was not bad-looking, indeed her features were regular and her complexion good, but she had a certain air of diffidence and dowdiness that made her liable to be overlooked. Her husband, on the other hand, was extremely good-looking, in an almost theatrical manner. Very fair, crisply curling hair, blue eyes, broad shoulders, narrow hips. He looked more like a young man on the stage than a young man in real life, but the moment he opened his mouth that impression faded. He was quite natural and unaffected, even, perhaps, a little stupid.

Mrs Gold looked gratefully at Pamela and sat down near her.

'What a lovely shade of brown you are. I feel terribly underdone!'

'One has to take a frightful lot of trouble to brown evenly,' sighed Miss Lyall.

She paused a minute and then went on:

'You've only just arrived, haven't you?'

'Yes. Last night. We came on the Vapo d'Italia boat.'

'Have you ever been to Rhodes before?'

'No. It is lovely, isn't it?'

Her husband said:

'Pity it's such a long way to come.'

'Yes, if it were only nearer England—'

In a muffled voice Sarah said:

'Yes, but then it would be awful. Rows and rows of people laid out like fish on a slab. Bodies everywhere!'

'That's true, of course,' said Douglas Gold. 'It's a nuisance the Italian exchange is so absolutely ruinous at present.'

'It does make a difference, doesn't it?'

The conversation was running on strictly stereotyped lines. It could hardly have been called brilliant.

A little way along the beach, Valentine Chantry stirred

and sat up. With one hand she held her bathing-dress in position across her breast.

She yawned, a wide yet delicate cat-like yawn. She glanced casually down the beach. Her eyes slanted past Marjorie Gold—and stayed thoughtfully on the crisp, golden head of Douglas Gold.

She moved her shoulders sinuously. She spoke and her voice was raised a little higher than it need have been.

'Tony darling—isn't it divine—this sun? I simply *must* have been a sun worshipper once—don't you think so?'

Her husband grunted something in reply that failed to reach the others. Valentine Chantry went on in that high, drawling voice.

'Just pull that towel a little flatter, will you, darling?'

She took infinite pains in the resettling of her beautiful body. Douglas Gold was looking now. His eyes were frankly interested.

Mrs Gold chirped happily in a subdued key to Miss Lyall.

'What a beautiful woman!'

Pamela, as delighted to give as to receive information, replied in a lower voice:

'That's Valentine Chantry—you know, who used to be Valentine Dacres—she *is* rather marvellous, isn't she? He's simply crazy about her—won't let her out of his sight!'

Mrs Gold looked once more along the beach. Then she said:

'The sea really is lovely—so blue. I think we ought to go in now, don't you, Douglas?'

He was still watching Valentine Chantry and took a minute or two to answer. Then he said, rather absently:

'Go in? Oh, yes, rather, in a minute.'

Marjorie Gold got up and strolled down to the water's edge.

Valentine Chantry rolled over a little on one side. Her eyes looked along at Douglas Gold. Her scarlet mouth curved faintly into a smile.

The neck of Mr Douglas Gold became slightly red.

Valentine Chantry said:

'Tony darling—would you mind? I want a little pot of face-cream—it's up on the dressing-table. I meant to bring it down. Do get it for me—there's an angel.'

The commander rose obediently. He stalked off into the hotel.

Marjorie Gold plunged into the sea, calling out:

'It's lovely, Douglas—so warm. Do come.'

Pamela Lyall said to him:

'Aren't you going in?'

He answered vaguely:

'Oh! I like to get well hotted up first.'

Valentine Chantry stirred. Her head was lifted for a moment as though to recall her husband—but he was just passing inside the wall of the hotel garden.

'I like my dip the last thing,' explained Mr Gold.

Mrs Chantry sat up again. She picked up a flask of sunbathing oil. She had some difficulty with it—the screw top seemed to resist her efforts.

She spoke loudly and petulantly.

'Oh, dear—I *can't* get this thing undone!'

She looked towards the other group—

'I wonder—'

Always gallant, Poirot rose to his feet, but Douglas Gold had the advantage of youth and suppleness. He was by her side in a moment.

'Can I do it for you?'

'Oh, thank you—' It was the sweet, empty drawl again. 'You *are* kind. I'm such a *fool* at undoing things—I always seem to screw them the wrong way. Oh! you've done it! Thank you ever so much—'

Hercule Poirot smiled to himself.

He got up and wandered along the beach in the opposite direction. He did not go very far but his progress was leisurely. As he was on his way back, Mrs Gold came out of the sea and joined him. She had been swimming. Her face, under a singularly unbecoming bathing cap, was radiant.

She said breathlessly, 'I do love the sea. And it's so warm and lovely here.'

She was, he perceived, an enthusiastic bather.

She said, 'Douglas and I are simply mad on bathing. He can stay in for hours.'

And at that Hercule Poirot's eyes slid over her shoulder to the spot on the beach where that enthusiastic bather, Mr Douglas Gold, was sitting talking to Valentine Chantry.

His wife said:

'I can't think why he doesn't come . . .'

Her voice held a kind of childish bewilderment.

Poirot's eyes rested thoughtfully on Valentine Chantry. He thought that other women in their time had made that same remark.

Beside him, he heard Mrs Gold draw in her breath sharply.

She said—and her voice was cold:

'She's supposed to be very attractive, I believe. But Douglas doesn't like that type of woman.'

Hercule Poirot did not reply.

Mrs Gold plunged into the sea again.

She swam away from the shore with slow, steady strokes. You could see that she loved the water.

Poirot retraced his steps to the group on the beach.

It had been augmented by the arrival of old General Barnes, a veteran who was usually in the company of the young. He was sitting now between Pamela and Sarah, and he and Pamela were engaged in dishing up various scandals with appropriate embellishments.

Commander Chantry had returned from his errand. He and Douglas Gold were sitting on either side of Valentine.

Valentine was sitting up very straight between the two men and talking. She talked easily and lightly in her sweet, drawling voice, turning her head to take first one man and then the other in the conversation.

She was just finishing an anecdote.

'—and what do you think the foolish man said? "It may have been only a minute, but I'd remember you *anywhere*, Mum!" Didn't he, Tony? And you know, I thought it was so *sweet* of him. I do think it's such a kind world—I mean, everybody is so frightfully kind to *me* always—I don't know why—they just are. But I said to Tony—d'you remember, darling—"Tony, if you want to be a teeny-weeny bit jealous, you can be jealous of that commissionaire." Because he really was too adorable . . .'

There was a pause and Douglas Gold said:

'Good fellows—some of these commissionaires.'

'Oh, yes—but he took such trouble—really an immense amount of trouble—and seemed just pleased to be able to help me.'

Douglas Gold said:

'Nothing odd about that. Anyone would for you, I'm sure.'

She cried delightedly:

'How nice of you! Tony, did you hear that?'

Commander Chantry grunted.

His wife sighed:

'Tony never makes pretty speeches—do you, my lamb?'

Her white hand with its long red nails ruffled up his dark head.

He gave her a sudden sidelong look. She murmured:

'I don't really know how he puts up with me. He's simply frightfully clever—absolutely frantic with brains—and I just go on talking nonsense the whole time, but he doesn't seem to mind. Nobody minds what I do or say—everybody spoils me. I'm sure it's frightfully bad for me.'

Commander Chantry said across her to the other man:

'That your missus in the sea?'

'Yes. Expect it's about time I joined her.'

Valentine murmured:

'But it's so lovely here in the sun. You mustn't go into the sea yet. Tony darling, I don't think I shall actually *bathe* today—not my first day. I might get a chill or something. But why don't you go in now, Tony darling? Mr—Mr Gold will stay and keep me company while you're in.'

Chantry said rather grimly:

'No, thanks. Shan't go in just yet. Your wife seems to be waving to you, Gold.'

Valentine said:

'How well your wife swims. I'm sure she's one of those terribly efficient women who do everything well. They always frighten me so because I feel they despise me. I'm so frightfully bad at everything—an absolute duffer, aren't I, Tony darling?'

But again Commander Chantry only grunted.

His wife murmured affectionately:

'You're too sweet to admit it. Men are so wonderfully loyal—that's what I like about them. I do think men are so much more loyal than women—and they never say nasty things. Women, I always think, are rather *petty*.'

Sarah Blake rolled over on her side towards Poirot.

She murmured between her teeth.

'Examples of pettiness, to suggest that dear Mrs Chantry is in any way not absolute perfection! What a complete idiot the woman is! I really do think Valentine Chantry is very nearly the most idiotic woman I ever met. She can't do anything but say, "Tony, darling," and roll her eyes. I should fancy she'd got cottonwool padding instead of brains.'

Poirot raised his expressive eyebrows.

'*Un peu sévère!*'

'Oh, yes. Put it down as pure "Cat," if you like. She certainly has her methods! Can't she leave *any* man alone? Her husband's looking like thunder.'

Looking out to sea, Poirot remarked:

'Mrs Gold swims well.'

'Yes, she isn't like us who find it a nuisance to get wet. I wonder if Mrs Chantry will ever go into the sea at all while she's out here.'

'Not she,' said General Barnes huskily. 'She won't risk that make-up of hers coming off. Not that she isn't a fine-looking woman although perhaps a bit long in the tooth.'

'She's looking your way, General,' said Sarah wickedly. 'And you're wrong about the make-up. We're all waterproof and kissproof nowadays.'

'Mrs Gold's coming out,' announced Pamela.

'Here we go gathering nuts and may,' hummed Sarah. 'Here comes his wife to fetch him away—fetch him away—fetch him away . . .'

Mrs Gold came straight up the beach. She had quite a pretty figure but her plain, waterproof cap was rather too serviceable to be attractive.

'Aren't you coming, Douglas?' she demanded impatiently. 'The sea is lovely and warm.'

'Rather.'

Douglas Gold rose hastily to his feet. He paused a moment and as he did so Valentine Chantry looked up at him with a sweet smile.

'Au revoir,' she said.

Gold and his wife went down the beach.

As soon as they were out of earshot, Pamela said critically:

'I don't think, you know, that that was wise. To snatch your husband away from another woman is always bad policy. It makes you seem so possessive. And husbands hate that.'

'You seem to know a lot about husbands, Miss Pamela,' said General Barnes.

'Other people's—not my own!'

'Ah! that's where the difference comes in.'

'Yes, but General, I shall have learnt a lot of Do Nots.'

'Well, darling,' said Sarah, 'I shouldn't wear a cap like that for one thing . . .'

'Seems very sensible to me,' said the General. 'Seems a nice, sensible little woman altogether.'

'You've hit it exactly, General,' said Sarah. 'But you know there's a limit to the sensibleness of sensible women. I have a feeling she won't be so sensible when it's a case of Valentine Chantry.'

She turned her head and exclaimed in a low, excited whisper:

'Look at him now. Just like thunder. That man looks as though he had got the most frightful temper . . .'

Commander Chantry was indeed scowling after the retreating husband and wife in a singularly unpleasant fashion.

Sarah looked up at Poirot.

'Well?' she said. 'What do you make of all this?'

Hercule Poirot did not reply in words, but once again his forefinger traced a design in the sand. The same design—a triangle.

'The eternal triangle,' mused Sarah. 'Perhaps you're right. If so, we're in for an exciting time in the next few weeks.'

CHAPTER 2

M. Hercule Poirot was disappointed with Rhodes. He had come to Rhodes for a rest and for a holiday. A holiday, especially, from crime. In late October, so he had been told, Rhodes would be nearly empty. A peaceful, secluded spot.

That, in itself, was true enough. The Chantrys, the Golds, Pamela and Sarah, the General and himself and two Italian couples were the only guests. But within that restricted circle the intelligent brain of M. Poirot perceived the inevitable shaping of events to come.

'It is that I am crime-minded,' he told himself reproachfully. 'I have the indigestion! I imagine things.'

But still he worried.

One morning he came down to find Mrs Gold sitting on the terrace doing needlework.

As he came up to her he had the impression that there was the flicker of a cambric handkerchief swiftly whisked out of sight.

Mrs Gold's eyes were dry, but they were suspiciously bright. Her manner, too, struck him as being a shade too cheerful. The brightness of it was a shade overdone.

She said:

'Good morning, M. Poirot,' with such enthusiasm as to arouse his doubts.

He felt that she could not possibly be quite as pleased to see him as she appeared to be. For she did not, after all, know him very well. And though Hercule Poirot was a conceited little man where his profession was concerned, he was quite modest in his estimate of his personal attractions.

'Good morning, madame,' he responded. 'Another beautiful day.'

'Yes, isn't it fortunate? But Douglas and I are always lucky in our weather.'

'Indeed?'

'Yes. We're really very lucky altogether. You know, M. Poirot, when one sees so much trouble and unhappiness, and so many couples divorcing each other and all that sort of thing, well, one does feel very grateful for one's own happiness.'

'It is pleasant to hear you say so, madame.'

'Yes. Douglas and I are so wonderfully happy together. We've been married five years, you know, and after all, five years is quite a long time nowadays—'

'I have no doubt that in some cases it can seem an eternity, madame,' said Poirot dryly.

'—but I really believe that we're happier now than when we were first married. You see, we're so absolutely suited to each other.'

'That, of course, is everything.'

'That's why I feel so sorry for people who aren't happy.'

'You mean—'

'Oh! I was speaking generally, M. Poirot.'

'I see. I see.'

Mrs Gold picked up a strand of silk, held it to the light, approved of it, and went on:

'Mrs Chantry, for instance—'

'Yes, Mrs Chantry?'

'I don't think she's at all a nice woman.'

'No. No, perhaps not.'

'In fact, I'm quite sure she's not a nice woman. But in a way one feels sorry for her. Because in spite of her money and her good looks and all that'—Mrs Gold's fingers were trembling and she was quite unable to thread her needle—'she's not the sort of woman men really stick to. She's the sort of woman, I think, that men would get tired of very easily. Don't you think so?'

'I myself should certainly get tired of her conversation before any great space of time had passed,' said Poirot cautiously.

'Yes, that's what I mean. She has, of course, a kind of appeal . . .' Mrs Gold hesitated, her lips trembled, she stabbed uncertainly at her work. A less acute observer than Hercule Poirot could not have failed to notice her distress. She went on inconsequently:

'Men are just like children! They believe *anything* . . .'

She bent over her work. The tiny wisp of cambric came out again unobtrusively.

Perhaps Hercule Poirot thought it well to change the subject.

He said:

'You do not bathe this morning? And monsieur your husband, is he down on the beach?'

Mrs Gold looked up, blinked, resumed her almsot defiantly bright manner and replied:

'No, not this morning. We arranged to go round the walls of the old city. But somehow or other we—we missed each other. They started without me.'

The pronoun was revealing, but before Poirot could say anything, General Barnes came up from the beach below and dropped into a chair beside them.

'Good morning, Mrs Gold. Good morning, Poirot. Both deserters this morning? A lot of absentees. You two, and your husband, Mrs Gold—and Mrs Chantry.'

'And Commander Chantry?' inquired Poirot casually.

'Oh, no, he's down there. Miss Pamela's got him in hand.' The General chuckled. 'She's finding him a little bit difficult! One of the strong, silent men you hear about in books.'

Marjorie Gold said with a little shiver:

'He frightens me a little, that man. He—he looks so black sometimes. As though he might do—anything!'

She shivered.

'Just indigestion, I expect,' said the General cheerfully. 'Dyspepsia is responsible for many a reputation for romantic melancholy or ungovernable rages.'

Marjorie Gold smiled a polite little smile.

'And where's your good man?' inquired the General.

Her reply came without hesitation—in a natural, cheerful voice.

'Douglas? Oh, he and Mrs Chantry have gone into the town. I believe they've gone to have a look at the walls of the old city.'

'Ha, yes—very interesting. Time of the knights and all that. You ought to have gone too, little lady.'

Mrs Gold said:

'I'm afraid I came down rather late.'

She got up suddenly with a murmured excuse and went into the hotel.

General Barnes looked after her with a concerned expression, shaking his head gently.

'Nice little woman, that. Worth a dozen painted trollops like someone whose name we won't mention. Ha! Husband's a fool! Doesn't know when he's well off.'

He shook his head again. Then, rising, he went indoors.

Sarah Blake had just come up from the beach and had heard the General's last speech.

Making a face at the departing warrior's back, she remarked as she flung herself into a chair:

'Nice little woman—nice little woman! Men always approve of dowdy women—but when it comes to brass tacks the dressed-up trollops win hands down! Sad, but there it is.'

'Mademoiselle,' said Poirot, and his voice was abrupt. 'I do not like all this!'

'Don't you? Nor do I. No, let's be honest, I suppose I *do* like it really. There is a horrid side of one that enjoys accidents and public calamities and unpleasant things that happen to one's friends.'

Poirot asked:

'Where is Commander Chantry?'

'On the beach being dissected by Pamela (*she's* enjoying herself if you like!) and not being improved in temper by the proceeding. He was looking like a thunder cloud when I came up. There are squalls ahead, believe me.'

Poirot murmured:

'There is something I do not understand—'

'It's easy enough to *understand*,' said Sarah. 'But what's going to *happen*? That's the question.'

Poirot shook his head and murmured:

'As you say, mademoiselle—it is the future that causes one inquietude.'

'What a nice way of putting it,' said Sarah and went into the hotel.

In the doorway she almost collided with Douglas Gold. The young man came out looking rather pleased with himself but at the same time slightly guilty. He said:

'Hullo, M. Poirot,' and added rather self-consciously, 'Been showing Mrs Chantry the Crusaders' walls. Marjorie didn't feel up to going.'

Poirot's eyebrows rose slightly, but even had he wished he would have had no time to make a comment for Valentine Chantry came sweeping out, crying in her high voice:

'Douglas—a pink gin—positively I must have a pink gin.'

Douglas Gold went off to order the drink. Valentine sank into a chair by Poirot. She was looking radiant this morning.

291

Agatha Christie

She saw her husband and Pamela coming up towards them and waved a hand, crying out:

'Have a nice bathe, Tony darling? Isn't it a divine morning?'

Commander Chantry did not answer. He swung up the steps, passed her without a word or a look and vanished into the bar.

His hands were clenched by his sides and that faint likeness to a gorilla was accentuated.

Valentine Chantry's perfect but rather foolish mouth fell open.

She said, 'Oh,' rather blankly.

Pamela Lyall's face expressed keen enjoyment of the situation. Masking it as far as was possible to one of her ingenuous disposition she sat down by Valentine Chantry and inquired:

'Have you had a nice morning?'

As Valentine began, 'Simply marvellous. We—' Poirot got up and in his turn strolled gently towards the bar. He found young Gold waiting for the pink gin with a flushed face. He looked disturbed and angry.

He said to Poirot, 'That man's a brute!' And he nodded his head in the direction of the retreating figure of Commander Chantry.

'It is possible,' said Poirot. 'Yes, it is quite possible. But *les femmes*, they like brutes, remember that!'

Douglas muttered:

'I shouldn't be surprised if he ill-treats her!'

'She probably likes that too.'

Douglas Gold looked at him in a puzzled way, took up the pink gin and went out with it.

Hercule Poirot sat on a stool and ordered a *sirop de cassis*. Whilst he was sipping it with long sighs of enjoyment, Chantry came in and drank several pink gins in rapid succession.

He said suddenly and violently to the world at large rather than to Poirot:

'If Valentine thinks she can get rid of me like she's got rid of a lot of other damned fools, she's mistaken! I've got her and I mean to keep her. No other fellow's going to get her except over my dead body.'

He flung down some money, turned on his heel and went out.

CHAPTER 3

It was three days later that Hercule Poirot went to the Mount of the Prophet. It was a cool, agreeable drive through the golden green fir trees, winding higher and higher, far above the petty wrangling and squabbling of human beings. The car stopped at the restaurant. Poirot got out and wandered into the woods. He came out at last on a spot that seemed truly on top of the world. Far below, deeply and dazzlingly blue, was the sea.

Here at last he was at peace—removed from cares—above the world. Carefully placing his folded overcoat on a tree stump, Hercule Poirot sat down.

'Doubtless *le bon Dieu* knows what he does. But it is odd that he should have permitted himself to fashion certain human beings. *Eh bien*, here for a while at least I am away from these vexing problems.' Thus he mused.

He looked up with a start. A little woman in a brown coat and skirt was hurrying towards him. It was Marjorie Gold and this time she had abandoned all pretence. Her face was wet with tears.

Poirot could not escape. She was upon him.

'M. Poirot. You've got to help me. I'm so miserable I

don't know what to do! Oh, what shall I do? What shall I do?'

She looked up at him with a distracted face. Her fingers fastened on his coat sleeve. Then, as something she saw in his face alarmed her, she drew back a little.

'What—what is it?' she faltered.

'You want my advice, madame? It is that you ask?'

She stammered, 'Yes . . . Yes . . .'

'*Eh bien*—here it is.' He spoke curtly—trenchantly. 'Leave this place at once—*before it is too late.*'

'What?' She stared at him.

'You heard me. Leave this island.'

'Leave the island?'

She stared at him stupefied.

'That is what I say.'

'But why—why?'

'It is my advice to you—*if you value your life.*'

She gave a gasp.

'Oh! what do you mean? You're frightening me—you're frightening me.'

'Yes,' said Poirot gravely, 'that is my intention.'

She sank down, her face in her hands.

'But I can't! He wouldn't come! Douglas wouldn't, I mean. She wouldn't let him. She's got hold of him—body and soul. He won't listen to anything against her . . . He's crazy about her . . . He believes everything she tells him—that her husband ill-treats her—that she's an injured innocent—that nobody has ever understood her . . . He doesn't even think about me any more—I don't count—I'm not real to him. He wants me to give him his freedom—to divorce him. He believes that she'll divorce her husband and marry him. But I'm afraid . . . Chantry won't give her up. He's not that kind of man. Last night she showed Douglas bruises on her arm—said her husband had done it. It made Douglas wild. He's so chivalrous . . . Oh! I'm *afraid*! What will come of it all? Tell me what to do!'

Hercule Poirot stood looking straight across the water to the blue line of hills on the mainland of Asia. He said:

'I have told you. Leave the island *before it is too late* . . .'

She shook her head.

'I can't—I can't—unless Douglas . . .'

Poirot sighed.

He shrugged his shoulders.

CHAPTER 4

Hercule Poirot sat with Pamela Lyall on the beach.

She said with a certain amount of gusto, 'The triangle's going strong! They sat one each side of her last night—glowering at each other! Chantry had had too much to drink. He was positively insulting to Douglas Gold. Gold behaved very well. Kept his temper. The Valentine woman enjoyed it, of course. Purred like the man-eating tiger she is. What do you think will happen?'

Poirot shook his head.

'I am afraid. I am very much afraid . . .'

'Oh, we all are,' said Miss Lyall hypocritically. She added, 'This business is rather in *your* line. Or it may come to be. Can't you do anything?'

'I have done what I could.'

Miss Lyall leaned forward eagerly.

'What *have* you done?' she asked with pleasurable excitement.

'I advised Mrs Gold to leave the island before it was too late.'

'Oo-er—so you think—' she stopped.

'Yes, mademoiselle?'

'So *that's* what you think is going to happen!' said Pamela slowly. 'But he couldn't—he'd never do a thing like that . . . He's so *nice* really. It's all that Chantry woman. He wouldn't—He wouldn't—do—'

She stopped—then she said softly:

'*Murder*? Is that—is that really the word that's in your mind?'

'It is in someone's mind, mademoiselle. I will tell you that.'

Pamela gave a sudden shiver.

'I don't believe it,' she declared.

CHAPTER 5

The sequence of events on the night of October the twenty-ninth was perfectly clear.

To begin with, there was a scene between the two men—Gold and Chantry. Chantry's voice rose louder and louder and his last words were overheard by four persons—the cashier at the desk, the manager, General Barnes and Pamela Lyall.

'You god-damned swine! If you and my wife think you can put this over on me, you're mistaken! *As long as I'm alive*, Valentine will remain my wife.'

Then he had flung out of the hotel, his face livid with rage.

That was before dinner. After dinner (how arranged no one knew) a reconciliation took place. Valentine asked Marjorie Gold to come out for a moonlight drive. Pamela and Sarah went with them. Gold and Chantry played billiards together. Afterwards they joined Hercule Poirot and General Barnes in the lounge.

For the first time almost, Chantry's face was smiling and good-tempered.

'Have a good game?' asked the General.

The Commander said:

'This fellow's too good for me! Ran out with a break of forty-six.'

Douglas Gold deprecated this modestly.

'Pure fluke. I assure you it was. What'll you have? I'll go and get hold of a waiter.'

'Pink gin for me, thanks.'

'Right. General?'

'Thanks. I'll have a whisky and soda.'

'Same for me. What about you, M. Poirot?'

'You are most amiable. I should like a *sirop de cassis*.'

'A *sirop*—excuse me?'

'*Sirop de cassis*. The syrup of the blackcurrants.'

'Oh, a liqueur! I see. I suppose they have it here? I never heard of it.'

'They have it, yes. But it is not a liqueur.'

Douglas Gold said, laughing:

'Sounds a funny taste to me—but every man his own poison! I'll go and order them.'

Commander Chantry sat down. Though not by nature a talkative or a social man, he was clearly doing his best to be genial.

'Odd how one gets used to doing without any news,' he remarked.

The General grunted.

'Can't say the *Continental Daily Mail* four days old is much use to *me*. Of course I get *The Times* sent to me and *Punch* every week, but they're a devilish long time in coming.'

'Wonder if we'll have a general election over this Palestine business?'

'Whole thing's been badly mismanaged,' declared the General just as Douglas Gold reappeared followed by a waiter with the drinks.

The General had just begun on an anecdote of his military career in India in the year 1905. The two Englishmen were listening politely, if without great interest. Hercule Poirot was sipping his *sirop de cassis*.

The General reached the point of his narrative and there was dutiful laughter all round.

Then the women appeared at the doorway of the lounge. They all four seemed in the best of spirits and were talking and laughing.

'Tony, darling, it was too divine,' cried Valentine as she dropped into a chair by his side. 'The most marvellous idea of Mrs Gold's. You all ought to have come!'

Her husband said:

'What about a drink?'

He looked inquiringly at the others.

'Pink gin for me, darling,' said Valentine.

'Gin and gingerbeer,' said Pamela.

'Sidecar,' said Sarah.

'Right.' Chantry stood up. He pushed his own untouched pink gin over to his wife. 'You have this. I'll order another for myself. What's yours, Mrs Gold?'

Mrs Gold was being helped out of her coat by her husband. She turned smiling:

'Can I have an orangeade, please?'

'Right you are. Orangeade.'

He went towards the door. Mrs Gold smiled up in her husband's face.

'It was so lovely, Douglas. I wish you had come.'

'I wish I had too. We'll go another night, shall we?' They smiled at each other.

Valentine Chantry picked up the pink gin and drained it.

'Oo! I needed that,' she sighed.

Douglas Gold took Marjorie's coat and laid it on a settee.

As he strolled back to the others he said sharply:

'Hullo, what's the matter?'

Valentine Chantry was leaning back in her chair. Her lips were blue and her hand had gone to her heart.

'I feel—rather queer . . .'

She gasped, fighting for breath.

Chantry came back into the room. He quickened his step.

'Hullo, Val, what's the matter?'

'I—I don't know . . . That drink—it tasted queer . . .'

'The pink gin?'

Chantry swung round his face worked. He caught Douglas Gold by the shoulder.

'That was *my* drink . . . Gold, what the hell did you put in it?'

Douglas Gold was staring at the convulsed face of the woman in the chair. He had gone dead white.

'I—I—never—'

Valentine Chantry slipped down in her chair.

General Barnes cried out:

'Get a doctor—quick . . .'

Five minutes later Valentine Chantry died . . .

CHAPTER 6

There was no bathing the next morning.

Pamela Lyall, white-faced, clad in a simple dark dress, clutched at Hercule Poirot in the hall and drew him into the little writing-room.

'It's horrible!' she said. 'Horrible! You said so! You foresaw it! Murder!'

He bent his head gravely.

'Oh!' she cried out. She stamped her foot on the floor. 'You should have stopped it! Somehow! It *could* have been stopped!'

'How?' asked Hercule Poirot.

That brought her up short for the moment.

'Couldn't you go to someone—to the police—?'

'And say what? What is there to say—*before the event*? That someone has murder in their heart? I tell you, *mon enfant*, if one human being is determined to kill another human being—'

'You could warn the victim,' insisted Pamela.

'Sometimes,' said Hercule Poirot, 'warnings are useless.'

Pamela said slowly, 'You could warn the murderer—show him that you knew what was intended . . .'

Poirot nodded appreciatively.

'Yes—a better plan, that. But even then you have to reckon with a criminal's chief vice.'

'What is that?'

'Conceit. A criminal never believes that his crime can fail.'

'But it's absurd—stupid,' cried Pamela. 'The whole crime was childish! Why, the police arrested Douglas Gold at once last night.'

'Yes.' He added thoughtfully, 'Douglas Gold is a very stupid young man.'

'Incredibly stupid! I hear that they found the rest of the poison—whatever it was—?'

'A form of stropanthin. A heart poison.'

'That they actually found the rest of it in his dinner jacket pocket?'

'Quite true.'

'Incredibly stupid!' said Pamela again. 'Perhaps he meant to get rid of it—and the shock of the wrong person being poisoned paralysed him. What a scene it would make on the stage. The lover putting the stropanthin in the husband's glass and then, just when his attention is elsewhere, the wife drinks it instead . . . Think of the ghastly moment when Douglas Gold turned round and realized he had killed the woman he loved . . .'

She gave a little shiver.

'Your triangle. *The Eternal Triangle!* Who would have thought it would end like this?'

'I was afraid of it,' murmured Poirot.

Pamela turned on him.

'You warned *her*—Mrs Gold. Then why didn't you warn him as well?'

'You mean, why didn't I warn Douglas Gold?'

'No. I mean Commander Chantry. You could have told him that he was in danger—after all, *he* was the real obstacle! I've no doubt Douglas Gold relied on being able to bully his wife into giving him a divorce—she's a meek-spirited little woman and terribly fond of him. But Chantry is a mulish sort of devil. He was determined not to give Valentine her freedom.'

Poirot shrugged his shoulders.

'It would have been no good my speaking to Chantry,' he said.

'Perhaps not,' Pamela admitted. 'He'd probably have said he could look after himself and told you to go to the devil. But I do feel there ought to have been *something* one could have done.'

'I did think,' said Poirot slowly, 'of trying to persuade Valentine Chantry to leave the island, but she would not have believed what I had to tell her. She was far too stupid a woman to take in a thing like that. *Pauvre femme*, her stupidity killed her.'

'I don't believe it would have been any good if she *had* left the island,' said Pamela. 'He would simply have followed her.'

'He?'

'Douglas Gold.'

'You think Douglas Gold would have followed her? Oh,

no, mademoiselle, you are wrong—you are completely wrong. You have not yet appreciated the truth of this matter. If Valentine Chantry had left the island, her husband would have gone with her.'

Pamela looked puzzled.

'Well, naturally.'

'And then, you see, the crime would simply have taken place somewhere else.'

'I don't understand you?'

'I am saying to you that the same crime would have occurred somewhere else—*that crime being the murder of Valentine Chantry by her husband.*'

Pamela stared.

'Are you trying to say that it was Commander Chantry—Tony Chantry—who murdered Valentine?'

'Yes. You saw him do it! Douglas Gold brought him his drink. He sat with it in front of him. When the women came in we all looked across the room, he had the stropanthin ready, he dropped it into the pink gin and presently, courteously, he passed it along to his wife and she drank it.'

'But the packet of stropanthin was found in Douglas Gold's pocket!'

'A very simple matter to slip it there when we were all crowding round the dying woman.'

It was quite two minutes before Pamela got her breath.

'But I don't understand a word! The triangle—you said yourself—'

Hercule Poirot nodded his head vigorously.

'I said there was a triangle—yes. But you, you imagined

the wrong one. You were deceived by some very clever acting! You thought, as you were meant to think, that both Tony Chantry and Douglas Gold were in love with Valentine Chantry. You believed, as you were meant to believe, that Douglas Gold, being in love with Valentine Chantry (whose husband refused to divorce her) took the desperate step of administering a powerful heart poison to Chantry and that, by a fatal mistake, Valentine Chantry drank that poison instead. All that is illusion. Chantry has been meaning to do away with his wife for some time. He was bored to death with her, I could see that from the first. He married her for her money. Now he wants to marry another woman—so he planned to get rid of Valentine and keep her money. That entailed murder.'

'Another *woman*?'

Poirot said slowly:

'Yes, yes—*the little Marjorie Gold*. It was the eternal triangle all right! But you saw it the wrong way round. Neither of those two men cared in the least for Valentine Chantry. It was her vanity *and Majorie Gold's very clever stage managing* that made you think they did! A very clever woman, Mrs Gold, and amazingly attractive in her demure Madonna, poor-little-thing-way! I have known four women criminals of the same type. There was Mrs Adams who was acquitted of murdering her husband, but everybody knows she did it. Mary Parker did away with an aunt, a sweetheart and two brothers before she got a little careless and was caught. Then there was Mrs Rowden, she was hanged all right. Mrs Lecray escaped by the skin of her teeth. This woman is exactly the same type. I recognized it as soon as I saw her! That type takes to crime like a duck to water! And a very pretty bit of well-planned work it was. Tell me, what *evidence* did you ever have that Douglas Gold was in love with Valentine Chantry? When you come to think it out, you will realize that there was only Mrs Gold's confidences and Chantry's jealous bluster. Yes? You see?'

'It's horrible,' cried Pamela.

'They were a clever pair,' said Poirot with professional detachment. 'They planned to "meet" here and stage their crime. That Marjorie Gold, she is a cold-blooded devil! She would have sent her poor, innocent fool of a husband to the scaffold without the least remorse.'

Pamela cried out:

'But he was arrested and taken away by the police last night.'

'Ah,' said Hercule Poirot, 'but after that, me, I had a few little words with the police. It is true that I did not see Chantry put the stropanthin in the glass. I, like everyone else, looked up when the ladies came in. But the moment I realized that Valentine Chantry had been poisoned, I watched her husband without taking my eyes off him. And so, you see, I actually saw him slip the packet of stropanthin in Douglas Gold's coat pocket . . .'

He added with a grim expression on his face:

'I am a good witness. My name is well known. The moment the police heard my story they realized that it put an entirely different complexion on the matter.'

'And then?' demanded Pamela, fascinated.

'*Eh bien*, then they asked Commander Chantry a few questions. He tried to bluster it out, but he is not really clever, he soon broke down.'

'So Douglas Gold was set at liberty?'

'Yes.'

'And—Marjorie Gold?'

Poirot's face grew stern.

'I warned her,' he said. 'Yes, I warned her . . . Up on the Mount of the Prophet . . . It was the only chance of averting the crime. I as good as told her that I suspected her. She understood. But she believed herself too clever . . . I told her to leave the island *if* she valued her life. She chose—to remain . . .'

Lightning Source UK Ltd.
Milton Keynes UK
UKHW021201050821
388320UK00007B/450